I0563401

What Might Have Been

by

Marianne Plunkert

Copyright Notice
This is a work of fiction. Names, characters, places, and incidents are either the product of the author's imagination or are used fictitiously, and any resemblance to actual persons living or dead, business establishments, events, or locales, is entirely coincidental.

What Might Have Been

COPYRIGHT © 2024 by Marianne Plunkert

All rights reserved. No part of this book may be used or reproduced in any manner whatsoever without written permission of the author or The Wild Rose Press, Inc. except in the case of brief quotations embodied in critical articles or reviews.
Contact Information: info@thewildrosepress.com

Cover Art by *The Wild Rose Press, Inc.*

The Wild Rose Press, Inc.
PO Box 708
Adams Basin, NY 14410-0708
Visit us at www.thewildrosepress.com

Publishing History
First Edition, 2025
Trade Paperback ISBN 978-1-5092-5993-9
Digital ISBN 978-1-5092-5994-6

Published in the United States of America

Dedication

In loving memory of Jack,
my very own stubborn Irishman

Acknowledgments

My heartfelt gratitude to Rhonda Penders, president and editor-in-chief of The Wild Rose Press, and her team for helping to make my lifelong dream a reality. I especially want to recognize Nicole D'Arienzo, historical managing editor, for handling the paperwork so efficiently, RJ Morris, who created the beautiful cover for this book, and historical editor Nan Swanson, whose attention to detail and thoughtful suggestions were invaluable as I pivoted from writing nonfiction to polishing this novel.

I am indebted to the Colorado Historical Society (now History Colorado), which served as both an inspiration and a primary research source for this book. I also garnered a significant amount of detail regarding the Sand Creek Massacre and its aftermath by reading Patrick M. Mendoza's book *Song of Sorrow: Massacre at Sand Creek* and Alvin M. Josephy, Jr.'s book *The Civil War in the American West.* And Fort Kearny State Historical Park in Kearny, Nebraska provided me with useful facts about wagon train travel as well as about the fort itself.

I am thankful for my dear friends, Nancy Zizic, Pamela Mayeda, Mitzi Lentz and Polly Putiri, and my brother-in-law, Ardin Goss, who all nagged me to finish writing this book when I stalled and took the time to read it and offer insightful comments, even though it is not their usual genre. Last, but not least, I owe an abundance of gratitude to my husband, Jack, who gave me his love and support throughout this process, including proofreading the final manuscript.

Chapter One

It was another in what seemed to be an unending string of hot, humid days in Nebraska City. Melissa sat aboard her uncle's buckboard and frowned up at the sun as though scolding it for its relentlessness. Passing her tongue over parched lips, she absently fingered the simple gold band that hung from a chain around her neck. The air was as heavy as thick soup, and there was not a hint of a breeze. She retrieved a handkerchief from her pocket to wipe the beads of perspiration forming on her forehead and the back of her neck. Weighed down by her long, thick, sun-streaked brown hair, the material of her homespun, high-collared dress stuck to her back, adding to her discomfort. It had taken her no more than half an hour to complete the errands with which her aunt had entrusted her, and she had been sitting here awaiting Uncle John's return for at least that same amount of time. She considered trying to hunt him down, but she knew he would delight in leaving her behind if he returned before she found him.

Her attention was thankfully diverted from her distress as a crowd gathered across the road from her. Bonnetless, as was her preference, she shielded her eyes with a hand in an effort to make out the figure standing on the wooden walkway addressing the motley gathering of men, women, and children.

"Ladies and gentlemen, my name is Watson

Calhoune." The speaker's weather-beaten face didn't hide his chagrin as he continued. "I've been asked to be wagon master for this here train, and I've agreed to do so. Reluctantly, I might add. But as most of you already know, the injuns have become a serious danger, and the army won't let any wagons pass without being one hundred men strong, so this is the only way I can get from here to where I want to go." Taking off his battered hat, he swiped his palm across his brow, pushing back his damp, straw-colored hair.

"How bad is the Indian trouble?" a timid female voice inquired.

"There's no sense pussyfooting around about it, ma'am," the wagon master replied. "You got a right to know what you're getting into. The Sioux are seeking revenge for the hanging of their leaders last fall up in Minnesota. They've convinced the Arapaho and the Apache to join with them against the white man, so we have triple the trouble. Even the women have not been spared during the massacres that have been occurring all over the place."

This last pronouncement provoked a loud murmuring among the crowd, and Melissa shifted uncomfortably. It had been accepted knowledge that the Indian tribes inhabiting western territories seldom killed white women.

"Lieutenant Bellamy and his men will help keep the train moving smoothly," Calhoune continued, indicating the three men who stood behind him on the walkway.

One of the three stepped forward. "For those of you who have not yet met us, please just call me Nat. And these two soldiers are Al and Tom. Our orders are taking us to Denver, Colorado Territory, and we have been instructed to help the emigrants on this train get there safely."

Melissa's eyes shifted to the speaker. She was surprised to see Federal Army issue attire, having detected a distinct drawl she would normally have associated with a Confederate soldier. Other than that, his appearance matched his voice. Both exuded strength. He would tower over her, and she was taller than most women. His waist-length blue jacket accentuated broad shoulders and slim hips. When he removed his hat as he began to address the crowd, black-brown curls the rich color of coffee beans sprang forth, softening the chiseled features of his face.

Lost in thought, Melissa was unaware of her uncle's return until the wagon shifted under his weight as he began to climb aboard. As she quickly scooted to the opposite end of the seat, she caught the skirt of her dress on a splinter and made a mental note to mend the small tear later. She had already let out the darts in the too-tight bodice, but she didn't have a large wardrobe and lacked the funds to purchase the materials to replace any garb.

"No need to sit so close to the edge, Missy," her uncle sneered as he reached an arm around her to draw her closer to him, his hand cupping her breast as he did so. "Wouldn't want you falling off the wagon now, would we?" he added snidely.

Melissa detected the smell of strong liquor on his breath as she jerked away, shooting him a threatening look.

"Is that any way to treat an uncle who has opened his home to you?" he asked, feigning offense as he grinned at her with tobacco-stained teeth. "Just you wait, Missy. Our time will come," he promised, rubbing his groin suggestively before urging the horse forward with the reins.

It was all Melissa could do to control her temper. If she didn't fear Aunt Georgina would suffer a consequence for anything her niece said or did, she would give Uncle John the tongue lashing he deserved, and then some.

As the wagon was pulling away, Melissa glanced back at the crowd still gathered and calling out numerous questions to the man who would be leading the way west. She felt her cheeks grow warm when she discovered Lieutenant Bellamy staring directly at her. Mortified, she turned back around. *How long had he been watching*? *How much had he seen*? Silently, she willed the horse pulling the buckboard to carry her away as speedily as possible.

****

"Can I help you with something, Aunt Georgina?" Melissa inquired as she entered the house that was now her home. Not waiting for a reply, Melissa placed the parcel she had carried from the wagon on the scarred, wooden table and pulled up a chair to join her aunt in shucking peas.

"I was able to get everything you had on the list except for the lye. Mr. Timmons doesn't understand it, but lye was missing from the last shipment, and he's temporarily out of stock."

"No matter," Melissa's aunt replied, unconcerned. "We have enough soap to make do as long as the next shipment doesn't take too long in coming. And if we run out, we run out. Leastwise, it's not an item that John will get het up over not having," she added flatly.

Melissa glanced up at her aunt. She could not

imagine herself living in fear of daily scoldings as her mother's sister did. However, Aunt Georgina seemed resigned to them, going out of her way to avoid angering her husband. John Hund treated his horse better than he treated his wife. Melissa felt sorry for the woman. Based on what she had observed since her arrival two months ago, Melissa believed he had married only to have someone help with the chores and satisfy his base sexual urges whenever the need arose. An unattractive man, both physically and in manner, he could not be selective, and Melissa suspected Aunt Georgina had thought she could do no better. Born with one leg shorter than the other, her aunt walked with a visible limp. If only she had realized how her own beauty shone from the inside out.

"Did you happen to have word from Alicia, dear?"

"No," Melissa responded sadly. "There was nothing waiting at the telegraph office for any of us."

Alicia, four years her elder, had married Jesse two years ago, after which the newlyweds had headed West, spurred on by the promise of gold. Under the circumstances, their communication to her had been understandably sporadic, but Melissa was beginning to worry whether the wires she had sent informing her sister of their parents' typhoid deaths had been received. Now, after learning about the trouble wagon trains were encountering, she wondered how she could possibly make the journey to join them when she did hear from them. Her mother, Catherine Sullivan, obviously unaware of her sister's plight, had, on her deathbed, directed her to use the little money left to travel to Aunt Georgina's home to await word from Alicia. Given Uncle John's increasingly abhorrent advances, Melissa was beginning to feel desperate.

****

Melissa excused herself quickly after supper, feigning illness, but the truth was that she could not cope with her uncle's lecherous stares. They seemed more pointed tonight than in the past and harder to ignore. In her room, she lost no time changing from her cumbersome street attire to a lightweight, white cotton nightgown. There were times she wished she were not female. How shackled women were with layers of clothing—victims of their own vanity. Throwing the dress she had just stepped out of over her arm, she grabbed the lap-bag containing her sewing tools from a peg on the wall and settled in the tattered wing chair beneath the tiny window in her room. After repairing the small rip in her dress, she worked on the hair wreath in her lap-bag, immortalizing strands from her mother and her father, until the light became dim and she fell asleep.

She had no idea how long she had slept when she was awakened by the loud rattling of the doorknob. She was still trying to clear the fog from her mind when the door was thrown open, and the corpulent body of Uncle John staggered in, undisguisedly inebriated.

"I tol' you our time woul' come, Missy," he slurred. "Tonight's th' night." Grinning, he began unbuttoning his pants as he started toward her. "I wan to introduse you t' sumone. Sumone yur gonna git t' know a lot bet'r."

Jarred completely awake by her uncle's appearance, Melissa leapt to her feet, ignoring the hair wreath as it fell from her lap to the floor. John Hund's bloated body blocked her exit and stood only a couple of feet from her. Instinctively, she moved around the small room to position the bed between herself and her adversary, her heart beating furiously in her breast. She had never expected her uncle would go this far. Since her arrival, he had cast lurid looks her way and surreptitiously let his hands glide across her most intimate body parts when he thought no one would notice, heady with his power over his niece. Initially horrified and humiliated by his actions, Melissa had learned to endure them. She had noticed that any reaction on her part seemed to give him more pleasure and encouraged him to act even more boldly. To trouble her dear Aunt Georgina would have been fruitless since her aunt's impotence regarding her husband's behavior was obvious. Temporarily, at least, Melissa felt trapped. She had no money left to support herself. She had hoped to have heard from Alicia by now. Until today, Uncle John had never violated her in public, and Melissa had always felt that if worse came to worst, she could easily escape her obese uncle. He probably realized that, too, since his advances had not yet gone beyond the fondling.

Holding his trousers up with one hand, her uncle was coming around to her side of the bed. With no room to dart past him, Melissa would be backed up against the wall in two more steps. Panic-stricken, she leapt onto the bed, hoping to flee through the door. As she did, she felt a hand grab her ankle, pulling her roughly to the floor. The quilt she clung to in desperation came with her but offered little protection. She felt the skin being torn from her knees and elbows as her body was dragged into position against the rough-hewn wooden floor.

Someone screamed. Melissa struggled to breathe as her uncle's massive body straddled her back. The weight against her lightened as the drunken man wrapped strands of her hair around his hand, painfully forcing Melissa to turn and face him. Once again pinned helplessly under her uncle's weight, Melissa squeezed her eyes shut, fearing the sight she'd see if she opened them. Terror seized her as she felt the cloth of her soft, white gown being yanked up above her waist. Her uncle's calloused hands invaded her most private region, rubbing her softness roughly as she bucked up, trying to free herself.

"Wild filly, ain't ya!" her uncle exclaimed in glee. Then, as though he were attempting to calm a terrified horse, "Ah, honey, it'll be good for you. Don't you worry none. I'm a mas'er at this. You'n me—wur gonna hav' a fine time. 'Sides, you owe me." John Hund's tone suddenly turned harsh again as he rent the top portion of the cotton gown.

Her breasts exposed, Melissa screamed again, this time cognizant that it was her own voice she heard.

"It's over, John."

Aunt Georgina's soft but firm voice came from the doorway. Melissa's eyes opened in time to see her uncle's face transformed by what could only be hatred. The look lasted so briefly she might have imagined it, though, for the next thing she knew, she was no longer burdened by her uncle's weight.

"Now, Georgie, it ain't what you thin'. I've bin tryin' ta administer t' our poor niece. Seems she's 'ad a misshap. Ain't tha' right, Missy?" Perhaps in an attempt to deny the obvious rejection by his niece, even to his own male ego, John Hund took an uncharacteristically defensive stance.

Before Melissa could respond, Aunt Georgina spoke again.

"No, John, not this time. No more lies. I've seen your leers, and yes, I've even seen you grope my niece when you thought I wasn't looking. I'm ashamed I haven't acted sooner. Forgive me, Melissa. I was afraid."

At her aunt's direct address, Melissa picked herself up to face the other woman, holding together her torn gown. She gasped as she noticed her aunt toted her uncle's rifle.

"You crippl'd bitch," John Hund, transformed to his old self, raged as he struggled to finish buttoning his pants. "You don' talk to me lak that. I've giv'n you food 'n' shelter when no one else'd have you. You owe me, and yur bitch niece owes me, too. I bin providin' fur her these last cup'l months, too."

"Don't come any closer, John," Aunt Georgina threatened.

Ignoring the warning, Melissa's uncle took two staggered steps toward his wife and lunged for the rifle, wrenching it from Aunt Georgina's grasp. As he did, the gun discharged, and Melissa's aunt fell to the ground with a sharp cry of pain.

"Aunt Georgina!" Melissa screamed as her uncle bent to the injured woman.

"This ish all yur fault, Missy," Uncle John accused as he straightened and started toward her again.

Spying the fire poker propped beside the empty fireplace, Melissa grabbed it and prepared to defend herself. Fortunately, the drunken man, although much larger, was no match for a younger, sober female. Mustering up every ounce of strength she had, Melissa struck him squarely on the side of his head. John Hund landed on the floor with a loud thud.

Seeing he was at least temporarily no threat, Melissa

hurried to her aunt's side and gave a silent prayer of thanks when she found the woman still breathing.

"Flee, child. Go to Alicia," her aunt managed weakly.

"But, Aunt Georgina, I can't leave you," the girl protested.

"Don't argue. John is dangerous to you. Take the money from the pantry jar. Please!" Melissa's aunt pleaded between long gasps. "Make haste, child, and forgive me."

Georgina Hund closed her eyes in exhaustion. Melissa planted a kiss on her plump cheek before hurrying to do as her aunt asked. The money jar, which was simply a canning jar Melissa's aunt used to squirrel away sums "for a rainy day," as she put it, was empty. Uncle John must have raided it earlier, as he often did before he went into town, and spent it on whiskey.

Poker still in hand, Melissa returned to her bedroom. Across the room, John Hund's body remained as still as it had been after her blow although she could see his bloated gut rise and fall slightly. Keeping a cautious eye on him, she stooped down to speak to her aunt, still lying in the doorway.

"Aunt Georgina," she cried mournfully as she sensed life had left the older woman's body.

Blinded by tears, Melissa used her fingertips to close her aunt's eyes and gave her one last kiss. Rising, she crossed the small room and stepped carefully over her uncle's body, alert to any chance he might be feigning his state of unconsciousness. As she retrieved the clothes she had been wearing that day, she spied the hair wreath lying to the side of her armchair. Scooping it up, she wrapped it in the clothing bundle and escaped into the night.

Chapter Two

Sparing no time for thought, Melissa changed out of her nightgown in the barn as quickly as her trembling fingers would allow, gathered up her skirts, and began to run in the direction of town. Her dress was an impediment, and she suffered new injuries to her already scraped knees and elbows each time she stumbled. With fierce resolve, she picked herself up, ignoring the pain, and continued on, hoping to put as much distance between her and John Hund as she could before he recovered his senses. Although a full moon made up for her lack of a lantern, the darkness still hindered her progress. The sound of angry, barking dogs coming from one homestead she passed caused her heart to leap into her throat, and she sent up a desperate prayer the sounds wouldn't result in their owner shooting wildly at an interloper. Not too long afterwards, her ears picked up the more frightening howl of coyotes reverberating in the distance, causing a brief chill to run through her despite the oppressive heat that had subsided only slightly with nightfall. The thick air continued to press down like a too-heavy blanket, finally causing her lungs to protest. Slowing her pace, she walked the remainder of the way as fast as she could, stopping once behind some tall scrubs to relieve a screaming bladder.

The dusty streets of Nebraska City, Nebraska, were mostly quiet when Melissa arrived. Now that she had reached her destination, she had no idea what her next move should be. Her driving thought had simply been to get away from the horror at her uncle's house as quickly as possible, but she had no doubt he would follow as soon as he regained consciousness and discovered her gone. *What to do*, she worried, as she realized it was her word against his. Her uncle was known in town, whereas she, who had come to Nebraska only two months ago, was not. *If only I could leave with the wagon train.*

As quickly as the thought entered her mind, Melissa accepted it. Although many of the travelers had left to camp on the outskirts of the town as they awaited their departure time, several wagons remained along the main street, their canvas-covered tops illuminated by the moon. Her sister and Jesse had set out in a similar conveyance, and she again wondered briefly why she had not yet heard from them before forcing herself to focus on the matter at hand. Perhaps she could stow away in an unoccupied wagon being used primarily to transport extra goods. As she began her search, some wagons were relatively easy to pass by, the inhabitants having tied back both the front and rear canvases in hopes of enjoying a breeze, however slight. She discovered this could not be counted on, however. When she approached a wagon with its canvases still down and began to lift the cloth door ever so slightly, a brusque voice demanded, "Who goes there?"

"Sorry, my mistake," Melissa whispered in reply, dropping the canvas as though it were a hot ash. She passed up a few wagons as she stole away as quietly as she could manage at a rapid pace.

As soon as she was assured her pounding heart would not give her away, she resumed her search for an uninhabited one. In most cases, the moon proved to be her friend again, shining a dim light through the canvas tops, enabling her to make out the contents of the wagons somewhat. She was disappointed, although not surprised, to discover that most of those designated to transport cargo were packed so tightly she would not have room to draw a breath even if she were able to press herself into any small remaining space. Although she felt like giving up, memories of the evening of terror spurred her on. She had no other choice.

She was forced to duck behind a wagon a couple times to avoid being seen by an inebriated customer stumbling out of a saloon before she finally discovered a wagon that appeared to have some extra space, with no heads apparent in the moonlight. Refusing to believe her good fortune, Melissa entered the wagon as slowly and soundlessly as she could, opening her eyes wide as she tried to see better in the dim interior that appeared to hold mainly boxes of supplies. As her eyes adjusted, she caught her breath. An elongated shape lay snuggled against one side of the wagon. *Could it be an unusually sound sleeper?* Empowered by a bravery borne from fear, Melissa crawled quietly up to the mass for closer scrutiny. She exhaled in relief when she discovered it was simply a bedroll with no body. *Well, I can provide the body*, she decided quickly. *Anyone planning to use it tonight would already be doing so.*

The task was not an easy one as Melissa unrolled and then tried to reroll the bedding around her long body, making certain no part of her was visible just in case its owner checked it out one final time prior to the morning's departure. The result was a hot, uncomfortable cocoon, but she was grateful for it, nonetheless.

Sleep evaded her as the events of the evening replayed themselves in Melissa's mind. She recalled her uncle's rough hands mauling her private regions and unconsciously squeezed her legs together at the thought. She saw her aunt's lifeless blue eyes staring back at her when she had returned to her that last time. Memories of her dead parents and the happy life she had shared with them and her sister floated by as though they had all been a dream. Silent tears of despair and desolation flowed down her cheeks as she realized how truly alone she now was. Thankfully, the tears gave way to sleep at some point because dawn was just breaking when she was awakened by discordant sounds and commotion.

"She must be around somewheres," a voice she recognized as her uncle's boomed out of the cacophony. "I'm offering a big reward. She done kilt my wife, she did, and took off with our savings." John Hund completed his speech with a description of his niece. He had sobered up since their encounter. Although she should not have been surprised, Melissa was horrified to hear his accusations against her.

"How big a reward?" a voice inquired.

"Big enough," John Hund replied. "Why? You seen her?"

"Well," the voice continued, "there was a girl poking around these here wagons in the wee hours. Woke me up. I couldn't see her plain-like, though."

"I knew it!" John Hund said, with the excitement of a hunter who has sighted his prey. "Who wants to help me search?"

"Whoa there, fella," a new voice interrupted. "I'm responsible for this here train, and nobody's going to be searching anything. We don't have time for that, and I don't want my travelers upset afore we even get started."

Melissa decided the speaker must be the same straw-haired man who had addressed the crowds the day before.

"Looky here," her uncle argued. "You don't understand, mister. My niece done murdered my wife, and I mean to find her."

"Ain't no concern of mine." The abrupt retort came quickly. "My job is to get this train moving, and *I* mean to do just that. Go take yur troubles to the sheriff."

Uncle John continued to argue, but his words must have fallen on deaf ears because Melissa heard no more from the wagon master. She held her breath, fearful her uncle would take it upon himself to start searching the wagons anyway. He must have thought better of it, though, because she finally heard retreating footsteps. Then only the rumble of indistinct voices remained, along with the whinnies, brays, and moos of the animals as they were being yoked to the wagons in preparation for the departure.

After several minutes had passed, she crawled forward quietly to peek out through the canvas flap opening, curiosity overcoming her fear. Her uncle had moved down the street and was now talking to none other than Lieutenant Bellamy. They were too far away for her to hear the conversation, but she could see the soldier nodding in agreement. Scared and confused, Melissa secreted herself in the bedding once again, resigned to endure the already sweltering heat in her hiding place. She had nowhere else to go, no one to whom to turn. She could only hope the owners of this particular wagon would be friendly and not too upset to find a stowaway.

She wondered who they were and where they had spent the night. Silently, she willed her heart to beat more softly. It seemed it would beat itself right out of her chest, and she worried that passersby could hear it. At the same time, she felt far removed from the world beyond her thin canvas shield. Hope-filled dreams, tearful goodbyes, Godspeeds, and children's queries were all within ear's reach and yet seemed so very remote.

Alert to any new sound or voice, she lay in preparedness. For what, she was not certain, but she felt it was surely better to be aware than to allow herself to be the victim of surprise. Every nerve in her body was activated as she waited for whatever might come next.

"Get much sleep last night, or did Rosie keep you too busy?" A voice that seemed to be nearing the wagon inquired.

"None of your business," the answer came. A lighthearted tone softened the effect of the words. "What about you, Al? Did your woman give you enough to keep you warm for the next couple of months?" Melissa felt fairly certain it was Lieutenant Bellamy's voice.

"I tried to commit every minute to memory to hold me over the long haul. Suzanne was most accommodating." After a short pause, the same speaker continued. "You sure we need to be heading out, Nat?"

"I'm sure. But if you care to stay, Al, you're free to do so. You know that."

"Nope. I'd follow you to the end of the earth and jump off with you, Nat. 'Sides, there's as good a girl in every port, right?"

"That may be true, but I don't think there're many ports where we're headed." Nat chuckled. "Have you seen Tom?"

"Tom found himself a woman, too. He must be having one helluva time. Here he comes now. Walking more bowlegged than ever," the voice belonging to Al chortled.

"Morning, Nat, Al," a new voice greeted. "We ready to get going?"

"Almost. Calhoune was just by doing a final check and said he'd be leading the way for the wagons already on the outskirts of town. He wants us to manage this group. We just need to hitch up the oxen and head out. Tom, would you handle the driving first?"

"Sure thing, Nat."

Melissa felt the wagon shift as someone—probably the man named Tom—climbed onto it. He seemed to be occupied by something on the outside, and Melissa almost began to breathe easier, thinking that perhaps she would be safe in her hiding place until they were well on their way. That thought was quickly dispelled when she heard him enter. Holding her breath, she listened as she sensed boxes being rearranged. Once, the intruder kicked her hiding place inadvertently as he moved about. She held her cry of pain captive and said a prayer of thanks when the man finished his inspection and returned to his outside chores. It wasn't too long afterward she felt the wagon begin to move forward slowly.

She had no idea how long they had been on the trail when the incessant rocking of the wagon came to a halt. The jubilant cheers she had heard from the other travelers as they were finally underway had been replaced by more subdued chatter although, even in her cocoon, she could sense the excitement in the air. Excitement she didn't share. Her bones and muscles ached from the chore of constantly bracing against the wagon's movements. She longed to be able to stand up and stretch. Becoming increasingly uncomfortable from the heat as the morning progressed, she had partially disengaged herself from the bedroll. Now she hurriedly rewound herself. She was physically and emotionally exhausted. And hungry. As the aroma of food anointed her senses, she wished she had partaken more heartily of her aunt's cooking the night before.

Her hunger was instantly forgotten when she realized someone was again entering the wagon. Abruptly, the bedroll was yanked off her, and she found herself staring into a face as black as the coal her father had mined.

"Thought you might be hungry, miss," her discoverer said, proffering a plate of beans and some hard tack. "An' you might be needing to use that as well," he continued, pointing to a bucket sitting atop some crates.

"No need to be skeared o' me, miss," the man said, responding to what must have been a look of sheer terror on her face. "I ain't gonna hurt you. I know what it's like to be in hidin'. I been there myself." Upon getting no response, he continued. "My name's Tom. What's yours?"

Still no answer.

"Well, if you ain't gonna talk, leastwise eat," he commented as his large black hands shoved the plate at her again.

This time Melissa took the dish. He continued his attempt at conversation as his ravenous stowaway ate.

"I knowed you was in here all along. You didn't do a very good job a' hidin' all your skirt, and when I kicked my bedroll, I knowed I had made contact with more than clothin'. I figured you was skeared enough, so I decided to let you be. I don't know what Nat and Al are gonna say about this, though, so you best be prepared for the worst. I'll hep you however I can."

The large black man was talking nonstop, no doubt in an attempt to soothe her, and Melissa did feel her heartbeat returning to normal somewhat. It was also becoming easier to swallow than it had been when she first took the plate he had offered.

"Want some more?" he asked, gesturing to the empty plate. She had devoured the meal.

Melissa didn't have time to respond before they were interrupted.

"Say, Tom..." Melissa's heart stopped as her eyes locked with those of the handsome lieutenant.

"What is this?" he demanded, his glare shifting to Tom.

"I found her stowed away in my bedroll, Nat. I figured she'd be hungry, so I brought her some food."

"Great. Just great!" Nat ran his fingers through his thick, wavy hair in exasperation. "What do you propose we do with her now?" Without waiting for an answer, Nat turned his questioning to the wide-eyed girl before him. "Just what are your intentions? Did you think you could remain hidden all the way to Denver? And what *right* do you have stowing away in *our* wagon?"

The barrage of questions stopped as Nat saw tears welling up in the frightened girl's eyes. After a few minutes of silence during which Melissa collected herself, Nat began again. This time more gently.

"Look, you can't stay with us. We're three men. There'd be nothing left of your reputation if it were discovered." An odd look suddenly passed over his face. It disappeared as quickly as it had appeared. "Your uncle claims you murdered his wife and stole some money. Is it true?"

Responding for the first time, she shook her head vehemently. Tears flowed silently and freely down her cheeks as the gate on her corral of emotions gave way. Lowering her head in a vain attempt to hide them, she admonished herself for not having a tighter rein on her emotions.

"Keep an eye on her, Tom," Nat ordered, with a look of what Melissa interpreted as disgust on his face as he exited the wagon.

"Don't you worry none, miss," Tom said after the lieutenant had left. "Nat won't do nothin' to hurt you. Now, I'll jus' sit outside a bit to give you a chance to use that bucket if nature demands. Call out when you're done, and I be emptyin' it for you."

Nat reappeared a half hour later and informed Melissa he had arranged for her to travel with the Averys, a middle-aged couple with two young children, Rachel and Joshua. A man of religion, Robert Avery hoped to establish a ministry in what he called the "wild country." As he motioned her to follow him, Nat explained that Melissa would be able to help Mrs. Avery with the cooking and the care of the children. Although she had no better plan in mind, it rankled her that this stranger had so arrogantly decided her fate for the next couple of months.

"And what right did you have to make these arrangements without bothering to consult me?" She lashed out at him, her brown eyes flashing angrily as she stopped dead in her tracks.

"I had every right, given that you presumed to use my wagon as a free ride out of town.

Of course, I might have demanded other payment," he shot back, turning and scanning her body in a way that made the meaning of his statement clear.

Melissa was too embarrassed to frame a response and resumed walking with her head down, feeling as trapped as any animal. *What had her uncle told him about her, and what must he think, having seen her uncle openly fondle her? Fine. She would travel with the Averys as cook and governess. But she would get even with this man who walked before her so self-assuredly. And once she got to Denver, no one would control her destiny again.*

Chapter Three

Melissa adjusted more happily to her new position than she had thought possible. The set daily routine suited her, enabling her to push unwelcome thoughts of the sorrow and horror she had recently endured to the back of her mind as she focused on the tasks at hand. She awakened each day just before dawn when she heard the emigrants on other wagons begin to stir, leaving Mrs. Avery and the children to sleep a bit longer. Mr. Avery, who made his bed under the wagon, rose about the same time and built a small fire before leaving her to prepare breakfast while he tended to his oxen and other necessary chores. Consisting of bacon, cornbread, and coffee, the daily fare was as monotonous as the trail had become. After a while, Melissa also incorporated johnny cakes and beans leftover from the previous night's supper into the morning menu. The children usually poked their heads out when they smelled the food cooking and scrambled out to join Melissa. If Mrs. Avery hadn't made an appearance by the time the meal was ready, which was often the case, Melissa prepared a plate for her to eat in the wagon.

The fire had to be extinguished and the wagon ready to roll again an hour or so later. Melissa learned to cook a little extra for the morning meal, which, accompanied by some of the dried fruit the Averys had among their provisions, served as lunch when the train halted briefly at midday. After the train finally stopped for the day, typically around four or five in the afternoon, Melissa again tended to the cooking and cleanup. And again, there wasn't much variety, but it was encouraging to see Mr. Avery and the children devour the dish she created with beans, rice, and bacon, served with cornmeal bread leftovers.

The only thorn was Mrs. Avery, who had scrutinized Melissa from head to toe with her dark, darting, beady eyes that first day before whining to her husband that she had no need of such help. Failing to get his attention with that, the following day she proclaimed she had had a dream that the girl had been sent by Satan. Fortunately for Melissa, Robert Avery was unimpressed by his wife's visions. Unwilling to engage in an argument with her, however, he simply bowed his head and walked away, leaving his wife to scream after him.

Despite her protests, Mrs. Avery was lazy and more than willing to relinquish her chores to Melissa, claiming a debilitating back pain caused by the relentless jostling of the wagon. Rachel, obviously starved for motherly attention for the first five years of her life, clung to Melissa immediately, and Melissa quickly fell in love with the child who became her shadow.

One evening while Rachel was helping Melissa prepare supper for the family, the girl abruptly proclaimed, "I hope I grow up to be as pretty as you."

Not having given her physical appearance much thought over the past couple of years, Melissa was initially both flattered and startled by the young girl's words. She had been too involved with other people's lives: helping her sister plan her wedding, helping her mother care for her dying father, and, finally, taking care of her dying mother alone. Although she had inherited her mother's high cheekbones and full, heart-shaped lips, she knew she wasn't the delicate beauty Catherine Sullivan had been. While her mother had been barely five feet tall, with coal-black hair and sparkling green eyes, Melissa had inherited her height from her father, along with his chestnut-colored hair. Her eyes were also brown, like her father's, but with elusive green flecks on their outer rims.

"My father used to have a saying: 'Beauty's only skin deep, ugly's to the bone. When beauty is dead and gone, old ugly will hold his own,'" Melissa finally replied.

Wrinkling her nose, the younger girl queried, "What's that mean?"

"Well, I think it means that if you're a good person on the inside, you will appear pretty on the outside, regardless of what you really look like. Haven't you ever known someone you didn't think was pretty until after you got to know them? And then you thought they were?" Melissa elaborated the point.

"No," the five-year-old replied emphatically, but she remained quiet and pensive for the rest of the evening.

Two-year-old Joshua was another matter. Melissa was amazed his mother could continue to ignore such a lovable child. Always smiling, with a stocky build that reminded Melissa of a tree stump, Josh amused himself when at camp by running from wagon to wagon and greeting its inhabitants with a palm-to-palm slap. Tom christened him with the nickname "Happycakes," which was quickly adopted by most of the other travelers as well. Josh clearly adored Nat, who often let the small boy ride several miles with him on the front of his saddle. For that, Melissa was grateful. While she tried to make up for his mother's indifference, the boy needed some male attention.

It wasn't so much that Robert Avery intentionally ignored his progeny. He often just seemed preoccupied and answered their questions absently. When Emma Avery, on the other hand, deigned to turn her attention to her children, it was always in the form of rebukes. They were giving her a headache with all their noise. Couldn't they play more quietly? What unappreciative children they were!

The rutted trail did not improve Mrs. Avery's spirits. She whined incessantly as she was bounced about in the wagon, declining to walk beside Mr. Avery as he coaxed his team of oxen along because the sun was too hot for her delicate skin. Like most of the other emigrants, Melissa much preferred walking alongside the wagon to the bruising ride inside, even though it meant constantly swatting away the no-see-ums on most days. She was grateful she hadn't developed any blisters, a common complaint of a lot of the other travelers. Occasionally, she and the children joined Mrs. Avery in the wagon when Rachel and Joshua got tired. Once, Melissa attempted to make a game of the constant rocking with the two youngsters, but it came to an abrupt end when Mrs. Avery backhanded Rachel across the mouth for giggling, cutting her young daughter's lip.

****

There had been no break from the sweltering heat in the few days since the journey had begun. The tall grasses growing along the trail waved mockingly in the slight breeze that failed to provide the travelers any comfort. Tom always joined her for a while during his daily rounds, intriguing her with his stories as he walked beside her while leading the children on his horse to give their little legs a break. He seemed to have designated himself her guardian angel, unlike Nat, who virtually ignored her existence. He explained he had been a slave on the Virginia plantation owned by Nat's father, Patrick Bellamy. Tom's mother had been Nat's nanny, and the two boys had grown up as brothers. Nat had taught Tom to read, against Patrick Bellamy's rules, and when Patrick had learned of the boys' misdeeds, Tom was the one who got whipped, not Nat. Tom had never blamed Nat, though, and Nat, feeling terrible about his friend's fate, was the one who put salve on the cuts made by the strap.

Most of the other emigrants snubbed Melissa initially. The gossip surrounding her had no doubt been embellished with each repetition, so Melissa could hardly blame them. She suspected her friendship with Tom led some tongues to wag harder. The war between the states aside, many Northerners shared the Southerners' belief that the Negroes should remain slaves. Many more did not think it proper for a black man and a white woman to be walking side by side.

Mavis O'Leary was an exception. Shortly after Melissa had been "assigned" to the Averys, she had excused herself to take care of bodily functions, which were screaming for attention. As she started for the sparse growth of foliage that would allow her at least some semblance of privacy, Mavis had appeared out of nowhere.

"Never ye mind. Take care o' yer business, and I'll watch for ye."

Startled, Melissa turned to observe a girl a few years her elder, with a thick mop of raven curls.

"I'll stand guard at the bushes with me back to ye," the girl continued, matter-of-factly.

"Thank you," Melissa collected herself enough to reply.

As they walked the short distance from the wagons, Melissa's self-appointed safekeeper identified herself.

"I'm Mavis O'Leary."

When Melissa offered no reply, Mavis continued. "And ye be the girl accused of murdering her aunt."

Inhaling sharply at the blunt statement, Melissa struggled to formulate a reply, but before she found the words, they reached their destination. Mavis bowed with a flourish, indicating to Melissa that the honor of use was all hers. Numbly, Melissa shrank behind some shrubbery as Mavis rattled on.

"Not to worry. Ye're not the talk of the train—yet. I'm quite good at puzzles, and I heard yer uncle asking around about ye—or someone who very nearly fits yer description."

Noting Melissa's despair as she reappeared beside her, Mavis sought to smooth things over.

"There now. I dinna believe the old man for one minute. He had a real shifty look to him if ye ask me. And I know me men. Been with all kinds. Fact is, I keep track by cutting notches in me leather belt here."

She laughed boldly at Melissa's shocked expression.

"I'm just tellin' it like it is. One thing I am is a straight shooter. Ye want honesty, Mavis'll give it to ye. Ye may not always like what ye hear, but ye can be sure it's the truth. And I expect the same of me friends."

Mavis had lowered her voice slightly and made the last statement in a warning tone.

"Speaking of men, there's a new notch I'd surely like to make," Melissa's new acquaintance said appreciatively.

Following the other girl's eyes, Melissa discovered she was referring to Nat. Nat seemed to have been looking in their direction as well. She felt a twinge of jealousy, which did not make sense. She hated the man who had coldly handed her off to the Avery family. Still, she could not deny his sensual allure. Even from this distance, Melissa could see his muscular thighs straining against the cloth of his trousers as he sat astride his mount. She must have made some unconscious sound of appreciation for what she saw.

"I see ye agree," Mavis chuckled. "Ye ever bedded a man, lassie?"

Melissa flushed as she shook her head no, remembering her uncle's attempted invasion of her.

"I thought not. Ye don't look the type. I do. Anyone with tits as big as these does."

Mavis threw back her shoulders to further emphasize the assets of which she was so obviously proud. Melissa had to smile. Mavis spoke of her breasts in the same manner that a farmer might boast about a prize watermelon he had grown. They were the only thing big about her otherwise petite frame. There was no doubt many men were enchanted by this dark Irish lass. Melissa felt like a wallflower next to her.

"Watch me land him, lassie." Mavis winked and started off in the direction of Nat, who had dismounted and was conversing with two other men.

****

"Nat's a fine man, miss."

Melissa blushed as she realized she had been distracted from Tom's latest story and was staring at Nat and Mavis, who seemed to be together frequently since the day Mavis had announced her intentions toward him. Nat was laughing. No doubt at one of Mavis's bawdy jokes. She had quite a repertoire of them, which a number of the men seemed to find quite entertaining.

"I knows you two didn't get off to a good start, but you oughta give him another chance."

"Like he gave me a chance?" Melissa retorted sharply. "Anyway, I don't recall his asking for one." She softened her reply upon seeing the chastised look on the Tom's face.

"You know, you reminds me of his sister." Tom adroitly changed the subject. "Nat jes' adores that sister of his."

"What're you two chawing about?" Alston Moore asked as he rode up and dismounted to walk beside them. Nat's other companion had gradually warmed up to Melissa as well, and the pair of them kept Melissa entertained with their constant bantering. Where Tom was tall, dark, and broad, Alston was shorter than Melissa by several inches, with a wiry build. His full, brown beard was in desperate need of taming, as was the thinning hair on his head, which seemed to point in as many directions as a weathercock. Melissa had initially found it difficult to look at him. One of his large, round, baby-blue eyes would wander off in another direction, and Melissa wasn't certain which eye to track. Sensing her discomfort, Alston matter-of-factly had pointed to his good eye.

"Follow this one, honey, and pay the other one no

nevermind. It goes its own way and keeps a watch out for any wild injuns for me."

The two men had Melissa laughing out loud as they recounted some of their past fiascos, each blaming the other for the outcome, when the spell was broken by Nat's sudden appearance.

"Calhoune wants to see us immediately."

Nat seemed to make a conscious effort to avoid glancing in her direction. Melissa also kept her eyes averted to avoid looking at him. Besides the cavalier manner in which he had dumped her on the Averys without her consent, he was obviously a traitor. No matter that he was a traitor to the Confederacy, which was a wrong cause. After all, a man who turned against his own kind was surely not to be trusted. Mavis could have him!

Chapter Four

The wagon train had proceeded north for the better part of a week, progressing slowly and erratically at first as the men grew accustomed to handling their oxen-pulled wagons. While many of the wagons were horse-drawn and some were mule-drawn, oxen were cheaper and stronger than horses and also cheaper than mules, at one-third the cost. Melissa had been despondent to learn that only six miles had been covered on the first day, worried that Uncle John might yet catch up with her. She breathed her first sigh of relief when, after the men had become less green-handed, the train was managing ten miles on a good day. Silently, Melissa prayed for even more distance between herself and her treacherous uncle. Why he had not followed the train when it pulled out of Nebraska City, she could only guess. Perhaps his certain hangover, the chastising he had received from the wagon master, and concern over his crops had all played a part. Maybe appearances drove him to give her aunt a decent burial. Certainly not love. Whatever the reason, Melissa was thankful.

She had initially enjoyed gazing ahead at the rolling hills as the wagons moved in a slow, steady stream toward a new future. The excitement of the other travelers was contagious. However, after the first week, the gently sloped hills gave way to flat, parched ground that seemed to extend forever. Although the level land made for easier handling of the animals and allowed the wagons to spread out across the fields, bobbing across the landscape like dancing mushrooms, the ebullience that had originally accompanied the train disappeared with the tree-covered mounds they had left behind. The emigrants' moods now seemed as dreary as the terrain ahead and as dry as the short, brownish grasses that covered it. There had still been no rain, and the humidity hung like a low cloud over the wagon train. Damp with perspiration, Melissa's clothes clung to her body, and she longed for a bath and the opportunity to wash her undergarments, at least, even though her dress sorely needed it as well. She supposed she could be thankful that its drab brown color disguised its filthiness somewhat.

She found the monotony of the landscape nearly unbearable as she trudged along beside the Avery wagon. Nor was she the only one experiencing travel fatigue, based on the short tempers that flared up frequently these days. One morning she heard one of the emigrants threaten to shoot a man in a nearby wagon for snoring too loudly the night before. Heated arguments between spouses carried across the plains, and mothers were heard issuing sharp reprimands to their children, who were given to more frequent periods of crankiness. Melissa suspected that was due to boredom, so she did her best to keep Rachel and Joshua entertained by engaging them in a game of finding clouds that resembled familiar creatures.

While they were playing this game one day, a great dark demon appeared in the distance. Before Melissa could react, a giant wall of dirt and debris advanced rapidly, rumbling louder and growing larger as it approached, turning the blue sky to ink black. Panicked screams and shouts competed with the howling wind as the travelers scrambled for the shelter of their wagons while the visibility quickly dropped to zero and a thick, dusty odor assaulted their nostrils. Maintaining an air of calmness she didn't feel as her hair was being painfully whipped around her and gritty pellets assaulted her body, Melissa hastily helped her terrified, crying charges into their wagon, crawling in behind them herself. Mr. Avery followed quickly after and hurriedly tightened the ropes of the canvas top in an effort to keep the demon out, ignoring Mrs. Avery's complaints of being too crowded. The other emigrants did likewise, but the canvas tops provided only minor protection. Children bawled and cowered in fear as the storm blew through ferociously, ripping loose the rope ties of some of the wagons, freeing the canvases to flap violently in the wind. Just as frightening were the sounds of the animals squealing and bellowing as they loudly stomped the ground. The adults, clinging to the nearest, heaviest item in the wagon to brace themselves, attempted to comfort the children. After what was probably only five to ten minutes, but seemed much longer, the monster exited almost as quickly as it had entered, leaving everyone and everything covered with a thin coating of grime as it continued on its journey. The air remained choked with dust several hours later, forcing emigrants to cover their mouths and noses as they crawled from their wagons to inspect for damage. Miraculously, most required only minor repairs that wouldn't prevent them from continuing forward.

Melissa was surprised to see Nat come riding up to check on the well-being of the Avery wagon almost as soon as the storm had passed through. She was overcome with a sense of relief at the sight of him. Despite the fact that she despised the man's arrogant, authoritarian attitude toward her, she had to admit she was glad to see him unharmed and realized that his mere presence made her feel safe. *Did his appearance mean that he might care about what happened to her after all?* Almost as soon as the thought entered her mind, she scolded herself for the ridiculousness of it. No doubt he was worried about the welfare of the Avery children, whom he clearly adored. He assured her that Tom and Al were fine and busy helping other travelers with some of their problems before he left to check on how Mavis had fared. A twinge of some emotion—certainly not jealousy—flitted through her when he mentioned who he was visiting next, even though she, too, wanted to be certain her friend had escaped injury. Her thoughts over the next several days seemed as hazy as the sky above, and it took just as long before Melissa no longer felt like she was chewing tiny bits of gravel mixed in her food.

****

Twenty-eight days into the journey, the emigrants arrived at Fort Kearny amid much happy hooting and hollering. They camped on the outskirts, looking forward to a few days of rest and renewal. Located on a slightly elevated piece of land a few miles from the Platte River, which the train had been following, the fort consisted of a number of sod, frame, and adobe buildings seemingly built in a haphazard manner around a large open area bounded by numerous cottonwood trees. A Union flag waved at the newcomers from its tall flagstaff in the center of it all. One of the buildings housed a blacksmith facility, which Colonel Stone, the fort's commander, generously allowed the travelers to use free of charge for repairs incurred during the dust storm. Soldiers were everywhere, and Melissa and the children took advantage of the security they provided, wandering some distance from their wagon when Rachel and Joshua spotted butterflies flitting among a bunch of wildflowers that had survived the heat of the summer and ran in that direction. Mr. Avery and several other men went duck hunting, leaving Mrs. Avery to rest in the wagon.

The sweet perfume-like scent of the milkweed flower was intoxicating as Melissa and the children grew closer to the draw for the butterflies, and the children asked if they might pick some of the round pink-and-white clusters of flowers to present to their mother. Smiling at the innocent resilience of the young who wanted to do something nice for a woman who did nothing but screech and yell at them, Melissa agreed. Perhaps it was an unconscious attempt to gain their mother's favor, her love? Melissa contemplated this as they headed back toward the wagon.

"She can remain here at the fort until a relative can send money for her return. I cannot be responsible for her presence on this train."

Melissa froze upon hearing the easily recognizable voice of the wagon master. First fear and then anger thundered through her as she realized that she was the subject of the conversation. Trying to remain calm, Melissa whispered to the children, "Okay, now, take these to your mommy. Be very quiet so you can surprise her. Won't your mommy love these pretty flowers and be happy?"

As the children scampered off, Melissa inched closer to the voices. She heard Mr. Avery declaring that he and his wife found her services invaluable only to hear Watson Calhoune reiterate that he did not wish to be responsible for the girl. He could be accused of white slavery, he contended, and in the midst of the Civil War, he was not certain what punishment that crime might carry. No, he would not risk it.

Melissa bristled at what she had heard. Again, others were attempting to determine her fate without consulting her. The nerve!

"Curiosity killed the cat—and you're much too pretty to die!"

Startled, Melissa gasped as she turned to see a Union soldier standing directly behind her. He was tall and slender, with shoulder-length hair that reminded her of the color of the sand on the Lake Michigan beach she and her family had visited one summer. His eyes were the elusive blue of a misty morning sky, and they twinkled as he teasingly challenged her with an amused turn to his lips.

"I'm Captain Precter. I didn't mean to embarrass you. Can we still be friends?" He flashed a boyish grin that said he was confident of her forgiveness. Captain Precter was obviously not accustomed to rejection.

"I...I must see to my charges," Melissa stammered after a moment as she hurried past the stunned man, confusion, humiliation, and inexplicable fear raging within her.

Jim Precter turned to watch her stumbling progress with a satisfied smile. He had been watching her surreptitiously since her appearance on the train. She matched the description her uncle had given, all right, and he was ready to return her for the sizeable reward the old man had offered. Having seen her, he wanted more than her uncle's money, however. He wanted her. She reminded him of an unbroken colt, and he was just the man to break her.

He had kept his distance until now to avoid arousing her suspicions. Once they had reached Fort Kearny, he dug out the uniform he'd taken from a soldier he had found it necessary to kill during a recent stagecoach robbery. He figured it would come in handy at some point, he thought smugly. Having the girl believe he was a captain stationed at the fort would make his task easier. And it might even make him more attractive to her. He smiled broadly at the knowledge that many women found him irresistible anyway, uniform or no. He played with them until they bored him. Yep, Jim Precter had a trail of broken hearts behind him. But this niece female seemed different, he reflected. He doubted he'd easily tire of her.

Precter had also overheard the debate on the fate of the girl. Striding purposely toward the fort, he rehearsed the story he had already devised to make him an easy choice for her escort back to Nebraska City. If all turned out as he planned, he'd get the girl and the reward money to boot.

Chapter Five

Watson Calhoune sat pondering the request of one of his train's organizers. In the nearly three weeks he'd worked with Nathanial Bellamy, he had grown to respect the younger man, but he wondered at the wisdom of this request. As wagon master, Watson had been informed of the stowaway on his train and was appreciative of the speed and efficiency with which Lieutenant Bellamy had handled the situation before Watson had even known the problem existed. He had observed the girl himself as she entertained her charges and admired the deftness with which she handled that eternal bitch, Emma Avery. He was certain she was not guilty of the theft and murder charges of which she was accused, and his brief confrontation with her uncle had been enough to convince him that he didn't like the man. Still, he wanted no trouble on this train. Dealing with all the whiners and serving as a mediator for the petty squabbles that had already erupted among some of the emigrants was hard enough. Hell, he wasn't cut out to be a nanny to this group. He had only agreed to lead the train because it seemed the only way he could get back to the Colorado Territory and his business of fur trapping, and now it looked like the train's progress would be delayed at least a week since the army would not let them advance farther until a scout party returned. Hostile Indians were rumored to have attacked a wagon train that left the fort five days earlier. A lone rider had come galloping into Fort Kearny the previous night with the announcement, requesting that the army send an escort to accompany what remained of the train to safety.

"Captain Precter at your service, sir."

Watson's thoughts were interrupted by the appearance of a man he recognized from his train. He was somewhat surprised to see the man in army attire. Noting this, Precter launched into a plausible explanation he had already concocted.

"I had to keep a low profile on the train, sir. I was assigned to gather information on some recent stagecoach robberies that have occurred in Nebraska recently. They are thought to be the work of Confederates, masking as Union soldiers, and I greatly suspect so-called Lieutenant Bellamy and his two cohorts of being just that. I have informed my superiors, and they will take care of matters from here," he lied. "Until they have decided how they will deal with it, they request that you not speak of this to anyone nor approach Bellamy about it, for fear of arousing his suspicion. They may want to put another tail on the three as the train heads west to find out what they're up to."

That should keep Calhoune from discovering his duplicity until it was too late, Precter thought smugly. He considered bringing up the subject of the girl, but decided it was wiser not to play all his cards at once. He had heard that the train's advance had been stalled, so he had time. Satisfied with the older man's silent nod in response and thankful he was not barraged with questions for which he might not have ready answers, he retreated in the direction of the fort. He planned to announce his presence to the commanding officer with yet another invented explanation he hoped would be convincing enough to allow him to continue his charade while the wagon train was camped there.

Watson Calhoune had questions all right. Plenty of them. After the soldier had departed, he considered the man's accusations. Truthfully, Watson himself had initially questioned Nathanial Bellamy's supposed devotion to the Union cause. Although the man wore Federal Army issue attire, Watson was aware that Confederate soldiers, reduced to rag-tags, often stole the clothing from fallen Federals, wearing the Union belt buckle upside down to express their derision. While Nat's belt buckle had been in the upright position, that didn't necessarily prove his innocence. Still, after being around Bellamy and observing him, he had come to like the man, and he wasn't too sure about this Precter fellow. The man talked too smoothly to suit him, and Watson Calhoune was a good judge of character. Damn, he didn't even care who won this ridiculous war. He only wanted to be allowed to go on with his own fur-trapping business. He decided to keep a closed mouth and a watchful eye. As for Bellamy's earlier request, well, he would decide on that later.

****

Melissa, having decided that Uncle John was not in pursuit, was thankful for the rest the delay would bring. Mavis had befriended one of the fort's laundresses, a simple woman named Sarah, who agreed to let them use her facilities to wash up. The tub of warm water set up in Sarah's tent was a welcome change to the quick, cold sponge baths Melissa was forced to use on the trail, which hardly seemed to remove any of the dust and grime of the trip. After giving her body a thorough scrub, she sank down to wet her hair, which remained knotted with dirt from the sandstorm. A comb she had designed using a small, generously twigged tree limb had been incapable of detangling it. The ability to finally wash the filth from it felt delicious.

She was reluctant to finish bathing and dress again in her only outfit, which had not been scrubbed and, at this point, must smell worse than a skunk. She had finally managed to launder her undergarments a few times on the trail, letting them dry while the wagon train was camped at night, but her outer garments would never have dried, and Mrs. Avery had not offered any of her precious wardrobe to Melissa, nor had any of the other women on the train. Most traveled with the barest necessities, Melissa knew. Mavis would have, but Melissa would have looked ridiculous in Mavis's clothes. They were very different in size.

She had resigned herself to donning her dirty dress when Sarah called to her from outside the tent's flap. "Missy, when you're done, I have a fresh dress for you to wear. A most handsome soldier—his name was Proctor, or something like that—gave it to me to give to you."

Proctor? Melissa knew no one of that name. *Precter? Could it have come from the captain she had met the day before? But why? And how had he known she would be here, in the laundress's tent?*

Regardless, Melissa was too grateful to question the gift or its sender and accepted the dress from Sarah through the flap of the tent. It was a simple, somewhat faded, calico blue dress. Though the laced cuffs of the white, detachable undersleeves were beginning to show signs of wear, the dress seemed quite serviceable, and it fit Melissa perfectly. Her benefactor must be a woman as tall as she, she reflected, for the dress modestly covered her ankles. The neckline, lower than Melissa was accustomed to, was trimmed in white lace, matching the lace on the sleeves and hem. Melissa hoped that enough of her was covered, as she yanked on the bodice to pull it farther up.

"Why, you look a sight better than when you went in there, Missy," Sarah exclaimed upon her exit from the close quarters of the tent. "That captain must be sweet on you to have gone to all the trouble. A real charmer, he is." She reached into her apron pocket. "And here, he gave me these to give to you, too."

Melissa was stunned as she gazed down at the two exquisite silver combs she now held in her hand. *Why? The captain hardly knew her!* She shook her head as though to shake the cobwebs out. Maybe she was just being too suspicious, given what she had recently endured at the hands of men.

"Here, let me brush that beautiful hair of yours. Lordie, I wish I had been blest with hair like yours, but God just didn't see fit, and it's not my place to question Him, I reckon."

Before Melissa could respond, Sarah had grabbed up her own brush and was tugging at the tangles of Melissa's long curls. It felt luxurious. The makeshift comb Melissa had created had been less than adequate, but it had served to remove most of the tangles so that she at least felt somewhat less unkempt. Now, the feel of the brush bristles gently stimulating her scalp was magnificent, and she thanked Sarah profusely before she left to return to the wagon.

"And just where have you been off to? These

children are a handful!" Mrs. Avery exclaimed before noticing Melissa's fresh look. "Where did you get that dress? Did you steal it? Mr. Avery will not be happy. And look at you, practically hanging out of it. You're beginning to look more and more like that whore, Mavis, you spend so much time with. I knew I was right. You're Satan's own! Mr. Avery is sure to believe it when he sees you in that get-up!"

Melissa's uplifted spirits were quickly deflated by the sharp needle of Mrs. Avery's tongue. Offering no response, she collected the children, who had been screaming gleefully as they chased each other around the wagon, and prepared them for their bedrolls.

"Gee, Melissa, you look beautiful," Rachel commented when she saw her.

"A bedtime story," little Joshua demanded as she tucked the little guy in while Mrs. Avery kept her nose stuck in her Bible.

"No! No more stories!" Mrs. Avery shouted at them. "Stories are just fantasies put there by the devil to tempt us to want more out of life than we actually deserve."

Melissa was taken aback by this outbreak. Had Mrs. Avery been listening covertly when she entertained the children with tales of her happier childhood days? Even so, Melissa did not think she had said anything that would be considered harmful. With a sigh of resignation, she kissed the children lightly and went out for some fresh air. It was the first evening since the wagon train had set forth that the evening temperature provided a slight relief from the intense heat and humidity of the day, and even Mrs. Avery's harsh criticisms couldn't trounce the fresh feeling Melissa enjoyed from having bathed and changed into a clean dress.

"There ye are!" Mavis called. "There's a dance going on in the fort, and there's many more men than women, so I've come to collect ye."

"Mavis, I don't really feel up to it right now," Melissa responded, wanting to take advantage of the relative peace and quiet surrounding the wagon train to sort through her thoughts. A lot of the train's occupants must be at the fort.

"What bloody nonsense," Mavis retorted, not one to take "no" for an answer. "Ye are in need of some merriment, and I mean to see ye get it. Besides, ye'll be a welcome sight for these men's sore eyes. That dress is becoming on ye. Much better than what ye had been wearing. Where'd ye get it? And those combs! Don't tell me old lady Avery finally found a heart!"

Mavis did not wait for a response as she tugged on her friend's arm, and Melissa didn't give one as she mutely followed the Irish lass toward the fort's entrance. Her spirits improved somewhat when she heard the music and laughter as they grew nearer.

Melissa was enjoying some cool punch near a table that was laden with roast duck—no doubt the rewards of the hunt the men had gone on earlier—boiled potatoes, and corn bread, the latter supplied by the few wives who had accompanied their husbands to the fort. Tom, she noticed, was accompanying the fiddler, a man she recognized from the train, on the harmonica. Mavis had joined the two and had captured the crowd's attention with a haunting rendition of "Danny Boy." Singing mournfully in a crystal-clear voice, she seemed far removed from the devil-be-damned friend Melissa had come to know. Melissa was not alone as she wiped the tears from her cheeks at the song's conclusion, amid all the appreciative cheers and whistles. One of the men called out a request for a livelier tune, and the mood was uplifted as Tom and the fiddler played "Nothing But a Plain Old Soldier," and dancers took the floor once again.

Looking around, Melissa spied Mr. Avery in a corner, talking quietly to a couple of the other men from the camp. It was no wonder he had not invited his spiteful wife to this small celebration. He was probably thankful to escape her waspish tongue, and since Mrs. Avery had not befriended any of the other women on the train, she probably didn't even know about the dance. Sinful, she would have called it, Melissa thought.

"That dress becomes you," a familiar voice interrupted. "I would have liked to have done better by you, but it was the best I could do on short notice. Corporal Mattox's wife was generous."

"Thank you," Melissa stuttered, touching the combs he had also presented to her, not quite knowing what else to say to Captain Precter. "It was thoughtful of you to send these items along with Sarah." Scanning the crowd, she inquired, "Where is Sarah tonight anyway? I haven't seen her."

"Why, ma'am, laundresses aren't invited to these things. Most are simple-minded women who follow the army and are grateful to be supplied with a place to sleep and some food in return for their services. Occasionally, a comely one will attract the attention of an officer and will advance her station in life, enabling her to sleep in a wood-floor barracks rather than sharing a small tent with another of her type."

Jim Precter had quickly educated himself in the ways of this fort by spending several hours shooting the bull with the fort's sutler, a man he discovered was as cunning as himself. The time was well spent, and it was there he had met Audrey Mattox, who had been only too happy to supply him with the dress that he'd had delivered to Melissa. All it had taken was some lavish compliments and a story he invented about Melissa's husband having abandoned the train and his wife in the middle of the night, leaving with all their possessions to return home. As an afterthought, Precter had purchased the combs from the sutler with his own money. Having shared several glasses of whiskey with the man, he had struck a good bargain for them. Besides, he expected to be well-paid for all his efforts.

Rankled by his cavalier dismissal of the kind-hearted Sarah, Melissa was about to respond when Mavis and Nat twirled by to the fiddler's tune, and Mavis cried at her to join in.

"Sounds like a right good idea to me, ma'am," Precter said, grinning and grabbing her by the waist before she could protest.

After a couple of rounds, Melissa's body relaxed, and she found herself enjoying the attentions of the handsome soldier, especially when she noticed Nat glaring at her when the two couples danced near each other. She wasn't sure what had provoked him, but she was happy to be the cause of whatever it was that made him angry.

"I've learned of the dilemma you're in, ma'am, and I think I can be of some help," the captain whispered into her ear as he pulled her body tighter to him than was comfortable. "May I call on you tomorrow?"

Before Melissa could respond, the two were interrupted by another soldier informing them that the call had come to change partners. The captain paired up with Mavis. Melissa was passed on from partner to partner and soon found herself face-to-face with a scowling Nat.

"Seems like you make friends awfully easy," he growled. "Who is that man?"

"Which man?" Melissa feigned innocence.

Nat's grip on her arm tightened.

"You know 'which man.'" He nodded in the direction of the captain.

"Oh, Captain Precter!" Melissa replied sweetly, as though she was oblivious to his anger. "I met him yesterday." Seeing his deepening scowl, Melissa could not resist the urge to provoke him further. "He's very charming, you know. Why, all the women he dances with look very merry when he's their partner." Maybe he was jealous at seeing Mavis dance with the captain, she thought.

On that note, Nat grabbed her roughly by the elbow and escorted her off the makeshift dance floor. Melissa started to pull away, then decided against making a scene. She glanced around for Captain Precter, but his back was to her, and Mavis was obviously keeping him entertained. Nat seemed not to notice the pair. Once outside the building, he released her elbow, and Melissa, determined to take the offensive, turned on him like a wild cat.

"I don't know why you feel you can treat me like this," Melissa cried, releasing her anger toward the man at last. "I'm a full-grown woman, not a child to be ordered about."

"Oh, that you are," Nat replied, allowing his gaze to rest pointedly on the creamy skin the new dress left exposed on her chest. "But as your protector, I have every intention of keeping you from getting yourself in more trouble than you know how to handle. Or perhaps you *do* know how to handle it," he added cryptically.

She felt her face turn as red as hot coals on a campfire. What *does* he think of me after seeing Uncle John's actions and then hearing his accusations? She attempted to cover her embarrassment with a further assault on him.

"My *protector*!" she exclaimed. "You call shoving me off to be a cook and nanny against my will and then ignoring my existence *protection*? Well, I don't need a protector. You're neither my father nor my brother, so I would be pleased if you would continue to ignore me. I can make my own way. And now, if you'll excuse me, I plan to return to the dance."

Melissa's mention of the word "brother" had hit a chord, and Nat mutely stepped aside. No, he wasn't her brother, and she did resemble his sister Emmie somewhat. Was it possible that his attraction to this woman that he was trying so hard to hide and suppress was due to memories of a much happier period in his life? Sweet Emmie! He hoped his brother, Alfred, was looking after her, despite what her recent letters revealed.

Emmie, only sixteen when the war broke out, had been the sole member of the family who hadn't been angry with Nat when he joined the Union army while the rest of his family and most of their friends fought on the side of the Confederacy. Nat had returned home once, when the fighting was nearby, to learn that Alfred had lost a leg to the war and had returned disabled to help their mother manage the family's plantation. Alfred was the lucky one. Reports were that both Nat's father and a younger brother had been killed. As their mother stood silently behind his older brother with weary sadness in her eyes, Alfred had informed Nat that he was no longer welcome there.

It was a tearful Emmie who had caught up with him, proffering a basket of goods she'd snuck out of the pantry while the ugly confrontation was ongoing, urging him to take care and to write to her when he could. But the feelings that stirred in him whenever he watched Melissa as she competently and without complaint went about her daily duties under the vigilant eye of that shrew, Mrs. Avery, were far different from those a brother felt for his sister. Truth was, he hadn't quite experienced such emotions before, certainly not with any of the women he had bedded. Although he had resented the unexpected baggage initially and had eagerly disposed of her, he had come to admire Melissa's grit.

The dress she had worn tonight was easily eclipsed by those worn by the other women, but it was a far sight better than the drab brown, puritanical dress in which she had been confined thus far on the trip and was more revealing of the gentle curves of her body as she moved gracefully in step with the music. And while her dress may not have been an attention-getter, her beauty certainly had been. Her freshly washed hair, held back by combs, fell in soft waves down to her waist. The flickering lights of the kerosene lamps had captured the sun-kissed highlights, creating the illusion of a halo. When he had at last allowed himself to be partnered with her, having maneuvered around it for most of the evening in an effort to keep himself in check, the soft scent of her body had nearly caused him to lose control.

So he had started an argument instead. It hadn't been

difficult. He hadn't enjoyed seeing her with that captain, and it was more than just jealousy. He had recognized the man from the wagon train, and he had been unsettled to see him in army attire tonight. Captain Precter, if that was his real name, had never given any indication that he was a member of the Federal army, a fact he found most unusual. He had told Mavis to glean whatever information she could from the man, and she had been delighted to be of service.

While he and Mavis enjoyed each other's company, there was a silent acknowledgement that they would remain friends and nothing more. For her part, Mavis was not unaware that Nat and her friend Melissa were attracted to one another, even if they were both too bullheaded to admit it, and despite her own behavior, she was a romantic and wanted the two of them to find each other. Too, she was heading West to find a man who had already struck it rich in the gold mines of the Colorado Territory, while Nat hoped that he could find enough gold himself to save the family plantation once his commitment ended.

His last two letters from Emmie had instilled more immediacy to his mission. She had reported that Alfred had turned to alcohol more and more to escape his depression over his missing limb. As a result, the affairs of the plantation were in disarray, and their mother had crawled deeper and deeper into the cocoon she had spun after learning of the deaths of her husband and youngest son. Nat could read between the lines and knew Emmie was striving to keep things going, but as the baby of the family, her position was not strong enough to do much. Their mother would listen to Alfred. Knowing Alfred's fondness for gambling, Nat felt certain the plantation was in imminent danger of being lost forever. If Union soldiers didn't find cause to burn it after they had foraged what they wanted of it, Alfred's excesses would eventually lose it for them. And there was nothing Nat could do to stop it. He only hoped he could strike it rich enough to be able to return and recoup what had been lost. Surely then he would be accepted back by his mother, if not by Alfred.

He had not yet told his family he had all but quit fighting for the Union cause. What difference did it make to them after having lost loved ones? And he would not switch sides and join the Confederate army, which is what they would have urged. Still, after watching a childhood friend die while fighting with the greybacks during the course of one of the battles, Nat knew he could no longer fight with the Union forces, either.

Upon recognizing Jeremy and seeing him fall after taking a hit, Nat had dropped to his stomach, crawling beneath the gunfire in an attempt to rescue his friend and remove him from the battlefield. He had not been fast enough. Jeremy's body had been stomped to death by charging horses from both sides. Sickened by the sight, Nat had eased his way to the edge of the battlefield, deep into a heavily treed area where he promptly threw up his breakfast rations. Alston and Tom found him there when they came looking for him after the enemy had retreated. Ever the loyal friends, they told Nat they would follow him whatever his decision.

His decision had not been an easy one. When he was five, he had seen his nanny, Tom's mother, whom he loved as much as his own dear mother, strung up between two trees and whipped by his daddy for some minor infraction until she was unconscious. At that young age, he had vowed he would help the slaves in whatever way he could. His boyhood friendship with Tom only intensified his desire. Still, Jeremy Jones and he had enjoyed a close relationship, too, fishing together and sharing other boyhood adventures. Nat thought Jeremy had been misguided in selecting his allegiance, but he knew his friend was not a bad person. If Nat were face to face in battle with another childhood companion or, worse, with his own father or brothers, could he do what was necessary? He knew the answer.

That was the argument Nat had presented to the commanding officer of his company as he, Tom, and Alston stood before Colonel Canus. Although the three could have probably just cut out and been assumed dead, Nat felt that he owed Canus something more than that. The man had always been fair-minded with his troops, treating them more like family than subordinates as some of the other high-ranking officers were rumored to do. The colonel's distress at the loss of any of his men in battle was obvious to all—and not because it meant fewer fighting soldiers. It was more personal than that.

After listening quietly with his bushy eyebrows raised, the colonel had sat in what seemed an interminable silence to the three soldiers standing before him. Finally, he spoke.

"Much as I'm loath to lose three good fighting men, what you say makes a good deal of sense. Tell you what. I have received word that our troops in the West need reinforcements. Seems the Indians in those parts have recognized the fact that the forts are less secure now that the army has been devoting its efforts to fighting the rebel forces. Their attacks on the wagon trains have become more frequent and more violent. The hangings of twenty-three of the Yankton Sioux leaders back in September hasn't helped matters. Never mind that the Sioux killed over three hundred Minnesota settlers and burned their houses. The Indians regard hanging as the most ignoble death, and they're bent on vengeance. I've already sent Captain Burrows and his company to the Colorado Territory, which has become a recent hotbed. The remaining nine companies, including yours, were to remain to continue the fight here, but I will authorize a transfer to Burrows' unit for you. I will sign the papers allowing you to ride out first thing tomorrow to join Burrows and his men."

****

"A halfpence for ye thoughts," a soft female voice broke into his thoughts.

"Mavis!" Nat was genuinely glad to see her. "Find out anything?"

"Only that ye had best be careful, Nat Bellamy, and watch ye back. I know me men, and that one 'tisn't what he presents himself to be. As charming as he might act, even I, Mavis O'Leary, woodna share a bed with a snake such as he."

Nat was amused at Mavis's righteous declaration, given that she had shared with him the story behind the notches on her leather belt, once they had become better acquainted. He was also even more concerned about Melissa since Mavis's statement reinforced his own feelings about the man.

As if reading his thoughts, Mavis continued, "I think ye'd best get in there and rescue ye lady from the hands of that rogue."

Mavis's words caught him by surprise. He had never confided his feelings for Melissa to her—or to anybody.

54

Hell, he hadn't even allowed himself to admit to them. But Mavis was nothing if not astute.

"Thanks, Mav, but I'll need an alibi. Care to join me in a dance?"

****

Melissa did not miss the arm-in-arm entrance of the couple as Mavis and Nat rejoined the festivities. She herself was again partnered with Captain Precter, who often held her uncomfortably close as they danced.

Why did she feel so ill at ease with this handsome, charming soldier who had presented her with a clean dress and clearly doted on her and so drawn to the man who alternated between issuing her orders and ignoring her? Deciding it must be due to her inexperience, she determined that she would offer her charms where they were appreciated and smiled gratefully at the captain as he twirled her around.

"I don't believe I ever answered your earlier request, Captain," Melissa suggested, slightly breathless from the dance in progress. "I would be most pleased if you would call on me tomorrow."

Captain Precter responded with the grin of a boy who had just caught a prized fish, dimples flashing charmingly, just as she was whirled into the arms of another partner.

Chapter Six

Melissa awoke the next morning with a sense of disquietude. Captain Precter had insisted on walking her back to her wagon when she had tried to escape the dance unnoticed. In truth, she had never been able to dismiss her confusion over her feelings for Nat. He had avoided her for the rest of the evening—purposely, she felt, since he seemed to remove himself from the dance floor whenever it seemed they might be thrown together as partners in the round dances—yet she felt his eyes upon her constantly. Was it only her imagination? Finally, being able to take no more, she had feigned a headache and excused herself from her current dance partner, eagerly seeking fresh air. Captain Precter must have observed her rapid retreat and had quickly caught up with her. Though she had wanted to walk back alone with her thoughts, she had not been able to think of a polite way to reject his offer. Happily, he had been nothing less than a gentleman as he escorted her to her wagon and had not attempted to intrude on her thoughts, although prior to leaving her he had reinforced the notion that he would call on her the next evening. *Why had she nodded in agreement instead of putting an end to it then and there? And why didn't she want to offer any further encouragement to this very attractive man who obviously could have his pick of many women?*

Rachel and Joshua were obviously enjoying the

trip's delay, spending their pent-up energy cavorting within the circle of safety provided by the wagons. Responding to their constant cries of "Watch me, Melissa" as they entertained her with their attempts at somersaults and cartwheels provided a welcome diversion for her troubled mind. She clapped and cheered at young Joshua's attempts to duplicate his sister's acrobatic efforts.

"Ye cut out before the dance was finished," Mavis said as she joined her friend.

"I guess I was a little tired," Melissa responded.

"I left right after ye myself, but I saw ye were enjoying the company of that captain, and I dinna want to interrupt anything. Are ye taken with him?" Mavis asked bluntly.

"Why shouldn't I be?" Melissa tried to elude the question.

"Be straight with me, lass."

Sometimes Mavis's perceptions were tiring, but she had been the only female on the train to befriend Melissa. The two were virtually outcasts. Melissa sighed, resigned to answering what she knew could be a string of further inquiries. Besides, maybe discussing her feelings with Mavis would help her sort things out.

"Well, he's handsome, attentive, and charming," Melissa began.

"But…?"

"But I don't know. Somehow, I just don't seem as taken by his charms as the other women do. Is something wrong with me?" Melissa was surprised to hear herself voice her secret, almost unconscious, concern. Had John Hund's actions ruined her so that she would never be able to have the type of feelings that Alicia had confided to Melissa she had for Jesse?

"I dinna think ye need to worry ye head over that one." Mavis laughed. "We have a wee voice inside us, though, that shouldn't be ignored. It can keep us out of trouble many a time if we heed it."

The somber tone with which Mavis delivered the last words was uncharacteristic.

"Have you ever been in love, Mavis? I mean, truly. Not just looking for another notch on your belt."

"Just once, lass. At least I thought I was. I gave the man me heart, and a whole lot more, if ye know what I mean." She gave a short derisive snort. "The wee voice practically screamed at me, but I chose to ignore it."

"What happened?" Melissa was so enthralled with this new revelation that she forgot her own problems for the moment.

"Oh, nothing terribly dramatic," Mavis responded, swatting away a band of no-see-ems that were on the attack as she spoke. "'Tis the age-old story. I was fifteen, and he was twenty-eight. Me parents owned a small shop in Ireland I helped tend, and I met him one day when he wandered in. He was the first man to tell me I was beautiful." Mavis paused as if she were remembering the experience of her first love.

"He came in often after that first day and won me over with all his attentions and compliments. Not that there was much winning to do. Ye may not believe it now, but at that time I was as naive as ye. Had a proper Catholic upbringing, I did. But such flattery from an older lad made me forget me parents' teachings and close me ears to that wee voice."

"At any rate," Mavis picked up the pace of her story, "one thing led to another, and I missed a couple of me monthlies. I was ashamed and terrified, but I felt that once he knew I was carrying his babe, he would make an honest woman out of me. I was wrong. I never saw him again."

"What happened to the baby?" Melissa inquired, mesmerized.

"I lost it after three months," Mavis replied sadly. "I had never told me parents me secret and never confessed me sin to the priest. Then, one day when I was working in the store, I felt such pain as you can't imagine. It brought me to me knees, it did. A customer came in and found me doubled up on the floor, me dress soaked with blood. He ran for the doctor, who arrived about the same time as me mom. Me secret was out then. The doctor said I would never bear another babe. The look of shame in me mother's eyes was almost as unbearable as the pain of me loss. Nothing was the same after that. As I lay in me bed recuperating, me parents made plans to ship me to America to live with an aunt and uncle in New York. Whether 'twas to spare me or themselves the humiliation, I dinna know. I met a man on the ship over, but I was a wiser person then. No man would use me again. I would use him." These last words were spoken with vehemence. "And I've done quite well for meself," Mavis finished in a lighter tone. "Love 'em, take their money, and leave 'em."

Seeing the look on her friend's face, Mavis returned the conversation to Melissa's concerns. "But ye are a different woman from meself. Ye've a kind, untainted heart. Ye'll fall in love, and ye'll know it when ye do. Just ye listen to that wee voice."

****

Melissa's "wee voice" was screaming at her as she

accompanied Captain Precter on a walk around the area that evening, her arm entwined in his. Still, she had agreed to allow him to call on her, and nothing untoward had happened. The air remained heavy and humid from the lack of rain, but it felt good to be stretching her legs, and the captain entertained her with stories of his life, many of which sounded highly implausible, even to Melissa's naive ear, but she allowed him to continue uninterrupted, glad she was not asked to reveal anything about herself.

"You know they're planning to ship you back to Nebraska City," the captain turned the conversation to a more serious one once he was certain they were out of earshot. "I figure that's not a situation you find appealing, or you wouldn't have joined this train to begin with."

Melissa offered no response, but he felt her muscles tense in the arm he held captive.

"The way I figure it, you're a damsel in distress, and I'd like a chance to be your knight in shining armor."

He gave her his most charming grin as he turned her toward him, putting his hands on her shoulders as he spoke. The grin was lost on Melissa, who remained silent before him.

"Well, would you care to hear my proposition?" He gently caressed Melissa's shoulders with his thumbs as if to massage an answer out of her.

"Yes… No… I don't know…" Melissa wavered, answering immediately in response to the touches that she inexplicably found repugnant.

"Tell you what. I'll explain my plan, and then you can think on it for a day or two." *Better not apply too much pressure right away. Many a fish is lost by an impatient fisherman*, he cautioned himself.

Neither of them noticed the man concealed by the trees as Captain Precter unveiled his scheme.

****

The sun seemed to be up before Melissa had even fallen asleep. What to do? The captain had promised to accompany her north, where he said she could safely catch a stagecoach to Denver. It was a roundabout way of getting there, but certainly better than being sent back to John Hund. Captain Precter claimed to have army business that took him there but had been evasive about exactly what that business was. And that wasn't the only thing she questioned. What about Indians? And why was the captain, who had just met her, offering to pay for her passage to Denver? What would happen to Rachel and little Josh when she left them in their mother's care? They would be heartbroken and feel Melissa had abandoned them, she was sure. And she *would* be abandoning them. Still, the bits of the wagon master's conversation she had overheard played themselves over in her mind. She had been grateful to hear Mr. Avery's support of her, but she doubted that he'd take any really strong stance. Goodness, he never even stood up to his own wife. The unbeckoned thought snuck in: *You won't see Nat again.* She forced it from her mind as quickly as it had come.

She was still pondering her decision as she completed her routine tasks, feeding the children a breakfast of johnnycakes and cleaning up the dishes, when Captain Precter rode up.

"Why, you outshine the morning sun itself," he greeted her.

"Good morning, Captain," Melissa replied stiffly.

"Please, call me Jim. After all, we're going to be riding companions."

Don't be too sure of yourself, Melissa thought, but said nothing.

"I've come to tell you that I'll need to be leaving sooner. My assignment has been moved up."

The last statement was probably the nearest thing to the truth that Jim Precter had ever told. He had seen the wagon master talking to the fort's commander this morning. The old coot had ignored his admonishment, and Jim Precter was closer to feeling a noose around his neck than he deemed was comfortable. He would lay low today, but he needed to cover a lot of miles tonight.

"How much sooner?" Melissa croaked out. She just couldn't make a decision this fast.

"I'll need to be leaving tonight. You can be ready. You don't have much packing to do anyway, from what I hear tell. What I'll do is meet you over yonder with an extra horse once everyone has turned in for the night." He pointed to a treed area some distance from the circled wagons. "Think you can manage it?"

"Captain, I won't be going." The man's pushiness had pushed Melissa right into an immediate decision. "I appreciate your offer, but I just can't leave the children. I wouldn't feel right."

Was it a look of anger that had appeared briefly on the captain's countenance as his face flushed? Melissa couldn't be certain. It might have just been embarrassment at the rejection. He seemed like a man who wasn't used to being turned down. A feeling of relief swept over her as he mutely tipped his hat and departed. She had made her decision, and the wee voice told her it was the right one.

Realizing that, for once, she had made her own decision about the direction her life would take, she embraced her newfound sense of contentment that evening as she sat in the moonlight after getting the children settled in their bedrolls. The silent, flitting lights of fireflies seemed to surround her, affirming her decision. No matter that there were still so many issues to be resolved. She felt strong. She touched the ring hanging around her neck—her mother's wedding ring—in a silent thanks to that parent for bequeathing her some of her strength.

The sound of pebbles landing near her feet interrupted her sense of satisfaction. Looking in the direction from which they seemed to have come, she saw nothing. A few minutes passed and then more pebbles. She thought she heard her name. Curiously, she walked over to the rock outcropping that lay just outside the circle of wagons. Again, she heard her name called, this time from a greater distance. Straining her ears for some hint as to the origin of the voice, she stepped behind the rock outcropping. Abruptly, she felt a hand clamped over her mouth.

"Keep quiet," a low male voice growled, "or I'll take you here and now."

What she sensed was a balled-up bandana was stuffed into her mouth until she gagged. She kicked backward, several times making contact with her assailant's shinbone, as her hands were wrenched behind her back and tied together, the rope cutting into her wrists. Using her tongue, she tried unsuccessfully to extricate the cloth wad from her mouth before her assailant roughly tied another kerchief around her mouth, holding the first in place and bruising her lips. Then, jerking her around, he slapped her so hard she lost her balance. Wide-eyed, she recognized her attacker just before her head hit the rock.

Chapter Seven

Melissa did not know how long she had been unconscious. When she awoke, she was being hauled over the front of a horse like a sack of flour, with her kidnapper in the saddle directly behind her. Her legs were bound now, too. Her head ached, and her mouth was so dry from the intrusive cloth that she started heaving involuntarily.

"Finally awake, are you? That's good. I like my women to be lively when I take them," Captain Precter said when he noted her movement. "And I've waited a long time for you. Longer than I had intended, but the opportunity to cart you back to your uncle never came until we arrived at the fort. There were always too many people nearby. Then I thought I might get you to come willingly, but I was—"

His words were cut off by a loud scream—or was it a bird screeching? Melissa couldn't tell. Suddenly, she was flung harshly to the ground as the rider and his horse took off at breakneck speed. She landed on her back, helpless as a turned turtle, with a jagged rock cutting painfully into the small of her back. Twisting her head, she saw the cause of Captain Precter's rapid departure, and her heart stopped. Indians! There were three of them, naked from the waist up, their faces and bodies covered with red and white stripes, and they were gaining on the soldier. Where had they come from? How had they sneaked up unheard, even if cloaked in darkness?

With another loud shriek, one of the Indians jumped from his horse, knocking her abductor to the ground. The Indian and the soldier wrestled on the ground while the other two retrieved his horse and were eagerly going through his saddlebags. Terrified, Melissa worked desperately at the bonds on her hands, attempting to free herself. She closed her eyes when she saw the glint of metal in the Indian's hand as Precter began weeping and begging. She did not want to witness a scalping—or worse. She opened them again when she heard animated voices speaking in a strange, guttural language. One of the assailants had pulled the captain's Federal Army jacket from his bags and was gesturing wildly as he spoke to the Indian straddling Precter's body, prepared to take his reward. The third Indian approached with a noose he had fashioned from a rope found in the other bag. Kneeling, he fastened the noose around the captain's neck. The other two turned his body, pulling tightly on the noose and choking their captive whenever he attempted to struggle. Using the ends of the rope, they tied his hands behind his back. They then bound his feet with another rope and lashed it to the saddle horn of his horse. Not once had the Indians looked in her direction, which gave Melissa hope. Maybe they would just leave her there to die. At least then someone might come and find her before she finally succumbed.

Her hopes were dashed as the three Indians mounted their horses, dragging the captain behind, and headed toward her prone body. One of the Indians dismounted, grunting as he stooped to run his hand through her hair. *Oh, dear God, he's going to scalp me!* Instead, he yanked at the chain that held her mother's ring and held it up, admiring it. He tied it, chain and all, to a leather thong decorated with colored feathers he wore around his neck. Melissa cringed to see her dear mother's ring touching the skin of such a savage as he grinned and pushed his chest out for the others to appreciate. This resulted in grunts of approval and more talk in the unintelligible language before one of them lifted Melissa up and flung her across the captain's horse.

****

Robert Avery approached Nat, Alston, and Tom as they shared the breakfast of biscuits, beans, and coffee Alston had prepared that morning.

"Have any of you seen Melissa? She's nowhere about, and Mrs. Avery is fit to be tied."

The trio exchanged looks.

"Nope, haven't seen her," Nat replied, more calmly than he felt.

"Guess I'll check with Mavis then."

After the preacher had departed, Tom was the first to break the silence.

"I cain't believe the girl went off willingly with that scoundrel."

"Well, Tom, you heard for yourself she was thinking of it when I had you follow her and Precter the other night," Nat replied. "I say good riddance. We've already had more than one setback in our attempt to catch up to Burrows' company. The girl would have just posed additional problems. She has made her own decision about her life, and we have our own mission," Nat continued with an argument that sounded unconvincing, even to his own ears.

Any response was cut short as Watson Calhoune approached the three men.

"Colonel Stone would like to speak to the three of you in his quarters immediately."

"What about?" Nat inquired, sounding more belligerent than he intended. He liked and respected Calhoune, but he didn't need any more problems.

"You'll find out soon enough," Calhoune responded, taking off in the direction of the fort, confident the three men would follow.

Nat was quickly able to dispel any suspicions the fort's commander had by producing the official papers that Colonel Canus had supplied them. At least one of the stagecoach robberies had been staged before the date on the documents. He explained that Burrows was reportedly heading to Denver where the Indian problems were becoming more heated. He had not been sure of the path Burrows had taken and had even held out hope that he would meet up with the company at Fort Kearny since it had seemed the obvious route. Why he had not reported immediately to Colonel Stone and inquired of any news of Burrows was less easy to explain.

It had been obvious Burrows was not there. Nat knew the man and would have recognized him. On the other hand, he did not know anything about Stone, except that he was the commanding officer of the fort, and Nat was not eager to be recruited into his service here in Nebraska. He wanted to get to Denver where he could at least ferret out information about the rumored abundance of gold to be found there, even if he was not immediately free to act on the information. And when he had seen Precter in uniform, he had wondered about the man's associations at Fort Kearny and had cause to doubt the leadership there if, indeed, Captain Precter was a member of the company that manned the fort. Nat could not tell the colonel that, so he simply explained that when he recognized that Burrows' company was not at the fort, he had felt it was in keeping with their mission to continue to accompany the wagon train to Denver where they would meet up with their new company. In the meantime, they would, in fact, be guarding against Indian attacks. *Guarding Melissa.* The thought crept, unbidden, into his mind.

As Nat spoke, he was interrupted by a corporal who presented the colonel with a recently transmitted telegraph wire.

"Well, Calhoune, seems your instincts were right. The Union army had no record of a Captain Jim Precter, but record-keeping has become a secondary consideration at this point in the war. Any warm body will do. So I double-checked on the stagecoach robberies he claimed he was investigating. Reportedly, they were carried out by a lone man who seems, coincidentally, to match Precter's description, for the most part. Only the last few of them were reported to be committed by someone in a Union uniform. But the buckle was turned upside down, leading the victims to conclude the robber was really affiliated with the rebel cause. Too bad about the girl. I checked around after you reported her missing to me this morning, and no one has seen Precter or her, which isn't surprising since you found his wagon emptied of the essentials. One of our horses was missing, also. I reckon he didn't feel he could get far on an ox." He included Nat, Tom, and Alston when he directed his next comments.

"I wish I could offer you some additional men for your protection, but our forces here have also been diminished due to the unrest farther west. I only ask that you wait a couple more days until the survivors of the previous wagon train return, and until we get a more complete report from our scouts regarding the situation. Then I might, at least, be able to spare a scout to accompany you—one who knows the Indian ways and language. Deal?"

"Deal," Watson and Nat responded in unison. What other choice did Nat really have? The colonel was right. If they left right now, there was a good chance the wagon train might never make it through, and he, Tom, and Alston would never make it to Denver. Too, he wondered at Melissa's fate now that Precter's true character had been revealed.

He wasn't alone in his concern. As they left the fort, Alston and Tom beleaguered him with entreaties.

"We gots ta go after them," Alston started. "They cain't have gotten far. From what's been said, there was only one horse and two riders."

"Even if'n she did go willingly," put in Tom, "she couldn't't've known what type of snake she hooked up with."

"True enough," Nat admitted. "But, if you recall, she told me the night of the dance that she didn't need or want my *protection*. So she's on her own."

"Now, Nat, neither of us was privy to that conversation, and while I don't doubt you heard what you heard, maybe you didn't hear what she really said," Alston put in. He was sure Melissa had the same feelings for Nat as Nat had for her, but both of them were too blamed stubborn to admit it.

"Are the two of you going to desert me for her, then?" Nat played on their emotions.

Alston and Tom looked uncomfortably at each

other.

"No, sir, yuse the boss," Tom replied.

An awkward silence accompanied the three men back to the wagons. Nat instructed Al and Tom to pack the saddlebags with the necessities they would need the moment the fort's commander gave the train the go-ahead to depart. He forced himself to focus on their mission to obliterate the visions of the golden-brown-haired, brown-eyed beauty that kept creeping into his head.

Mavis didn't help.

"What's this about Melissa's being kidnapped?" she inquired immediately as she sauntered up to their wagon.

"Don't know much about it," Nat replied. "Far as I know, she went willingly."

"I dinna believe it! And neither do ye, Nat Bellamy, if ye'd only listen to ye heart for once. Miss has a good head on her shoulders. And I told ye she had misgivings about Precter. I canna believe she wouldna have listened to her wee voice."

Nat rolled his eyes. Mavis had talked to him about listening to some "wee voice" before. It was all hocus-pocus to him. In fact, he found it hard to reconcile the hard-talking, brazen Mavis with the soft-hearted woman she sometimes seemed to be. Good grief! He was of Irish ancestry and was somewhat familiar with the culture's superstitions, but this native Irish gal was something else.

"Well, if ye're not intending to do something about it, I sure am." Mavis strode off toward the fort with a saucy toss of her head.

Chapter Eight

No one in the wagon train was prepared for the attack that came later that morning, so complacently were they camped on the outskirts of the fort. A band of yelping savages descended from the north, bearing tomahawks, bows and arrows, and flaming torches, which they threw onto the wagons and into the fort as women and children screamed and ran helter-skelter, seeking cover. Grabbing their firearms, the men dove to position themselves to best fend off the attackers. Devilish fingers of flame surrounded the emigrants as they sought to escape the heat and certain death. Animals pulled at their restraints, blowing and bellowing. A few broke loose and escaped into the wooded area. Some of the emigrants ran toward the center of the circled wagons. Others, seeking refuge outside the circle, were immediately killed by the charging Indians. Shots rang out from the fort. Chaos reigned. Obscenities accompanied the gunfire as wives and children huddled behind the men fighting desperately to save them. Their backs to the fort, Nat, Tom, and Alston positioned themselves next to Calhoune, behind one of the wagons that had escaped being torched. Several of the assailants had already penetrated the circled wagons. Robert Avery fell as he crouched in front of his wife and children, rifle in hand in an effort to protect them. Nat took aim at the Indian who had dealt Avery his death blow. He hit his mark, but not before a stray arrow struck down Rachel as well. Sobbing hysterically, Emma threw herself over the dying bodies while little Josh clung to her skirt, his small body shaking convulsively as tears rushed down his red cheeks, wetting his shirt. A second Indian swooped both the woman and the boy onto his horse and rode off in the direction from which he had come, releasing a piercing war cry as he evaded a barrage of bullets.

It seemed that for every Indian killed, two more arrived. The ground was littered with the dead and dying, and there looked to be more white bodies than there were dark. There was nothing Calhoune and the three soldiers beside him could do but fire their rounds of ammo and reload as rapidly as possible. Except for the occasional muttered curse, they did so in silent concentration. Nat observed a couple of men crawling under the burning wagons in an attempt to escape south across the Platte River, only to be greeted by a volley of arrows. The attack seemed to be coming from both directions. Hearing pounding hoofbeats, Nat glanced quickly over his shoulder. Soldiers were firing their weapons as they rode out of the fort's perimeter, trying to get to the circled wagons. Nat knew some would have to remain within the fort's boundaries to protect it. The army's troops were divided.

"Come on!" Calhoune barked urgently as he dropped to his belly and crawled back under the floor of the wagon they had been using as cover.

The three men followed suit. From their new position on the opposite side of the wagon, they could pick off the Indians from behind as the savages rapidly advanced to repel the reinforcements from the fort. One of the Indians, noticing their movement, charged at them, tomahawk drawn, while another one, seeing the intended targets, began shooting arrows in that same direction. Alston fired at the second Indian, missing, and an arrow embedded itself in Tom's arm. Watson's shot was true, felling the Indian, whose horse squealed in fright and took off in the opposite direction. A bullet from Nat's weapon brought down the tomahawk attacker. As the Indian slid off his mount, Nat grabbed at the reins of the horse, restraining it. While Alston and Watson covered for him, he deftly tied the horse to one of the wagon cleats and quickly rejoined the other three men. As more soldiers fanned out from the fort, the Indians found themselves attacked from behind and before. The looks on some of their faces suggested they had been caught by surprise, and upon hearing a guttural command, they retreated, lessened greatly in number.

"Nat, look 't this," Alston exclaimed.

The Indian that Watson had killed wore a ring on a leather thong tied around his neck—a ring Tom, Alston, and Nat easily recognized.

Chapter Nine

Melissa awakened to someone tugging at her hair. As she drowsily opened her eyes, she stared into coal black eyes only a few inches from her own. She gasped at the sight of the old squaw and held her breath against the stench invading her nostrils. Greasy, gray hair hung limply to the old woman's shoulders, and her bronze-colored face was more wrinkled than a grape that had been forever forgotten on the vine. A smile revealed the few discolored, broken teeth the old woman had left as she put her bent index finger to her lips, indicating that Melissa was to remain silent. Seeming content that Melissa had gotten her message and would comply, she removed the bandana still binding Melissa's mouth. Immediately, Melissa started retching involuntarily as the old woman watched silently. When Melissa's body seemed to have settled itself, the elderly squaw dipped a cloth into a clay bowl, tugged Melissa's head back with her hair, and squeezed out the rag into Melissa's mouth. While the cool, fresh water never felt so good on Melissa's parched, cracked lips, she initially choked on it. The old woman repeated the process a few more times before quietly collecting her bowl and retreating into one of the teepees.

They had arrived at the Indian encampment sometime during the night. Melissa had been tied, sitting, to what seemed to be a stake that had been driven into the ground. She had sensed, rather than seen, that the captain was alive when they had arrived. *Was he still?* Miraculously, she had at some point fallen asleep with her head resting on her chest. Throughout the night, she had awakened to the sound of harsh Indian voices, followed by inhuman screams, which might have come from Jim Precter. Each time she expected to be next, but, for some reason, she had so far been spared. Shortly after the final time she had heard any voices, she thought she heard a body being dragged across the ground. As she studied her surroundings in the daylight, she saw no sign of the captain. *Was he dead?*

The camp was awake. A band of Indians, painted similarly to the three Indians who had captured her, rode off shrieking ferociously as the women and children in the camp stood watching. One of the riders' horses came dangerously close to her, its hoof almost landing on her bound feet. The savage grinned as she quickly scooted her feet to avoid the impact. Her sudden movement sent a stabbing spasm through her lower back, magnifying the throbbing pain that had been her constant companion since she had regained consciousness after the captain's attack. No doubt the hours of being carried like a sack of flour on horseback and sleeping tied to a stake had aggravated the initial injury incurred when the captain abducted her.

With the men gone, the women went about their tasks. A couple of them sat on their heels and were using small stones to grind something that looked like grains in larger, bowl-shaped stones. Another using a sharpened stone to scrape the hair off what appeared to be a deer hide that had been stretched out on a frame and staked to the ground. Still another was rubbing a greasy-looking substance on the hide of an animal Melissa couldn't identify, given her angle. A faint smell of dried blood assaulted her nostrils. One young mother was tending her baby. Some older boys were engaged in what seemed to be target practice with their bows and arrows. Several curious young children came up to inspect Melissa. One of them—a male child of about five— rubbed his dirty fingers through her hair. The old squaw appeared from a nearby tepee and grunted something at them that shooed them away.

What, exactly, were they intending to do with her? Melissa had heard stories of Indians making captured women their wives, and she shuddered at the thought. The stench of the Indian who had ridden behind her on the way to this camp would have made her vomit had she not had the gag in her mouth. As it was, bile had accumulated in the back of her throat, and she had had to take several deep swallows to keep from choking to death on it. Suddenly, she remembered Watson Calhoune's words to the emigrants who would be traveling with him: *even the women were not spared. Dear God!*

As the day wore on, the sun's heat became nearly unbearable. The old squaw had returned several times. The first few times, she had repeated the process of feeding Melissa water. The last time she had come with a bowl of something that tasted like watery cornmeal, scooping it up with two fingers and putting it in Melissa's mouth. Melissa would have turned away at the sight of the bony, crooked appendages with filthy nails, but she was too famished to reject the nourishment. She knew she had to stay alive somehow. When the bowl was empty, Melissa tried to communicate her now excruciating need to relieve herself to the old woman, but the squaw couldn't, or wouldn't, understand. Unable to control the urge any longer, Melissa was forced to urinate as she sat there bound to the stake. While her insides felt better, the acidic moisture now trapped next to her skin by her clothing was burning her, and the malodor of it radiated up to her nose, deepening her humiliation.

The band of Indians returned later that day. It seemed there were fewer of them than had ridden out. The lead horse carried an extra rider—or was it two? Melissa couldn't tell. As the riders came closer, she heard the crying. *Joshua? It couldn't be!* The rider halted his horse at the old squaw's tent, pulling a woman and the boy who clung to her off the horse onto the hard ground. *Mrs. Avery?* The woman was crying softly and lay in a fetal position, clutching her child. Melissa heard only mewing sounds emanating from her. The boy started howling louder as the Indian pried him from his mother's grasp. The savage shook him harshly before throwing him down to the ground, kicking him in the head until the crying stopped.

"Nooo!" Melissa screamed helplessly as she watched little Joshua being cruelly bludgeoned.

Hearing her cry, Joshua's assailant stomped over to her and slapped her hard, whipping her head to the side as he yelled something in his guttural language to the other Indians. Two of them then approached her with their knives. *This is it. Please let my death be speedy, God,* she prayed frantically. A mixture of both relief and shock shot through her as the knives were used to cut the ropes that bound her to the stake. The savages dragged her over to where the woman and her child lay. She could see that Joshua was still breathing—barely—his cherubic face mangled. Part of his skull had been cracked open.

"Bury him." The order came from a second Indian who had joined the first as his interpreter.

"But…he's still alive!" Melissa managed to stammer through her terror. The first Indian emitted what sounded like a growl and slapped her again. The old squaw came and grasped Melissa's arm with a strength that belied her years, while a second Indian woman, who appeared to be only a few years older than Melissa, pulled Joshua from his mother's arms and handed him to Melissa. Seemingly oblivious to the events that were unfolding, Mrs. Avery continued making her mewing sounds. As the two Indian women led her away from the village, Melissa made an effort to comfort the unconscious little boy she held against her bosom. The thought of escape passed through Melissa's mind, but she couldn't bring herself to leave precious Joshua alone with these foreign people in what would be his last hours on earth. After trudging what Melissa estimated to be about a quarter of a mile, they reached an open site, devoid of trees, but peppered with multicolored wildflowers that had survived the drought of the summer. The younger squaw found a large, sharp-edged rock and began using it to scrape the foliage off the land and make the beginnings of a gravesite. Melissa could feel Joshua's faint heartbeat against her chest.

"He's alive!" Melissa exclaimed, pressing the old squaw's hand to Joshua's chest to make her point.

In response, the old woman squeezed Melissa's hand and looked into her eyes with what seemed to be sympathy. She stooped down, picked up a large rock, and hit Joshua's head with it before Melissa knew what was happening. Joshua's body slumped farther into her arms, his heartbeat no longer present.

"Oh, Joshua," Melissa whispered, holding him close and sobbing into his dead body as a collage of memories of an alive, happy-go-lucky toddler paraded through her mind. "You savages! I hate you!" She spewed the words at the two women who were now working together on the gravesite.

Glaring harshly at her, the younger woman left her work and walked over to Melissa.

"We savages?" Her face contorted in bitterness. "White man come many moons ago. He want make trades. The elders make trades. White man and Indians happy. Smoke pipes and drink magic juice of white man together. Maybe white man not so happy, though. When white man left, he take me with him. I not many moons old and playing in stream, away from eyes of village. I scream; no ears hear. White man treat me worse than my people treat dogs. You no believe? Look!" The woman slipped her buckskin dress off her shoulders revealing a pattern of scars on her breasts that could only have been made by cigarette burns. "And this what only one white man do. Your people steal our buffalo, taking only what pleases them at the time and leaving the rest behind to rot. Buffalo our food, clothing, shelter. White men assault our land just as the one white man assaulted me. White men savages!" she finished.

As Melissa gaped in horror and disbelief at the sight before her eyes, the older woman approached her and pried the young boy's dead body from her arms, handing her the rock she had been using to dig the grave and motioning for her to do the same. Melissa dropped the rock in defiance and turned to run. There was nothing she could do for Joshua now. The younger woman caught up with her quickly, unimpeded by the yards of clothing which tangled in Melissa's legs as she ran.

"No good. You must do." The younger Indian commanded. Surprisingly, her voice was not angry as Melissa would have expected, but had a sympathetic tone.

Knowing now that the woman spoke some English, Melissa tried to reason with her.

"Look. I've done nothing to harm you or your people. Please…let me go," she pleaded.

"No good. You must do," the other woman simply repeated as she tightened her grasp on Melissa's arm.

Melissa swung her free arm to strike a blow at the woman's face. The woman averted her swing and, enraged, pulled a knife from her buckskin boots.

"You will do," she commanded as she threatened Melissa with the knife and forced her, crawling, back to the gravesite. "Boy would not see next moon," the Indian woman grunted to Melissa in what seemed to be an attempt to explain her actions as she stooped to help with the grave.

The ground was hard, and it had taken most of the afternoon for the three women to dig a hole deep enough to protect Joshua's body from being immediately dug up and eaten by animals. Why they should even care was beyond Melissa's comprehension. As the two Indian women led her back to their encampment, she felt as lifeless as the little boy they had just buried.

Upon their return, Melissa saw Captain Precter for the first time since they had arrived at the village. He was tied, standing, to a stake that had been driven deeply into the ground in the middle of the camp. His neck, waist, arms, and legs were bound to the stake, allowing for only minimal movement. His badly beaten body was naked and had been smeared with a black, tarry substance. Several of the Indian women and children were taking turns poking him with a stick they had held in the coals of a nearby firepit until it was red hot.

"You lie, white man, like all white men," the Indian who had commanded her to bury Joshua screamed at Precter. "My brother and many others dead from your lies. You say white man's guns easy to steal. Not guarded. This not true. Now you will die, too."

"No, no! I didn't know. Something must have happened since I left the fort. They must have gotten reinforcements after I left! I swear, there were only ten men at the fort when I left it; the rest had gone out to help wagon trains that had been ambushed!" Captain Precter screamed the words between howls of pain. "Release me, and I will return to you with guns from the fort. I promise!"

Melissa gasped at what she knew were lies on both counts. The Indian was not taken in this time.

"White man's promises mean nothing." The Indian spit on the bound man to emphasize the point.

Melissa had advanced within Precter's view.

"My wife, there," he exclaimed hurriedly when he saw her, nodding in her direction. Seizing on another opportunity for salvation, he declared, "I give her, my most precious possession, to you as a hostage to keep if I don't return with the guns." His sentence ended with a screech of pain as a red-hot stick met one of his nipples.

Melissa was about to render a violent protest, not against the man's torture, but to his words, when the

Indian's next words cut her off.

"Hah! She already ours—to be used however and whenever we wish. You do not *give* her to us, white man. We take her. You can do nothing about it. Perhaps we will let you watch before you die." With a deep laugh, the Indian retreated, the captain screaming profanities after him.

Shrugging off the two females who held her, Melissa advanced on Precter.

"How dare you! May you burn in hell!" She was tempted to take one of the burning sticks being used to torture him and use it herself. Before she gave in to that temptation, the two women dragged her away. She had a glimpse of Mrs. Avery, who was now tied to the same stake to which she herself had been bound. The woman had ceased sobbing, but had a vacant look in her eyes, seeming not to recognize Melissa even as she passed close by. When they approached a teepee that seemed larger than most of the others, the Indian women halted. An older Indian emerged from it, a magnificent headdress of feathers adorning his long, graying hair. He wore a buckskin loincloth and a buckskin vest, decorated with blue and white beads and white feathers. Following him was a younger Indian man, about her own age, Melissa guessed. A multicolored-beaded band with three feathers arising from its crown held back his straight, shoulder-length black hair. He, too, wore a loincloth, but his copper-colored chest was naked, displaying rippled muscles with strong arms folded on top of them in a defiant gesture as he stood before her with his muscled legs spread.

Upon a command from the older Indian, the younger Indian advanced toward her with a knife, ripping the buttons from her dress, exposing her chemise. Shocked, Melissa immediately attempted to pull her dress together, but the two females grabbed her hands and held them behind her back with amazing strength. The younger Indian then cut through the thin material of the chemise with remarkable accuracy, exposing her bare breasts without grazing her skin. The older Indian grunted his approval. As an audience gathered to view the spectacle, tears of humiliation filled Melissa's eyes. Undaunted, the young brave grinned and slashed through the bottom portion of her dress and her petticoats until Melissa stood naked before them, shivering with trepidation but afraid to move for fear she might exact a slash that would be fatal. This time the younger brave grunted. He approached her and cupped her full breasts in his hands, his deep brown eyes looking straight into hers as though to search her soul. She met his eyes in an attempt to hide her fear, but her body, with a mind of its own, tried to shrink away from his touch as the two women behind her continued to hold her firmly in place.

Chapter Ten

When Nat saw the ring around that savage's neck, he felt like his own heart had been torn out. He'd had time to wrench it from the dead body and pocket it just as the fort's calvary charged after the retreating Indians. Retrieving the horse he had restrained, Nat joined the chase. Alston, seeing Nat's intention, found his own horse close by and unharmed and caught up with him. The two left Watson and the injured Tom to pick up the pieces with the other wagon train survivors.

The troops killed a few more savages in their pursuit, but most of the remaining Indians, being excellent horsemen and more acquainted with the land over which they rode, managed to escape. The calvary lost their trail and turned back. It was possible the savages would circle back to the fort, and only a skeletal force remained there to protect it and what was left of the wagon train. Nat and Alston decided to continue on in hopes of picking up the trail once again. Neither spoke, but each knew that Melissa's fate weighed heavily on the other's mind. Nat also hoped to find Joshua—the little boy had captured his heart—although he had to admit he didn't much care what happened to the boy's mother. After another couple of hours, though, Nat wondered if they should also return to the fort. Observing the sun, Nat reckoned it to be about six o'clock, and it seemed they had been travelling in circles. Dusk was approaching and would further inhibit their ability to pick up the trail on the unfamiliar terrain. Perhaps tomorrow he could convince the colonel to supply him with some additional manpower to go after the savages. *But tomorrow might be too late*, his heart told him, urging him forward.

Surprisingly, Alston, with his lazy eye, was the first to spot the smoke that signaled they were approaching *something*, at least. They continued cautiously and, peering over a small mound, found themselves looking onto what was, indeed, an Indian village. But was it *the* Indian settlement they had set out to find? Exchanging a look of agreement, both men dismounted, tying their horses securely to two trees that were part of a sparse grove on this side of the embankment that separated them from the village. They continued on foot, crouching down and trying to be as soundless as possible.

They had been able to make some distance when Alston, several feet in front of Nat, caught his foot on a half-buried tree root and landed face down on the ground. The noise alerted the Indian assigned to guard duty. Fortunately, the Indian's attention had been focused on some activity in the village, so he had been slow to react. By the time he did, Alston had regained his footing and stood glaring defiantly at the Indian. Meanwhile, Nat had quickly secreted himself behind a tree and was now silently closing in on the Indian from behind, preparing to shoot even though the gunfire would alert the village. Looking into Alston's eyes, the Indian's own eyes widened as though he were staring into the eyes of a demon, and he took two steps backward. Seeing the savage's momentary lapse, Nat was swift to close the distance and levelled the butt of his rifle at the Indian's skull. Both Nat and Alston exhaled loudly as the enemy fell with a muffled grunt.

From their new vantage point, they could see a woman tied to a stake, and Nat immediately recognized Mrs. Avery by her clothing. As his eyes scanned the scene, he saw another individual tied to a stake, although he could not discern if it was male or female. The hapless victim appeared to be nude, but its body was abnormally disfigured. *Melissa?* The frightening question entered his mind as his eyes searched for evidence that his mind was wrong.

There was a scurry of activity taking place at the left side of the village, and Nat commenced breathing again, not realizing he had stopped. In the center of a gathered crowd stood a woman with waist-length, golden-brown hair. Her back was to him, and she was being restrained by what seemed to be two Indian women, but he was certain it was her. One of the savages stood before her in what appeared to be a threatening posture. Damn! He didn't have much time to plan. Looking over at Alston, Nat saw that Al had taken in the scene, too.

With an urgency in his voice, Nat whispered, "We need to move fast! I'm going back to get my horse. When I come riding through, I'll need you to create a diversion. Anything—just so I can get Melissa out of there."

Wide-eyed, Alston nodded silently in agreement. That girl was too good and too kind, and it was no telling what the savages would do to her next.

"Stay here and keep low," Nat whispered the command as he retreated as quickly and silently as he could to where their horses were tied. He returned, leading his horse, several minutes later.

"Here. Take this repeating rifle the calvary gave us before they left. It should be fully loaded, which means you can shoot sixteen rounds before you need to reload. I will continue on foot until I'm close enough to catch them off guard when I charge in. When I make my move, fire your first two or three shots from here, then move and fire another few rounds. It's best they think there are more than two of us. Try to make it back to your horse before you run out of ammunition. I put the second Henry repeater they left us in the rifle sheath on your horse. It, too, should be fully loaded. Don't move in a straight line, but be careful as you move. I doubt even Indians are dumb enough to leave but one guard, although they may have developed a false sense of security once they realized the calvary had retreated." Nat nodded in the direction of the Indian who still lay motionless on the ground a few feet away. "Keep moving and shooting for as long as you can, but when they collect themselves enough to start coming, get the hell out of here. Ride as fast as you can for the fort, hear? No matter what happens!"

Nat hated asking Alston to cover for him in this way. Al was not a good shot—never had been, with that bad eye of his—so if the Indians caught him by surprise… But he didn't see any other option. As he stealthily walked his horse even closer to the Indian encampment, he looked back to see Alston readying himself to follow the instructions. Fortunately, it appeared that the village was so intent on the scene being played before them they were oblivious to any movement on their outskirts. His heart fell as he now saw that Melissa stood nude before the threatening brute. He had intended to be a little closer before he attacked, but the sight of Melissa, vulnerable in the midst of the savages, spurred him into action.

The sound of two gunshots diverted the villagers'

attention from the scene they had been enjoying. As the Indians scattered to mount their horses and charge in the direction of the gunfire, Nat had enough time to sweep in and scoop a surprised Melissa onto his horse. Riding away from the direction of Alston's shots, Nat heard the steady pace of hoofbeats immediately behind, telling him at least one of the Indians was in hot pursuit even while the remainder of the warriors raced in the opposite direction. *Get out of there fast, Al,* Nat prayed silently.

"Are you okay?" Nat finally whispered in Melissa's ear.

"Yes," Melissa stammered in answer, not quite certain it was the truth, but feeling comforted by the strong arms that held her close even as she shivered at the sound of the echoing shots emanating from the village behind them. Suddenly, she remembered her nudity and felt a blush that quickly and furiously extended from head to toe.

"Damn you, woman, but you're more trouble than you're worth!" Nat's voice had turned angry as a jumble of emotions jockeyed for position in his heart. He was relieved Melissa seemed to be physically unharmed, and God, her naked body was beautiful and felt good pressed against him. His manhood rose despite their current situation. At the same time, he was worried about Al's fate and about his own capability of outdistancing the skilled riders who were in hot pursuit behind them. He knew himself to be a good horseman, but the Indians' reputation on their steeds was known far and wide. The fact that he was riding farther away from the fort—and safety—heightened his concern.

"Then just drop me here!" Although that was the last thing Melissa wanted, she vented all her pent-up anger, frustration, humiliation, and fears as she began sobbing uncontrollably.

"Oh, so you liked the caresses of that young savage," Nat couldn't help but taunt. For all their sakes, he had to dispel the feelings in his groin her warm, naked body was creating. Unconsciously, in an attempt to do so, he clung to his anger as tightly as Rachel had sometimes clung to her penny doll when she had been rejected by her mother. Melissa's only response was the stiffening he felt in her body.

The hoofbeats behind were closing on them. Melissa heard a zinging sound and then a soft thump. Nat's moan followed just as she felt his body slump over her, the reins slackening in his fingers. Frantically, Melissa grabbed the reins, but she was no match for the horseman behind her. The Indian quickly caught up and pulled her body from the animal onto his own horse. Carrying his limp body, Nat's horse continued undirected.

Seconds later, another Indian joined them. Melissa was surprised to see it was the younger woman who had helped her bury Joshua. The female threw Melissa a blanket, which she gratefully used to cover herself, and began speaking in her foreign tongue to the warrior. The two seemed to be arguing. Finally, the young woman spoke in her halting English to Melissa as the other Indian set her back on the ground.

"You free now. Gray Fox my brother," she said motioning to the warrior who had turned his horse around and was racing back to the Indian encampment. "I suffer at white man's hands. Gray Fox know. White woman help me escape back to my own people. Now you return to your people. I repay. Great Spirit will like. Maybe favor us in big buffalo hunt."

"But how?" Melissa had no idea of where she was or how she would be able to reach safety.

"Go that way to river," the Indian woman pointed, "and follow river north to fort." She departed as abruptly as she had spoken the words.

Although she had not considered the young woman her friend, Melissa had a strange sense of bereavement as she set out on the lonely path. *What had happened to Nat? Will I come upon his dead body? Is the calvary nearby?* She had heard the gunshots coming from the opposite side of the Indian village just before Nat rescued her. *Will I be able to meet up with them? If not, can I even find the river that the young woman told me to follow? Enough! I will not become a whiner and sniveler like Mrs. Avery, God save her soul. I, and only I, am in control of my own destiny now, which is what I have longed for. I should be happy I still have sturdy shoes upon my feet, if little else.* She automatically reached to touch her mother's ring and remembered sadly it was no longer there. She was truly on her own. Determinedly, she pulled the Indian blanket tightly around her body, knotting it at the top and bottom to keep it semi-closed around her, squared her shoulders, and marched on with as much dignity as her mind could muster. She was thankful the savage had not yet cut her brogans from her feet when she had been rescued.

She quickly learned the river was probably much farther than she had imagined. The young Indian woman had obviously directed her to a point that would be some distance from the village. Night had fallen hours ago. Still, she trod on, to the buzz of the cicadas that seemingly surrounded her. Shivering at the distant howl of coyotes, she pushed herself to keep going, both for her sake and for Nat's. *Please be alive*, she prayed. As she picked her way through the darkness, she hoped she remained on the same course. The half-moon offered some light, but not enough to allow her to avoid the occasional slap by a low-hanging branch. The resulting scrapes to her face continued to sting. Her bruised back throbbed in pain, and her thighs were screaming in protest as she continued to force them forward. Her mouth was so dry she would have been grateful to have that old squaw appear before her again to squeeze drops of water into it from an old rag. She pulled up blades of grass and chewed on them in an effort to placate her body's scream for moisture. The physical and mental exhaustion she felt was taking its toll. If she could just lie down and go peacefully, she decided she would almost welcome death. With that thought, she lay still when she stumbled over yet another tree root and fell, having no idea where she was.

Chapter Eleven

Day was just breaking when the sense of someone hovering over her awakened her. Wearily, she opened her eyes, with the unhappy feeling that she was somehow still alive.

"Missy! Are you okay? Where's Nat?"

Alston! At the sight of her old friend and the mention of Nat, Melissa was suddenly wide awake. As she sat up, she reached behind her to massage a pain in her lower back and noticed Alston was now looking away uncomfortably. She was mortified to see her blanket gapping in the middle, exposing a great deal of her body. With as much dignity as she could muster, she rearranged it to cover all she could. Between the sips of water Alston offered her, she recounted the events of the preceding day somewhat incoherently, while tears of relief at seeing him flowed down her cheeks.

"Nat told me to head for the fort, but I couldn't leave the two of youse out here alone, so's I headed in that direction, but once I'd crossed the river, I slapped the mare on the behind, knowing she'd go back to where the train was, and walked back down the river so as not to leave a trail. If I hadn'ta, they'da catched me anyways."

"Is the river close?" Melissa recalled feeling she'd never find it.

"'Bout a quarter mile down the ways is all. Once I knew I was past the village, I decided to try an' find youse off the beaten path." He beamed. "And here you are! Now's all we gotsta do is find Nat."

Given what she had revealed about Nat's fate, Melissa decided Alston was the eternal optimist. Still, she wanted to grab hold of that optimism and ride it like a wild horse. She just didn't know how.

"I told you, he's dead." She stated with less certainty than she had previously held.

"Hell...I mean, heck, no, he's an Irishman!" Alston responded with an exuberance beyond Melissa's comprehension. "He's got more lives than a cat!"

Melissa only prayed Alston was right as he decided to walk the riverbank in search of his friend. Alston explained that it was likely Nat's horse had headed toward the water.

"But you cain't walk around like that, Missy." Alston took off his shirt and handed it to her, revealing a sparse growth of graying brown curls on his pale chest. "Here, puts this on, too. It'll at least cover more of you."

Gratefully, Melissa accepted the shirt, while hoping the exposure to the sun would not leave Alston with a blistering sunburn. The shirt barely fell below her waist, but she was able to knot the Indian blanket at her waist so her body was modestly clothed.

By the time the sun was directly overhead, they had been trudging up and down the riverbank for hours with no sign of Nat or the horse, and Melissa had begun to despair again. Alston must have noticed her fatigue and suggested they sit for a spell under one of the cottonwood trees near the river. He caught fresh water in his canteen as it flowed over a large rock near the river's edge and offered the cool liquid to Melissa along with a piece of beef jerky he pulled from his pants pocket.

"Afore I let my horse go, I had the presence of mind to grab some of this out of my saddlebags. I was afeard to try an' carry the heavy bags with me. It would've slowed me down in my search for the two of youse, and them injuns are smart. They most likely would have noticed the horse carried a much lighter load from the hoofprints and would've figured they'd been tricked and come after me. Hopefully, my own body weight, slight as it is, won't make that much difference."

Alston must have noticed she was preoccupied with her own thoughts and likely hadn't heard a word he said. "Don't worry, Missy, we'll find him."

"It's just that he risked his life to save mine," Melissa said by way of explanation. She didn't want Alston to get the impression that she actually *cared* about Nat.

Alston nodded. "He done saved my hide, too. He an' Tom found me drunk in a gutter one night whilst they was on a mission to get more supplies for their regiment, and I would've froze to death if Nat hadn't taken me to his warm hotel room. It was him convinced me to join the cause and give up the booze. He's about as good a man as walks this earth, and he's got a heart as big as that there prairie we've been crossing. He really cares about folks, not like some of those snot-nosed rich boys I met up with once I joined the regiment. He was grievous concerned about you when you turned up missing, I can tell you. Couldn't hold him back from coming to find you." Alston deviated from the truth a bit, but he had decided these two mules needed a little nudge.

Melissa savored the revelation but declined to comment on it. Instead, she asked, "Why were you lying drunk in a gutter?"

"Because the bestest thing in my life—my wife, Trudy—died giving birth to our first child ten years afore. The baby died, too, and I felt like I had nothing more to live for. After I buried the two of them, I started drinkin' and never stopped. Trudy was special. She loved me, even with my wayward eye, which I know puts off most folks. Hell—I mean, heck—even my own ma and pa was somewhat ashamed of me. They never did say so in so many words, but I could tell bys the way they acted. Trudy—well, she treated me like a man wants to be treated, from the very first."

Melissa wasn't certain she should ask the question, but she was curious and couldn't resist. She ducked her head so Alston might not notice her face reddening. "How does a man want to be treated?"

Alston's eyes opened as wide as saucers at the query, and a small smile crossed his countenance. He was silent for a bit before he responded.

"Why, just like a woman wants to be treated, I imagine. Men want to feel loved and cherished and have their opinions respected." He shook his head and grinned. "My Trudy was good at it. Not a day went by when she didn't declare her love for me and tell me I was the handsomest man she had ever met. Now, I knew from looking in a mirror that weren't true, but I always hoped maybe I really was in her eyes. And Trudy had a mind of her own, too. She was one smart woman. Looking back, I see she was smart enough to get me to change my mind on some things I was wrong about while letting me keep my self-respect, what little there was of it."

"My father's favorite saying was, 'Beauty's only skin deep,' and over the years I've realized how right he was," Melissa responded. "You *are* a handsome man,

Alston, and Trudy *was* a smart woman to recognize it. I hope I find that kind of love one day," she ended wistfully.

"Oh, you will," Alston responded confidently. "'Course, you're really beautiful on the outside, so you'll have the problem of being courted by those who're only interested in being able to show you off like a pretty trinket. You'd best shy away from them. Now, Nat—"

Blushing at the compliment but not liking the direction Alston was heading, Melissa interrupted. "Do you think you'll ever marry again?"

"I doubt it. I've slept with some whores since then." Seeing Melissa's face, he quickly apologized. "I'm sorry, Missy. But a man does get lonely for those things. I don't feel like I'm being unfaithful to Trudy none 'cause she'd understand. She'd understand, too, if I took me another wife, but the woman would have to be somethin' awful special. An' Trudy will always have a special place in my heart. The woman would have to understand that, too."

They sat for a few minutes, each absorbed in their own thoughts. Alston finally broke the silence.

"It's possible the horse threw him before it got to the river. Being an injun horse without a rider, it probably headed back to the Indian village. Maybe we should scour the area some distance from the river."

Dusk was approaching again, and Melissa had no idea how many miles they had gone, zigzagging to and from the riverbank, trouncing through tall grasses, pushing aside low branches, and climbing over fallen limbs. Alston had demanded they not split up. It wasn't safe for her, he had insisted. Her legs ached even more than they had the night before, and by now she felt certain Nat was dead. The thought left her aching elsewhere in her body. *Had he truly cared for her and not known how she felt about him as he lay dying? If only she had abandoned her pride and let him know her true feelings! It all seemed so petty now.*

Her thoughts were interrupted when she heard Alston cry out Nat's name. She ran the several feet it took to join him, nearly tripping over a moss-covered limb. As she approached, she saw Nat, lying on his stomach, an arrow protruding from his back. His shirt was coated with dried blood, and his body was still.

"There's a heartbeat, so's he's still alive, but he's lost a lot of blood. We's got to get him help quick, but first we's got to get that arrow out afore infection sets in," Alston proclaimed. "We're gonna need strips from that shirt you have on," he added apologetically.

Melissa turned her back, her hands shaking with anguish as she removed the garment while Alston proceeded to cut off Nat's bloodied clothing. She re-knotted the blanket around her shoulders and handed Alston the shirt he had lent her. Alston tore one strip, doused it with canteen water, and applied it to the gaping wound around the arrow to cleanse it. Melissa pointed out a big gash on Nat's forehead as well.

"Musta hit his head on a rock when he lost the horse," Alston mused as he moved to wipe the blood from Nat's forehead. "It don't look serious, just a graze. Looks like the arrow got him just to the right of his right shoulder blade. That's good. There's no vital organs in the way." Melissa inhaled sharply as she watched Alston push the arrow through Nat's body so that the arrowhead came out his chest.

"Only way to get it out," Alston said in explanation.

"The arrowhead is jagged and could've broken off in his body if I'd a tried to pull it straight out like it was." He proceeded to break off the visible head and then pulled the arrow shaft out from the back. As he began cleansing both wounds, he instructed Melissa to tear more strips of cloth, which he wrapped tightly around the injured man's body.

"Help me move him over yonder." Alston pointed to a flat spot that was closer to the riverbank and offered some trees for protection and concealment. He grabbed the injured man under the arms while Melissa carried him by the legs. Nat groaned.

"Good thing he's out cold right now." Alston observed as they gently placed Nat's body on the ground. "Do you know how to shoot?" Alston's question surprised her.

"A little. My father set up a target practice for my sister and me when we were younger. He said women needed to learn to defend themselves, too. But I was never very good at it," she admitted.

"Well, here's Nat's gun," he said, tossing it to her. "I 'spect you'll be able to use it well enough if the occasion arises. He sure won't be able to." He jerked his head toward Nat. "I have to hightail it back to the fort. I can cover more distance if I'm alone, and someone has to stay here with him. Make more strips out of that shirt and change the bandage when you see it bleedin' through. I'll be back with help soon as I can."

Before Melissa could protest, Alston broke into a trot. For a man who must be nearing forty, he certainly was spry. She bent to her patient. Although the evening was still uncomfortably muggy and warm, Nat's face felt cold, and she noticed he was shivering. *Had he gone into shock?* She remembered from somewhere that an injured body needed to be kept warm. *What to do?* There was nothing with which to cover him except… Removing the blanket from her body, she cautiously lay down beside the unconscious man and wrapped her arms and legs around him before pulling the blanket over them both.

Now nude, with her breasts pressed against the rippling muscles of his chest, Melissa felt an unfamiliar warmth move rapidly through her entire body, settling, it seemed, in the uncharted place between her legs. *What would it be like to have this man make love to her?* She could hardly believe the thought had entered her mind and tried to push it out, but there was no escaping the growing sensations that seemed to be overtaking her body. Enjoying the feeling, she nestled her body closer to his. *Please don't die, Nat!* Her mind kept repeating the phrase as she fell asleep.

She awoke with a start to the sound of a coyote's howl somewhere in the distance. Her jerk must have stirred Nat. He groaned and seemed to be saying something.

"Emmie."

Melissa wasn't quite certain she had heard correctly. She placed her ear closer to his mouth.

"Emmie, girl, I won't let you down."

Although the words were slurred and slow, Melissa was certain that's what the injured man had said. She felt as though somebody had doused her with the cold water of the nearby river. *Dear God, Nat already has a woman in his life—someone he obviously cares for deeply. And to think I was fantasizing about him only a few hours earlier.* The thought made her blush. She shifted her body slightly away from his, but kept her arms and legs wrapped around him, giving him her warmth. After all, he had saved her life. It was the least she could do for him. Once Alston returned with help, she would leave and never look back. Tears spilled from her eyes as she reconciled herself to the fact that Nat's actions had been born only from kindness, not love for her as she had dared let her heart hope. *How mean life can be! Just when I finally admit to myself that I love this man, I learn he loves another.*

Determinedly, she forced her mind in a different direction. Rather than wallowing in sorrow, she would plan for her future. Sleep found her as her mind turned over various possibilities.

Chapter Twelve

Nat was dreaming. He had entered the door of a large, cheery house. While it wasn't the house in which he had grown up, it was his home. Three children came running up, eager to greet their father upon his return. Emmie was there, too. Wiping her hands on her apron, his wife sprang from the kitchen to greet him with a smile and a kiss. He loved his life now, and he loved his wife. Her long, golden-brown hair smelled so good as it brushed his face, tickling his nose.

Tickling his nose. He tried to reach up to scratch it but found he couldn't move. His right arm throbbed with pain, and he sensed something on top of him holding him down. It felt like…a body! He struggled to open his eyes. One of his eyelashes brushed against hair, some of which he felt cascading down his chest. A slim, naked arm was thrown over his torso, and long, slender legs were entwined with his. A soft patch of pubic hair brushed against his hip. *Melissa! What was she doing here, and where were her clothes?* His mind flitted to the last thing he remembered. He had felt a searing pain as an arrow hit him, knocking the air out of him. He'd just rescued Melissa from the Indian encampment and was trying desperately to outdistance his pursuers. *Was she alive?* Focusing, he was relieved to feel her steady heartbeat against his chest. His chest was bandaged, he noticed. *Did she do this? And where did she get the cloth to do so?* The last he remembered, she had not a stitch of clothing. *God, her body was lovely!* Although his left arm was pinned down by her head, he managed to move the fingers of his bandaged right arm, gently caressing the soft locks of her hair. She looked so vulnerable and angelic lying there, and it felt good to have her body pressed against his. Alston and Tom were right. He *was* in love with this woman. He fully admitted it to himself. Like it or not, he realized he could not let her go. He'd figure out a way to allow her to accompany them to Denver, and from there…well, he'd think of something. He shifted to relieve the stiffness in his back. Suddenly, he was staring into surprised, green-flecked brown eyes.

"You're awake!" The joyful look on her face was quickly replaced by one of horror as she became acutely aware of her state of undress. Flushing, she jumped up, grabbing the blanket that had become tangled in their legs, and covered herself. Her sudden movement caused a searing pain in Nat's shoulder. He grimaced and emitted a loud groan.

"I'm…sorry." Melissa stammered. "It's just that I…well, your body was so cold, and I didn't know how else to keep it warm so you wouldn't go into shock." *Now he must really be convinced I'm a trollop!*

"I appreciate it greatly." He flashed her a pained grin, which Melissa quickly interpreted as lecherous. She remembered his delirious words of the previous night.

"How are you feeling?" She asked stiffly, her voice taking on a coolness that left Nat confused.

"Okay, I guess, considering the circumstances. My shoulder and right side hurt like hell. My whole body feels like a herd of buffalo stampeded across it, and, ouch, a shooting pain goes through my head whenever I try to move it," he said as he attempted to adjust his position. "My mouth feels like it's stuffed with cotton. I can definitely say I've had days I've felt better."

Despite herself, Melissa had to smile at his lighthearted understatement.

"Let me get you some water. Are you hungry? Alston left us with a few strips of beef jerky." Alston had also left Melissa with his canteen, explaining he was able to bend down at the river to quench his own thirst and she would need the vessel to transport water to Nat.

"Alston? He was here?" He was curious to learn what all had taken place while he had been unconscious, and Melissa promised to fill him in.

Returning with fresh water, Melissa tried to lift Nat's head gently so he could get some of the cool liquid into his parched mouth. He winced as she did so and ended up dribbling much of the water down his chest, wetting the blood-soaked bandages.

"Try again. We'll have to change the strips of cloth anyway, and I have to cleanse the wounds."

As Melissa helped Nat replenish his body fluids, she related what had happened since he had stolen her away from the Indians. She told him about the young Indian woman and about Joshua's fate, watching his eyes fill with tears as she did. She was certain Captain Precter was dead, and Nat confirmed the body he had seen tied to a stake through his binoculars looked very much so. Mrs. Avery, she thought, had gone mad, and Melissa asked Nat what he thought her fate would be.

"Well, she might be used as a slave for a while, and then the Indians will try to get ransom for her, I imagine. That seems to be a pattern for them."

Melissa shuddered at the thought. Mrs. Avery had

behaved in a mean-spirited fashion toward her, but she wouldn't wish that fate on anyone.

"Can you roll to your left side with my help? That way I can remove the soiled bandages."

Nat complied, struggling to hold himself up on his left elbow so she could reach around him. Melissa was silent, doggedly ignoring the muscles in his back and chest as she worked. This man belonged to another woman. Nat finally broke the silence.

"I have something to tell you," he said in a subdued voice.

He's going to confess his devotion to the woman named Emmie. Melissa couldn't bear to hear it.

"Maybe you'd better save your strength," she responded.

"No. I'd rather tell you now than have you find out later," he insisted as Melissa braced herself mentally. "The Indians attacked the wagon train the other day. A lot of the wagons were burned to the ground, and a lot of lives were lost. Rachel died, and so did Mr. Avery." Knowing Alston, Nat realized Melissa wouldn't be aware of their fate. Alston wouldn't have wanted to upset her more than she already had been when he found her.

Melissa shut her eyes tight against the news and began blinking rapidly in a vain attempt to keep the tears from falling. As soon as she felt she could speak again, she had to know.

"And Mavis and Tom?" She nearly screamed the words through her tears, angry at God, the world, and the Indians.

"Tom took an arrow in his arm, but it will heal just fine. He's recovering at the fort, which is why he couldn't join us. Mavis and I had an argument shortly before the attack. Last I saw her, she was stomping off toward the fort, so hopefully she was safe inside. I didn't see her during the fighting."

What did you and Mavis argue about? Melissa wanted to ask. *Did you finally tell her about Emmie?*

"By the way, where's my old shirt?" Nat asked as she finished wrapping the clean bandages around his body, her breasts brushing against his bare chest as she leaned over and stretched to reach around him. Nat wondered how anyone could look so good clad in a shapeless blanket. He felt a longing deep in his groin.

"Alston had to cut it off of you. What's left of it is up there a way." Melissa nodded in the direction from which they had moved Nat's body.

"Would you be kind enough to bring it to me? I'd go myself, but…" He gave her a helpless grin that deepened the thin valleys on either side of his mouth and increased Melissa's heartbeat. She hastened to fulfill his request lest he hear the rapid pounding.

Her heart had slowed somewhat by the time she handed him the wad that used to be his shirt. With his left hand, he dug into a pocket and handed her…her mother's ring.

"Wh…where did you get this?" she asked, gripping it tightly in the palm of her hand as though she feared losing it again.

"I took it off an Indian I killed. That's how we knew where you were. Well, not exactly where, but we suspected what your fate had been."

Melissa had assumed that Alston and Nat had followed Precter's tracks, leading them eventually to the Indian village. She had thought they must have understood Precter had kidnapped her. But now… She

106

suddenly realized Nat probably thought she had gone off willingly with the captain, and she opened her mouth to explain, then shut it tightly again. *It doesn't matter. It never mattered. We'll be going our separate ways shortly, and I'll never see him again anyway. I'll go to Denver and find Alicia and Jesse and start a new life for myself.*

After helping Nat prop himself up against a tree in a more comfortable position, she and Nat shared some beef jerky while he related what he remembered about what had happened after their separation. The arrow's blow must have had enough force to knock him out temporarily. Recovering consciousness at one point as he felt himself slipping off the horse, he had tried to regain control of the animal, but the loss of blood had sapped him of the necessary strength. The steed had easily thrown him off, and the last thing he remembered was hitting his head on a rock as he fell.

"I guess the combination of the blood loss and the blow to the head put me out for a long time. When I finally woke up, I was still disoriented and couldn't fully recall what all had happened. When I saw you lying beside mc, I was afraid *you* were dead."

The recollection of *how* he had found her beside him made Melissa blush furiously. Unconsciously, she pulled the blanket more tightly around her body and nervously fingered the ring she now wore around her neck again.

"That ring must be very important to you. I've never seen you without it. Does it have a story?" Nat had noticed Melissa's discomfort and wanted to turn the conversation to something that might make her feel more at ease.

"It was my mother's wedding ring. It's all I have left

of her," Melissa responded sadly. Prompted by Nat's casual questioning, she proceeded to tell Nat about her happy life with her loving parents and her sister, Alicia. She told him how she had had to bury both parents and how she had ended up in Nebraska City with her aunt and uncle. She stopped short of telling him about her lecherous Uncle John. He had seen what he had seen, heard what he had heard, and could draw whatever conclusions he might. She didn't have to try to convince anyone—especially not Nat—of her innocence.

"Hey, I'm sorry about even asking you the question about your murdering your aunt when I first saw you stowed away in our wagon," Nat said softly when Melissa stopped talking somewhat abruptly. "I just had so much on my mind and saw you as a further complication. But I watched you with the Avery children, and I admired how adroitly you handled their hatchet-faced mother's sharp tongue. No one as gentle as you could ever be capable of such a deed. From the one brief conversation I had with him, your uncle seemed like a man I'd delight in punching out."

Nat decided against revealing he had observed how her uncle had put his hands on her that day in Nebraska City. He had witnessed Melissa's reaction and had come close to chasing down their cart and having it out with the man right then. But, not knowing Melissa, her uncle, or the townspeople, he had felt it was totally possible he was mistaken and figured he had best keep his nose out of it. He feared telling her at this point would catapult her into silence, and he was enjoying their quiet conversation and the gentle lilt of her voice as she spoke.

As she mentally relived the time she had spent in her aunt and uncle's home, Melissa's eyes welled with tears.

She thought of poor Aunt Georgina's fate and wondered if the woman had welcomed death as an escape from the horror of her life with John Hund. Things had happened so quickly since then she had mostly been able to avoid dwelling on the past. She felt Nat's good hand reach out to hers and give it a firm squeeze as if in sympathy for what she had gone through, although he couldn't possibly know. Keeping her hand in his, he began entertaining her with humorous tales of his life on the plantation, some of which she had already heard from Tom. Melissa remembered Tom had mentioned a beloved sister, so she asked about his siblings. A cloud came over his face.

"I had two brothers and a baby sister. One of my brothers died in the war, along with my father," he stated flatly. He hadn't even told Alston the story of his ejection from the family. Tom knew, but he had sworn Tom to secrecy. "You know, I'm feeling a little bit tired now and would like to get some rest," he ended.

Disappointed with the sudden termination of an enjoyable conversation—*he is so easy to talk to*—Melissa helped Nat back to a reclining position. She pulled some leaves off trees to construct a makeshift pillow so his head wouldn't be lying on the hard ground and sat silently beside him as he drifted off to sleep. Once he seemed to be resting comfortably, she decided she'd best find something they could eat when he awoke. They had consumed the last of the beef jerky, and it was no telling when Alston would arrive with help. Although she had gone fishing several times with her father and figured she might be able to fashion a fishing pole out of one of the tree branches and knot some of the used bandages for line, the thought of eating raw fish made her lose her appetite. Alston had warned her not to build a fire, lest the Indians spot the smoke and find her and Nat. She carried Nat's gun with her, but only for protection. She wasn't sure she could hit an animal even if it stood still, and besides, the gunshot might be heard. Maybe she could find some berries.

Returning about an hour and a half later, empty handed, she found Nat lying in a semi-conscious state. Beads of sweat were pouring down his face, even as he murmured he was cold, and his body shook as though chilled. *What to do?*

"Nat, I'm going to check your bandages," Melissa said in the calmest voice she could muster. She didn't want to alarm him, but Alston had warned her about the possibility of an infection setting in, with blood poisoning, especially since they had had nothing but water with which to cleanse the wounds. Her hands shook as she struggled to remove the strips of cloth without causing him a lot of pain. *Dear God, puss is oozing from the wounds, and I have no idea what I should do!*

She ran to the river to fetch clean water and the bandages she had left there. Before she had begun her quest for food, she had had the foresight to wash the bloodied strips of cloths from the first changing as best she could without soap, scrubbing them furiously against a rock in the river and leaving them to dry in the sun.

"It's okay, Nat, I'll keep you warm," she continually consoled as she changed his makeshift dressings with trembling hands. Nat's only response was an unintelligible mumble. He seemed to be slipping deeper and deeper into oblivion. Removing the blanket from her body, she again curled up beside him, enfolding him in her body warmth as she tightened the covering around them. Lying there, she considered Nat's reaction when asked about his siblings. *Had his father and brother been fighting for the Union or the Confederacy?* She knew Virginia had been split. *Had he been responsible for their deaths? Was it guilt that had caused his face to cloud over?* Then she prayed again that God would spare Nat's life—for her and for Emmie.

"Melissa, dear sweet Melissa."

Melissa must have succumbed to sleep at some point, but the sound of her name awakened her. Nat's forehead was beaded with sweat, and she raised the blanket to wipe the moisture from his face. His body felt moist and cold, and she inched closer, trying desperately to instill her warmth in him. *He had called out her name in his delirium!* The night before, she would have felt joy, but now she felt only despair. He must be grateful to her for nursing him through this—if, indeed, she could—but his first love was for this woman Emmie, and as much as she had come to care for him herself, Melissa would never try to steal a man from another woman.

****

Awakening as daylight beckoned, Melissa's first instinct was to check for a heartbeat in her patient. She was gratified to sense one. Gently, she untangled herself from his inert body and, taking care not to disturb him, tucked their only blanket around his body. Still asleep, he immediately shoved the blanket to his waist, revealing his chest, its dark curly hairs damp with sweat. The bandages were soaked, and Melissa knew she needed to change them. Since he seemed to have little use for the warmth of the blanket, she clad herself in it once again before going to the river for fresh water, maneuvering gingerly to avoid slipping on the muddy banks. Nat was still slumbering heavily when she returned. Struggling, she managed to roll him onto his left side and began to unwrap the soaked, soiled cloth from his body. He barely stirred, which alarmed her. The area around his seeping wounds was now a scarlet red, and Melissa prayed help would come quickly.

Her anxiety heightened, she alternated between sitting beside her patient and pacing the surrounding area. The sounds of birds chirping depressed rather than cheered her. How could they be so merry when she was so sad? She imagined the squirrels chattering in the trees above were discussing Nat's fate among themselves.

It was late afternoon when she heard hoofbeats. Grabbing Nat's rifle, she hoped it was the help she had prayed for and not Indians. As she clutched the weapon, her stomach felt like it was touching her backbone so great was her hunger. She had tried to appease it by drinking voluminous amounts of water, but she was more worried about Nat. He needed nourishment, and she was unable to provide any. She herself was growing weak and beginning to feel faint. Only the knowledge that Nat needed her to take care of him kept her from succumbing. Her heart thudded against her chest as she shielded her eyes and tried to identify the riders in the distance without revealing her location. The combination of the sun in her eyes and the dust being kicked up as they approached made it difficult, but she could tell there were a large number.

"Missy!"

Joyous upon hearing Alston's voice, she stepped out from her hiding place, waving and calling out to him.

Chapter Thirteen

A full week had passed since Nat and Melissa were rescued. After loading Nat into a wagon, Alston, Watson Calhoune, and a couple of the calvary, including a medical doctor, accompanied them back to the fort. The remaining calvary attacked the Indian village, burning their teepees in much the same way as the Indians had burnt the wagons. Mrs. Avery had been killed by one of the Indians as she ran screaming toward the rescuers. Hearing the soldiers boast about how they had caught the savages by surprise and that most of the braves had been with the village at the time, Melissa wondered about the fate of the old squaw who had taken care of her and the younger woman who had ordered her brother to let Melissa go. *Were the white men any kinder in their attack than the Indians had been? Had they spared the women and children?* Somehow, she doubted it, and the words of the young Indian woman echoed in her ears. Perhaps all men were savages, regardless of their color, in the throes of battle. The whites were fighting to protect their own as they attempted to make their homes in this wild country. At the same time, the Indians were fighting to protect their lands from the white invasion. And things were hardly better back East where people purported to be more civilized. There, whites fought against whites, brothers and fathers against brothers and fathers. She had heard the rumors of plantations being burned and women raped by the Union soldiers. Horrors of what befell Northern women when the rebels gained ground in a battle had not escaped her ears either. While Melissa did not believe in slavery and she had not quite understood it when she had heard her father talking about how the Southern states claimed they were fighting for something called "states' rights," she wondered if anything was worth all the bloodshed. Everything had seemed so simple less than a year ago. The North was right; the South was wrong. The whites were righteous in driving the savages from the land they had always inhabited; the savages were, after all, a dirty, inhuman bunch—closer to beasts, really. Such were the beliefs with which she grew up. But the young Indian woman had given her back her freedom, even if out of a sense of repayment for another good deed. Now nothing seemed so black-and-white anymore.

"Good news! The colonel has given us permission to continue west now that another train has joined us." Mavis's voice broke into her thoughts. "I thought maybe ye and I could ride together in my wagon. We're told we must prepare to leave in the morning before other tribes get word of our recent destruction of that village a few days ago, though. Ye *are* coming, aren't ye?"

Mavis's wagon was one of several that had escaped major damage in the Indian attack. To be sure, there were a few unclaimed wagons now, their owners and their dreams buried in this unfamiliar land. The Averys' wagon had been burned to the ground. Several of the surviving members of the train had banded together and, taking some of the wagons still intact after the attack, had already headed back East, their visions of a better life out West shattered. A fiery Scotsman named MacCormack had led them, against the better judgment of Colonel Stone. But even more emigrants were arriving, replacing those who had departed. Just yesterday, the fort's guards had announced the approach of another wagon train, and Mavis and Melissa joined others to watch their advance. The billowing white canvases, some approaching twelve abreast, were spread across the prairie looking like fluffy, low clouds, as another set of hopefuls arrived. Watson Calhoune had been more animated than Melissa had ever seen him. He was restless and eager to get back to the Colorado Territory before the first snow, Melissa sensed. She had heard that MacCormack's group had met up with the new bunch and that the tales of their misfortunes had convinced some of the would-be western pioneers to return with him. Most, judging by their numbers, had continued. Melissa had made her decision to continue, too. There was nothing for her back East. She knew some of the people from their wagon train who had lost some or all their family members, as well as their worldly possessions, were forging forward as well. Their fortitude in the face of such severe adversity both astounded her and gave her strength. If they could manage to make a new life for themselves despite it all, so, too, could she.

"Thanks, Mav, I appreciate that. Yes, I'm coming." Melissa had been worried that Calhoune would send her back as he had originally intended, but he had apparently changed his mind.

"I understand Nat, Tom, and Alston are coming, too, though Nat is a wee bit unhappy about being relegated to riding along on the seat of a wagon for a while. Doctor Carson said his wounds are healing nicely, but he doesn't want Nat handling any reins and reopening them." Mavis glanced slyly at her companion as she brought up the topic.

"What Nat is or is not happy about is none of my concern," Melissa replied tersely.

Upon his initial examination, Doctor Carson had reported that blood poisoning had not yet set in but said the wounds had become severely infected. He had cleaned them with alcohol, stitched the gaping holes left by the arrow, and rewrapped the area, claiming he could do little more. The body would have to heal itself, and Nat's had obviously done a remarkable job. Melissa had seen him walking, albeit slowly as though still in pain, around the fort yesterday with his jacket thrown over his shoulders to provide room for the massive bandage wrapped around his breast and right shoulder. Immediately drawn to the curly dark hair on his chest, which tapered as it met the waistline of his trousers, she scolded herself, averted her eyes, and turned to walk in the opposite direction, pretending not to hear when he called her name.

Mavis was not to be put off. "Hmm. I noticed ye dinna once visit him in his convalescence. Yet Sarah tells me ye've asked her for news of his health when ye've gone to her tent. What exactly happened whilst the two of ye were alone together?"

"Mavis, please. You're a dear friend, but I just don't want to talk about it."

"Okay, grand. Well, 'tis best we get started packing up the wagon," Mavis replied, adroitly changing the subject. "I bought some supplies from that greedy sutler. He wanted a dear price, but I negotiated with him a bit."

Mavis's grin told Melissa exactly what type of negotiations Mavis had engaged in. Salvaging what they could from the damaged wagons, the surviving train occupants had divided the usable supplies among themselves, but shortages had to be made up with purchases, and Melissa had heard the sutler was charging ten times the normal price, knowing of the travelers' needs.

She felt fortunate she now had three serviceable dresses among her belongings. The officer's wives, Audrey Mattox among them, had taken her into their homes when she had returned in such a scraggly state with only a blanket covering her body, exclaiming over the ordeal she had been through and sharing what they could of their personal belongings as they plied her with questions about the Indians, eager for the bit of sensationalism. Melissa was grateful for their help but had no wish to revisit her experiences. She had answered their questions without embellishment and was thankful when the women, obviously realizing her fatigue and her reluctance to talk about it, gave up. Mrs. Mattox and another wife who was about Melissa's size had donated the dresses along with two sets of undergarments.

The remainder of the day was a bustle of activity as the wagons were prepared for departure the next morning. The new arrivals restocked supplies and helped others finish repairing the wagons that had been damaged but were still deemed in good enough condition to make the trip. Despite all their recent ordeals, spirits were high. That evening the military wives prepared another banquet as a farewell to the travelers, with whom some close friendships had formed during the nearly two weeks the wagon train had been stalled there. Tom, having quickly recovered from his own wound, pulled out his harmonica, and voices joined to sing the familiar

Stephen Foster song, "Camptown Races" as well as others they all knew. Calhoune and the wagon master of the new train, a large man who introduced himself as Jake Seymour, instructed their combined charges on what to expect in the days that lay ahead. The wagons would continue to follow the Platte River to Julesberg, which was a good two weeks' journey if all went well. At Julesberg, they would take the southern trail along the South Platte into Denver. Water should not be a problem. With any luck, they would arrive in Denver by mid-September, hopefully before the first snowfall. After Tom finished playing a soulful rendition of "Amazing Grace" as a tribute to their fallen companions, Melissa left the gathering to pay a final visit to Sarah's tent to thank her for her friendship. She had already revisited the grave sites of Mr. Avery and young Rachel, placing freshly-picked wildflowers upon the mounds of dirt marked with simple wooden crosses on which someone had taken the time to whittle their names. Graves of the others killed in the massacre bore similar crosses.

She hadn't gotten a quarter of the way to her destination when she felt a strong hand come from behind to encircle her upper arm. Frightened—she hadn't heard anyone following her, possibly due to the din of the farewell gathering—she swung around and, fist drawn, was ready to attack the assailant with her free hand when she saw it was Nat.

"You should know better than to sneak up on someone like that, especially in your condition," she scolded, lowering her arm.

"Want to tell me why you've been avoiding me?" Nat countered. "I've been wanting to thank you for saving my life."

"Alston did that. He pulled the arrow out and tended to it. All I did was change the bandages as he instructed."

"And used your own soft body to keep mine warm," Nat reminded her, his eyes sparkling with mischief as he used his grip on her arm to pull her closer. Melissa could see his intent as he lowered his head.

"Nat, I—" Her words were cut off as his mouth met hers. His lips felt soft and warm against hers, and she unwillingly responded. His mouth captured her lower lip, gently pulling on it and teasing it with kisses. As she opened her mouth to issue a weak protest, he entered it with his tongue, exploring it tenderly, forcing her own tongue to respond. Dazed by the foreign sensations, Melissa caressed his neck with her slender fingers as their tongues performed their own secret dance, their movements alternating between delicate and intense. The dance ended as Nat sought to capture her upper lip, and Melissa could feel his hardened manhood pressing against her pelvis when he grasped her buttocks in his large hand, pulling her body even closer. Lost in an unfamiliar world, Melissa was willing to follow his lead anywhere. Running her hands over his lower back, she reveled in the feel of his powerful muscles. Suddenly, a loud cheer came from the building they had just left, breaking the spell. *My God, what am I doing?* Bringing her hands to the front of his chest, she pushed away.

"No!" She cried, tears forming in her eyes as she turned and ran from a stunned Nat.

****

At daybreak, the wagons were rolling again. Melissa sat beside Mavis as the petite woman expertly took charge of the reins. That Mavis was strong enough to handle the team of horses pulling her farm wagon astounded Melissa, but then so many things about Mavis amazed her. Tom stopped to check on their well-being as he rode by, directing the wagons into manageable rows. Alston was driving their wagon with Nat riding beside him in foul temper, Tom reported good-naturedly. Tom's arm was still tender, but he hoped to be able to spell Al on the wagon reins in a couple of days.

Fortunately, Mavis seemed unaware of the flush Melissa felt creeping over her body as the smaller woman concentrated on making the animals go in the direction Tom had instructed. *What happened to me last night? I behaved like a common harlot!* She couldn't tell if the warmth spreading quickly through her body was due to remorse or rekindled memories of the night before when she had so brazenly pressed her body closer to Nat's. She felt nauseous and sick at heart. Her actions had, no doubt, confirmed Nat's opinion that she was a loose woman. First, he had seen her with her uncle; then he believed she had run off with that captain; and now he had first-hand knowledge of how easily she succumbed to lustful pleasures. *Had he said anything to Alston or Tom?* She remembered hearing the three of them jokingly discuss their nightly exploits the morning she had awakened as a stowaway in their wagon. The thought heightened her embarrassment. Mentally, she revisited the recent brief encounter with Tom. *Had he looked at me any differently?* She didn't think so, but she couldn't be certain.

****

Nat grumbled an apology to Alston after leveling a stream of curses at the older man when the wagon hit a rut, throwing Nat's injured shoulder hard into one of the wooden bows supporting the Conestoga's canvas.

"What's ailing you, Nat?" Alston had a look of alarm. "Them stitches get torn?"

"Damnable woman!" Nat growled.

Alston's only response was a relieved grin, which aggravated Nat more. He'd been haunted all morning by the sight of Melissa's tears when she had turned and run from him. Hell, he hadn't violated her in any way, although he had to admit he would have liked to do just that last night. He sensed she was inexperienced and had planned to move slowly so as not to frighten her away. God only knew what pain her uncle had inflicted on her. He would strangle the man with his bare hands if he ever got hold of him. He had been pleasantly surprised when she had reacted so passionately toward him.

He'd only had experience with one other "lady" before, a Southern belle who was the daughter of a friend of his mother's. At his mother's urging, he had called on her a few times. He had to admit Amanda had been comely, but she was also vain and self-centered and prone to playing coy. When he had kissed her as they strolled in the manicured garden behind her family's mansion, finally realizing that's what she wanted all along, he'd felt like he was kissing a rattlesnake. Her lips had been dry and cold. Since then, he'd only relieved himself with so-called loose women, avoiding the respectable ones. At least they were honest about their feelings, or lack thereof, and they exuded a certain lusty warmth.

He'd assumed all "ladies" were like Amanda. But he'd found Melissa irresistible. The feel of her lean, long body sprawled nude across his kept floating through his mind while he had been bedridden, causing him some embarrassment whenever an unexpected visitor popped his head in to see how he was faring. He'd had to see if she tasted as good as she smelled. She'd tasted even better, he thought with a smile. And, if he didn't miss his guess, she could prove to be a fine blend of "lady" and "harlot"—feminine and refined, yet down-to-earth and passionate. Well, he reconciled himself, they'd be in this damn caravan together for another month or more. That should be enough time for him to get her to trust him. He'd keep his distance for the first week or so. He didn't want to scare her off again.

He had gotten Calhoune to agree to let her come along on the condition that he, Tom, and Alston would be responsible for her. He suspected her recent plight at the hands of that fake captain and then the Indians had softened Calhoune's heart a bit. When they got to Denver, the three soldiers would have to report to Camp Weld, but he'd see Melissa settled there with her sister and brother-in-law. And after he had fulfilled this damnable commission, he would offer for her hand. He'd saved enough from his army pay to establish a little nest egg that would help him and Tom and Alston get started in the mining business. Visions of a comfortable log house with a roaring fire and a woman with golden-brown hair and green-flecked brown eyes greeting him when he came home had taken up residence in his mind.

He had wired Emmie from Fort Kearny to let her know of his whereabouts. Right now, he could only hope Albert had gotten hold of his senses, though he doubted it. Regardless, he'd take care of Emmie. He'd have her take a stagecoach to Denver today if he thought it was safe, but between robbers and Indians, she was probably better off where she was for the time being. Satisfied he had solved the issues at hand, with a word to Alston he crawled into the bed of the wagon, pulled his cap over his eyes, and went to sleep.

Chapter Fourteen

Although she had taken the reins of her father's horse-drawn carriage upon occasion, it took several days for Melissa to learn how to handle a whole team of horses. She was glad to be able to give Mavis's arms a rest, however, and controlling the beasts took her mind off the monotony of the trip as the autumn-gold hue of the prairie seemed to stretch endlessly ahead. It also took her mind off other matters. Since leaving Fort Kearny, she had not spoken to Nat, although she had glimpsed him from time to time when the wagons were stopped. It looked like he was moving around better, a fact confirmed by Tom and Alston when she overheard them talking to Mavis. He seemed to be avoiding her, no doubt having decided she was simply a whore and no longer interested him. She tried to tell herself it didn't matter. He had his life, which included a woman he loved, and she would make her own life. But she couldn't lie to her heart. She missed the friendship she sensed had developed between them that afternoon when they had enjoyed such an easy conversation. He had expressed a genuine interest in what her life had been like before she had joined the train, and his responses had been so gentle and caring. *Oh, Mama,* she thought, clutching her beloved ring, *what have I gotten myself into? How does one cure a broken heart? I wish you were here to talk to!*

"Storm coming!" Alston rode by, alerting the

members of the train who may have been oblivious to the dark clouds in the distant horizon. "Calhoune says these prairie storms move fast and furious, so best be prepared."

Watson Calhoune obviously knew what he was talking about. After she had secured the wagon's flaps to guard against the oncoming downpour, Mavis walked beside the wagon to stretch her body. Melissa had the reins when the clouds, which had seemed so distant, were suddenly directly over them, drenching the travelers as the storm raged. The temperature had dropped several degrees, and Melissa's teeth started chattering as she sat trapped in her cold, wet clothes. She heard Mavis's cry as her friend ran toward the wagon to seek shelter. The darkened sky was lit up by a burst of lightning that accompanied a loud clap of thunder. At the sound, one of Melissa's horses bolted, and the others followed suit. Standing up, she braced herself against the seat to get more leverage, pulling hard and desperately at the reins to try to regain control. She could barely see as the rain came down in torrents and the wind whipped strands of her wet hair across her face. The horses continued to race forward, passing wagons drawn by oxen and mules, animals that seemed to have been undaunted by the sudden loud sound. Other emigrants yelled instructions to her as she flew past, instructions lost in the wind. The wagon rocked perilously as it gained speed over the rough terrain. Nearly losing her balance, Melissa could only scream silently in terror while she concentrated on her attempt to gain control of the runaways. Suddenly, a body flung itself off one of the wagons to land astride a lead horse.

"Pull those reins as hard as you can and, when the

horses start to slow, set the brake," the man shouted back at her as he pulled on reins at the front of the team.

After what seemed like an eternity but had probably been only a few minutes, the horses slowed and the wagon came to a standstill. Melissa had managed to keep her wits about her and follow the man's orders throughout the ordeal, but now that the terror of the ordeal was over, her body was wracked with uncontrollable sobs.

She felt strong arms encompassing her body as she let all her pent-up emotions flow through her tears.

"Hush, Sweetness, hush." Melissa was vaguely aware it was Nat's voice and it was Nat rocking her as her hysteria continued along with the storm. The downpour strengthened in intensity, and with it came pellets of solid matter.

"Damn! Hail! I've got to unhitch those horses. They're liable to bolt again, and the brake will be useless. I'll be right back. Best you get into the wagon," Nat coaxed gently as he opened the flap and motioned for her to enter the shelter of the canvas.

Within minutes he reappeared. "I tied them to the back of the wagon. They won't like riding out the storm there, but there's no shelter here on the prairie, and at least they won't take us on another unwanted ride," he said as he climbed into the wagon and encircled her quivering body in his arms once again.

"Mavis…" Melissa spoke her friend's name as a question.

"She's okay. When your wagon went out of control, she found shelter in another."

The hail was coming down harder, and balls of ice, some the size of small plums, tore through the canvas covering. Nat and Melissa scooted to the back of the wagon where the canvas was still intact.

"I'm sorry for being such an idiot and panicking as I did," Melissa apologized.

"You're not an idiot, and you handled the situation well, especially given your inexperience. You're one helluva woman," Nat responded huskily as he lowered his mouth to hers, seeking to taste the honey once again.

"Nat, no," she murmured in weak protest. Using all the willpower she could muster, she grasped his shoulders to push him away, remembering his injury when she felt him flinch.

"Nat, you're hurt! Have the stitches torn? Take off your shirt!" Melissa had fully recovered her senses and was gently pulling off his wet shirt as she spoke.

"Good idea," Nat said with a grin. "In fact, I think both of us need to get out of these wet clothes," he added in a sultry voice.

Satisfied that the stitches had held, Melissa narrowed her eyes as she gazed into the clear blue sea of his. "Well, you might have pulled some already tender muscles, but it seems like the damage is minimal," she responded, ignoring his comment.

"I'm serious, Melissa. And it's not like I haven't seen it all before," he could not resist adding. "It wouldn't do for either of us to come down with pneumonia."

Unable to argue with the wisdom of those last words, Melissa ordered him to turn his back while she rid herself of her own wet clothes and wrapped a blanket around herself, thinking that she would wait to don fresh, dry clothes when the danger of immediately soaking them had passed. Nat had taken off his boots and was beginning to strip off his trousers in full view of Melissa. Shocked, she threw him a blanket.

"Cover yourself," she commanded. Nat raised his eyebrows at her as though to say it wasn't necessary so far as he was concerned, but he mutely gave in to her demand and wrapped the blanket around his waist, leaving his chest bare.

"Come here." It was Nat's turn to issue a command. Melissa was about to refuse when he added a gentle, "Please. You're getting wet again."

It was true. The hail had stopped as suddenly as it had begun, but rain was still pouring through the holes in the front part of the canvas. The only dry spot was where Nat now sat, and Melissa settled herself down next to him, wrapping the blanket tightly around herself as she pulled her knees to her chest, encircling them with her arms.

"That's better," he commented as he wrapped an arm around her shivering body.

As tempted as he was, he vowed he would not take advantage of her vulnerability, even if it killed him. This was not the time or the place. Using every bit of will power he could dredge up, he pulled away once she had stopped shaking and, kneeling before her, tucked her blanket around her more tightly. Melissa didn't know whether to feel relieved or disappointed.

"The rain seems to be letting up, so I suppose we should get dressed," he whispered hoarsely, his breath kissing her face like a gentle breeze. "I love you, Melissa," he added in a voice so soft Melissa wasn't certain she had heard him correctly as he pulled her into a quick, tight embrace before releasing her again, leaving his hands resting on her shoulders.

His declaration startled her, and she searched his face for any sign of insincerity. She studied the eyes locked on hers. Brilliant blue eyes. Bluer than the sky on a clear summer day. Long, soot-colored eyelashes, slightly curled at the tips, gave him a perpetual look of mischievous boyishness. She lifted a finger to trace the slight creases on his face that deepened as he smiled at her explorations. *Yes, she loved him, too, she was certain. Mavis's wee voice couldn't be denied. But she would never tell him. He already had a love—possibly his first love—maybe even his wife. What about Emmie?* She considered asking but was afraid of the answer. She tried to squelch the jealousy she felt, and her stomach churned as images of Nat with another woman flashed through her mind. *This is wrong!*

"Please, let me up," she pleaded.

Now Nat was the confused one. He had watched a myriad of emotions fly across her beautiful face as she had studied him. He thought he had seen bewilderment, then love, and then…desperation? Or was it anger? She had not responded to his declaration of love, but he was certain she felt something more than friendship for him. Frustrated, he relaxed his hold on her and moved aside. Immediately bolting up, she clutched the blanket to her.

"I know, I know, turn my back," Nat teased gently as he turned around and moved farther away to allow her the privacy he knew she was about to demand. *I will win her trust, and I will marry her*, he silently vowed to himself.

****

Calhoune and Seymour passed the word that the wagon train would remain where it was for a day to allow the emigrants to repair the damage done by the hail. A day's delay would also give the ground a chance to dry some so wagon wheels would not get stuck in the mud as they continued. Mavis stood on an overturned pail to reach the canvas with her needle and thread as Melissa stood by her side, working to patch one of the several other gashes.

"What I wouldn't give ye for ye height at times like this!" Mavis exclaimed in frustration as she nearly toppled off her perch.

"And I've always yearned to be short like you." Melissa smiled at her friend. "Tallness in a woman is not fashionable, you know. Men prefer women your size." She imagined Nat's Emmie was a petite, feminine-looking creature.

"I'm thinking there's one man on this train that likes ye figure just fine." Mavis declared bluntly, giving Melissa a knowing look.

Pretending to check her handiwork from another angle as she felt her face redden, Melissa turned away. The two women continued to work in silence. Melissa's thoughts kept returning to the scene in the wagon a few hours before, as they had ever since Nat had pulled on his wet clothes and departed, giving her a quick kiss on the cheek. Although she hadn't seen him since, the lingering memories still caused a warmth to spread over her. Resolutely, she pushed them out of her mind.

"Whew! I feel like I've got lead weights in my arms," Melissa exclaimed as she rubbed her limbs that ached from holding them above her head so long as she stitched.

"What I wouldn't give ye for a hot cup of tea," Mavis said, jumping off the bucket after she'd completed her last stitch.

"Me, too, but it's unlikely there's any dry timber to be found to build a fire to heat the water," Melissa responded forlornly.

Mavis studied her friend closely. "I'm thinking ye are concerned about something more than not being able to enjoy a hot cup of tea, at the minute." When Melissa did not respond, Mavis continued brightly, "Tell ye what. We'll prepare a feast for supper. We have some jerky here, some biscuits left over from breakfast, some cheese we bought from that unscrupulous sutler at Fort Kearny, and some candied dried fruits for dessert. We'll wrap ourselves in blankets and share secrets like two schoolgirls."

Melissa's increasingly heavy heart didn't leave her hungry for any of Mavis's suggestions, but she couldn't bring herself to squelch her friend's ebullience as Mavis began gathering the items necessary to prepare the repast. Once done, Mavis threw her a blanket and drew one over herself as she tied into a piece of the jerky, inviting Melissa to do the same.

"Did ye ever in your wildest imagination be thinking that ye'd be doing what ye're doing now—traveling on a wagon train heading west—when ye was growing up? Did ye ever be thinking that ye might be captured by Indians or handling runaway horses?" Mavis queried to break the silence.

"No." Melissa replied, recalling that she had expected to live with her parents until the day she met a respectable man, fell in love, and married him as Alicia had done with Jesse. She had envisioned herself living in a house with a white picket fence, happily hanging out laundry as her children chased each other around the yard, screaming gleefully and tugging at her skirts from time to time. *When had that image changed?* When she had moved in with Uncle John and Aunt Georgina, she realized. In her naiveté, she had never considered that all marriages weren't as happy as those of her parents and her sister and brother-in-law. During the short time she had lived with Aunt Georgina, she had sensed that if her dear aunt had had some kind of trade to turn to, she might have left her abusive husband. Now she was dead, and her death made Melissa determined to become a self-sufficient woman. Even if she fell in love and chose to marry in the future, if the man didn't treat her well, she could leave him and make her own way in the world. Nat's handing her off to the Averys without giving her a say in the matter still rankled her. *What gall! No one will ever determine my life's course again!*

"I was never thinking I'd end up as I am, either," Mavis continued as she munched on a piece of cheese. "I'm thinking I still have a wee bit of the romantic in me, in spite of all that's happened. Someday I'd like to meet me a gentleman I can trust with me heart—to give me whole self to, to share me life with. But I'm what most would call 'soiled goods' now," she ended despondently.

"Really, Mav?" That admission astounded Melissa. Mavis was the most independent woman she had ever met, and she admired that, even though she didn't quite agree with her friend's cavalier attitude toward using sex as a method to achieve what she wanted.

Recovering from her own musings, Mavis warned, "Now don't ye be spreading it around that I've gone soft in the heart. I can't have me reputation ruined," she ended with a grin.

"Mavis," Melissa hesitated, not certain how to phrase her question or whether she should even ask it.

Her mouth was dry as she tried to swallow a piece of biscuit. "You've had a lot of experience with a lot of different men, right?"

"Ye can count on it. Ye've seen me belt." Mavis had returned to her usual bold self.

"Has a guy ever not—I mean, have you ever been naked with a guy who didn't try to…to…well, you know." Melissa grabbed a piece of the jerky and began chewing vigorously to cover her embarrassment.

"Bloody, no! I always leave me men well satisfied. That's how I get what I want from them. I told ye that," Mavis chuckled with self-satisfaction as she licked the sugary residue of the candied fruit off her fingers. Sensing Melissa's dismay with her response, she inquired, "Why do ye ask?"

"No reason in particular." Melissa wanted to be alone with her thoughts. "I'm feeling weary from the day's events, Mav. I think I'll turn in early, if you don't mind. I'm sorry I'm not better company."

Mavis stared at her friend as Melissa wrapped herself in her bedroll. She'd give a pot of gold to know what had transpired between Melissa and Nat during the time they were sheltered in this wagon together. She sensed Nat had strong feelings for Melissa, and she for him. Something wasn't right. She shrugged. *It's not me funeral*, she reminded herself.

****

Melissa, feigning sleep, fought desperately to organize her thoughts. Organization had always comforted her. While Alicia's drawers had been stuffed with unfolded undergarments that often peeked out, and their closet floor had been littered with her scattered shoes, Melissa had always carefully folded her belongings and lined her shoes up neatly, like little soldiers. She had promptly mended torn stockings and other apparel and, as a result, had on many occasions lent her older sister her belongings when Alicia had discovered her only clean garments were torn. Melissa hadn't minded. She was just thankful she knew her own belongings were in order. She always felt she could meet any situation head on as long as she was organized. Now she sought to put some structure to her thoughts.

Point one: *She loved Nat Bellamy. No*, she argued with herself. She only thought she loved Nat Bellamy. Truth be known, her feelings were probably no more than lust. Point two: *Nat had been kind and caring.* She had experienced this firsthand and had seen him exhibit it toward others. She remembered how much little Josh had loved him. *And he was loyal.* Tom and Alston had regaled her with enough of their stories to convince her of his undying loyalty to them. And hadn't he come to her rescue when it seemed no one would?

This is getting me nowhere! She admonished herself. *If I'm to get over him, which I must, I need to concentrate on his bad points, not his good.* Point three: *He is domineering and overbearing. His wife would never be allowed to be her own person.* She was certain of this, given his callous handling of her when he had learned she was a stowaway on his wagon. Point four: *He was a traitor.* Even though she now knew he had actually fought for the Union, he was from the South. Undoubtedly, he had fought against friends, if not his own family. *So much for loyalty. And what about Emmie? He is betraying her whenever he attempts to pursue me. A man such as that cannot be trusted. Even if I were to succumb willingly to him, I could never be sure he would not betray my love with some other woman in the same way.*

There, she had cleared her mind and was thinking rationally again. She congratulated herself. She now had the ammunition she needed to resist her own heretofore seemingly uncontrollable desires for him. Mavis, as worldly as she seemed, was wrong. The "wee voice" one heard was born from one's emotions. Emotions led to muddled thinking. Mavis herself had admitted she was still a romantic at heart, and that was not what Melissa wanted for herself anymore. She was no longer the young girl she had been when she and Alicia had frivolously fantasized about the men they would each meet and marry. She was, and needed to be, a sensible and self-reliant woman now. Confident she had solved the problem at hand through her methodical thought process, Melissa finally slept.

****

The following day was bright and sunny, lifting everyone's spirits, including Melissa's. The wagon masters determined that since all the broken wheels and canvases had been repaired by noon, the train should try to make a few miles in the remaining daylight hours. Too many precious days had already been wasted, putting them behind schedule. Luckily, all the emigrants had the area around Denver as their ultimate destination, so they need not worry about having to cross the treacherous Rocky Mountains. Still, an early snowfall, even on the prairie, would make their trip difficult.

The train moved slowly as the drivers steered to and fro to avoid the biggest ruts left by the downpour. Tom, Alston, and some other men appointed by Calhoune and Seymour were busy shouting orders to keep the wagons in some semblance of order. Nat was at the reins of his own wagon.

Melissa saw the approaching Indians first. Since her recent experience, she had strained her eyes to focus on every tree and rock outcropping, sometimes visualizing lurking hostiles where there were none, letting herself breath again as their wagon approached close enough to dispel her fears. This time she knew it was not her imagination. She spied the men with feathered headbands on horseback maneuvering toward the train just as Alston was passing by.

"Indians!" Her voice squeaked out as she pointed her finger in their direction.

Alerted, Alston followed her finger and immediately spurred his horse forward to find Calhoune. The command to halt came shortly thereafter. The travelers, some with guns at the ready, sat tensely aboard their wagons, watching as Calhoune and Seymour approached the band of twelve Indians on their own horses. The group was too far away to be able to hear what was taking place, but both the Indians and their leaders were gesturing furiously. Finally, the wagon masters returned. The word was spread. The Indians wanted horses in return for passage over their land, and Calhoune and Seymour had agreed to the bargain. Several of the men argued with the two leaders.

"We don't owe them dirty savages nothing," one man put forth. "We already paid for our passage with bloodshed at Fort Kearny!"

Another agreed, adding, "This here's the United States property. We should make *them* pay! *We* got *them* outnumbered now."

"Yeah, make *them* pay." A chorus arose.

Calhoune's booming voice took command of the quickly escalating chaos. "These here Indians don't belong to the same tribe as them that attacked us. These are Lenape. They're a peaceful tribe. Somewheres about thirty years ago, they were relocated here from back East by the U.S. government, so they believe this land is theirs, and their request for a toll is not that unjust. We have extra horses to give them, and then we can proceed without worry of further bloodshed."

"All injuns are alike. The only good injun is a dead injun. I say let's take 'em." As the speaker raised his rifle to level it at the band of Indians, Seymour drew his pistol and shot the man in the arm, causing him to drop the weapon. His wife, who sat beside him, cried out and reached to inspect his wound.

"You're a fool, Miller," Calhoune said angrily to the man who was now clutching his arm with a surprised look on his face. "You think there aren't more of them out here than them twelve who showed themselves? Indians aren't stupid. You just about got us attacked! Seymour and I are the wagon masters here. If you don't like our decisions, then pull out and make a go of it on your own. That goes for any of you who feel like Miller here does. I won't be responsible for losing more lives because of the idiot actions of a few."

Silence followed Calhoune's speech. Finally, some of the men untethered the horses tied to the backs of their wagons to give as a peace offering. Miller glared at them as they did so.

"Cowards, all of you. Well, I'm no yellow-belly," he spat. "We're only a day from Julesburg, by my reckoning. We can find our own way easily from there. Who wants to join me? Annie, take the reins," he commanded his obviously reluctant wife as he wrapped his bandana around the flesh wound to stop the bleeding. "I said, take the reins, woman," he repeated as he backhanded her for not responding immediately, ignoring mumbled protests from a few of the witnesses.

Recovering from her husband's slap, Annie maneuvered their wagon forward to forestall any further abuse. Several whoops of encouragement were heard from five other wagons that proceeded to follow Miller's lead. Calhoune only shook his head as he and Seymour continued to collect horses from the remaining emigrants and deliver them to the waiting Indians. Melissa saw the Indians nod in agreement as they accepted the offering and peacefully retreated in the direction from which they had appeared. Calhoune and Seymour returned to the train and called a meeting, during which each of the leaders repeated Calhoune's warning that their orders were to be obeyed without question. Anyone who did not wish to abide by these rules could catch up with Miller and the others. Not one wagon moved. Both Seymour and Calhoune had previously agreed that this most recent trauma, coming so soon on the heels of the hailstorm, would leave the travelers tense and spent. No good could come from attempting more miles today. Avoidable accidents could occur. Reluctantly, they also announced a halt to the train's progress until the next morning.

Nat rode up to Mavis's wagon almost immediately. "You two all right?" While the question was directed at both women, his eyes rested solely on Melissa. He knew she had to have been terrified, given her previous experience with Indians, and Alston had told him she had been the first to spy them.

"Just as fine as a warm spring day," Mavis answered

brightly for the two of them.

"Melissa?" Nat wanted to hear the words from her.

His concern for her was met with a glower. "As Mavis just told you, we're fine," she replied curtly.

A look of boyish bewilderment flashed across his face at her brusque response, followed quickly by a scowl just before he turned his horse and rode back to his own wagon. Melissa felt a brief sense of shame upon observing his initial puzzled look over her snappish response. *No,* she cautioned herself, *don't feel sorry for him. He is, after all, a traitor.* She caught Mavis's curious look out of the corner of her eye but offered no explanation, and Mavis, wisely, did not pursue the matter.

****

They had been on the trail the next day for three hours when they came across the razed wagons and bloodied bodies. The travelers had been shot to death— some by bullets, some by arrows, some by both. Even though his scalp had been removed, as had those of the other victims, and his eyes gouged out, Miller's body was still recognizable. Some of his body parts had been severed. His wife's body lay over his, dried blood caked on the back of her garment where a bullet had entered to end her life. Melissa cried out upon looking at the scene of needless deaths. She was particularly distraught when she saw Annie's body. *If only she hadn't been so submissive. If only she had stood up to that blackguard husband of hers and refused to go on.* Unable to take in anymore of the brutal spectacle, she ran from the site and promptly proceeded to lose her breakfast in some nearby scrub oak. She felt a firm arm encircle her waist and a warm hand hold her forehead as she continued retching.

She felt comforted initially, as she had when her father had done the same thing when she was sick as a child, but after she was spent, embarrassment crept over her, and she turned to face the source of her solace.

"It's all right, Sweetness. I know exactly how it feels," Nat said in sympathy, his hands now resting comfortably on her shoulders. He remembered only too well the time he had found Jeremy, too late to save his boyhood friend.

Resolving not to be taken in by the false shimmering gleam in his eyes this time, Melissa spat out her retort. "You *have* no feelings, you bastard." Stunned by her words, Nat dropped his hands, and Melissa spun off toward Mavis's wagon. He stood there momentarily, staring at her retreating form and trying for the life of him to think of what he had done to cause such a vicious change in the woman he loved. *Thought he had loved*, he corrected. Perhaps he hadn't come to know Melissa as well as he thought. The language she had just used wasn't the language of an innocent. He might very well have pegged her all wrong. If so, he consoled himself, the woman was one helluva actress.

Graves were dug for the bodies of the victims, prayers recited, and the wagon train moved ahead. Melissa was struck by the realization that life, just like the train, continued on, no matter what. Her parents' deaths, within a month of each other, had made her feel like she didn't want to live anymore either. But, somewhere deep inside her, she knew she must. *Perhaps it's just an innate desire of every human being to survive*, she thought. But then she remembered Mrs. Davis, a neighbor of her parents who had been left a young widow at the age of twenty-three. Hours after learning of her husband's death, Mrs. Davis had taken her own life, using his straight razor to slash her wrists. The razor had been among the personal belongings returned to her by the soldier who had reported his death. Melissa shook her head. *Will I ever understand life?*

She continued mulling this over during the lulls in the conversations she had with Mavis as they followed the rest of the wagon train across the prairie. Mavis had reverted to her brazen personality and rambled on with tales of her exploitation of men, reveling in the fact that she had learned how to get pretty much anything she wanted from them. While Melissa dearly loved Mavis, she really wasn't interested in hearing all the gory details. They had upset her initially, but she had become immune to them. Nevertheless, for her friend's sake, she managed an appropriate shocked response whenever one seemed called for.

They reached Julesburg that same day and took the opportunity to restock on fresh meats, fruits, and vegetables. Their supply of game, killed shortly after their departure from Fort Kearny, had been sparse and was now depleted. The circumstances encountered had prohibited further hunting excursions. Melissa voiced her embarrassment at being unable to help Mavis pay for the purchases that would feed them both on the remainder of their trip, but Mavis quieted her with a simple wave of her hand.

"Does not the Bible say 'feed the hungry'?" she asked. "I haven't much paved me path to heaven in me ways thus far. Mayhap God will shed some amount of pity on me for me good deeds now," she said, grinning at Melissa. "Besides, I've taken a liking to ye," she added warmly. Melissa could not help but smile back.

The wagon train crossed the river at Julesburg to continue down the South Platte River fork. Fortunately, the river was low due to a smaller amount of rainfall than usual, and no mishaps occurred, although some families had been forced to leave more of their precious possessions behind before the river was crossed to avoid getting bogged down on the river's bottom. Earlier in the journey, Melissa had been appalled when women were compelled to leave sacred keepsakes along the trail to lighten the load so the wagons could continue at a reasonable pace. Cedar chests, dining room tables, and other precious possessions, many of them heirlooms, had joined those of previous emigrants in littering the trails west. Now, with all the other horrors experienced, she realized this should be the least of their worries and considered those women who protested these losses to be somewhat immature, regardless of their age. She was thankful, however, that her only valuable possession remained around her neck, and she clutched the ring for good luck. She refused to dwell on the fact that it was Nat who had returned it to her.

A little over a week later, the wagon train reached Fort Morgan with no mishaps along the way. While there was a threat of hostile Indian activity reported in the area, the forts had received more reinforcements since the horrendous Hungate massacre that had occurred just outside of Denver in June, Melissa learned. That and the Indians' experience against the new howitzer guns, which could rapidly fire many shots at a time without reloading, was thought to be the cause of the current uneasy peace. "Like the calm before the storm," Melissa had heard one of the men at Fort Morgan say. The wagons circled outside the fort, but the atmosphere was still tense. The revelry that had occurred when they reached Fort Kearny was not repeated. The occupants of each wagon built their own campfires and cooked their own food, retiring early, eager to resume their trip to Denver, their final destination.

The commander of the fort sent reinforcements with the train to escort them safely to Denver, and the tension diminished visibly at the sight of the five military men riding in front of the wagons. Whether it was due to the increased soldier escort or for some other reason, the train was not attacked.

****

A few days later the mountains came into view, eliciting exclamations of awe from the travelers. Even at this distance, the peaks reigned majestically over the prairie. Excitement bubbled over at the realization they must be nearing the end of their journey, and hoots of glee arose from the wagons. Calhoune and Seymour spread the word that, barring anything unexpected, the train would arrive in the Queen City of the West in just another four days' time.

Mavis turned to Melissa. "Well, lassie, this journey's about to end for both ye and me. I'd like ye to do me a favor if ye feel like it."

Melissa was surprised by the request. She truly had nothing to offer Mavis in repayment for all her kindnesses. "Just ask. I'll be happy to do it."

"Well, I've told ye me life's stories to the point of boring ye, I know. I'm thinking I'd like to hear yer story if ye've a mind to tell it to me."

Melissa had been very unwilling to discuss her past with anyone, and her face flamed at the thought of revealing any of it, even now. However, Mavis had been a dear friend, and since Melissa had not been able to pay her own way on this trip and had relied on Mavis's support, she felt it only fair she indulge her friend in this request. Taking a deep breath, she told Mavis about her parents' deaths; about Alicia and Jesse, whom she hoped to meet up with soon; and even about Uncle John and Aunt Georgina, her uncle's attack, and Aunt Georgina's untimely death.

As Melissa recounted her story, Mavis was uncharacteristically silent for the most part, allowing herself only to take a hand off one of the reins briefly to give Melissa's a squeeze of consolation when Melissa told of her parents' deaths and then, later, of that of her aunt. She had not been able to refrain from exclaiming, "That bloody bastard!" when Melissa revealed her uncle's treachery, but she had held her tongue throughout the rest of her friend's monologue, in fear she would clam up for whatever reason, and Mavis dearly wanted to hear her tale. Even though there wasn't that much difference in their ages, she had come to think of Melissa as a kid sister. Melissa was so naive in so many ways. Perhaps, had she not been, Melissa would not have befriended the likes of her. She might have realized her friendship with a "loose woman" would cause her to be the object of even more scorn from most of the women on the train. *Nay, I dinna truly believe that. Melissa has a good heart.*

Mavis remained quiet for a couple of minutes after Melissa had ceased talking. "I'm sorry for what ye've been through," she finally said in all sincerity. "I'm thinking, though, that like meself, ye'll be stronger for it. And soon ye'll be reunited with yer family. Ye'll not be forgetting me once ye get settled with yer sister, will ye?" She added with a mock look of warning on her face, "Ye can visit me in Denver, ye know. I'm thinking ye've become like family to me, and I canna afford to lose another family. Surely, I'll understand if ye dinna want to remain associated with the likes of meself, though," she added dejectedly.

"Oh, Mavis, how could you think that?" Melissa exclaimed, putting her arm around her diminutive friend's shoulder and giving it a hug. "In fact, I know Alicia and Jesse will love you. You can come and join us on the holidays for a big family feast. You've become part of my family now, too, you know."

Mavis pretended the tears running down her cheeks were caused by the dust being kicked up by the animals' hooves.

Chapter Fifteen

Cheers rose from all the wagons as they rolled into Denver in late afternoon. Calhoune and Seymour relayed instructions for them to halt their wagons next to the banks of the South Platte. A creek ran off the river, dividing the city into what seemed to be two distinct parts. Tents dotted both sides of the creek. To the east lay the sprawling town of Denver, which, as far as Melissa could see, looked flat, brown, and treeless. The flat lands seemed to end abruptly at the foot of the massive mountains that had heralded Denver's proximity to the travelers. Closer now, they looked like giant gods to Melissa, with their gleaming imperial white crowns of snow. Melissa was awestruck by them and marveled at the fortitude of those who dared to cross them in their wagons as they headed farther west.

"Bloody beautiful!" Once she had set the brake on the wagon, Mavis's gaze also fixed on the mountains.

Calhoune's booming voice drew their attention away from the spectacular view, and the two women joined the other emigrants who were gathering around the wagon master.

"This here's where we part company. Yonder is known as Cherry Creek. The Arapaho named it for the chokecherries that grow wild on its banks." He pointed to the body of water Melissa had observed. "Used to be Denver City to the northwest and Auraria to the southeast, but a few years ago, the two communities combined to form what is now known as plain old Denver, the capital of the Colorado Territory. Those of you that don't have no folk here can set up camp on either side of the creek if you take a liking to. I know some of you have come looking for gold. The Ferry Street ferry over yonder will carry your wagon across the Platte for your journey farther into the goldfields. Good luck to ya! Those of you who are thirsty will not find a lack of saloons to whet your whistle, and you can hook up with a woman there to handle whatever else ails ya. Good luck to ya, too!"

The last was met with loud whoops from the men to the indignation of some of the more "proper" women travelers as Calhoune returned to his wagon to go his own way. Tom and Alston had picked their way through the crowd to where Melissa and Mavis stood.

"Well, ladies, it's been a pleasure," Alston began, seeming almost embarrassed, scrunching up his hat in his hands as he spoke.

"We havta be reporting to Camp Weld now," Tom continued. "Don't rightly know how long we'll be around town before we head out after either the rebels or the injuns. You gonna be okay, Missy?"

"I'll be just fine, especially once I find Alicia and Jesse," Melissa said as she took the big black hand in her smaller, pale white one and gave it a squeeze she hoped would convince him that she truly *would* be okay. "Thank you two for being such good friends!"

She stood on tiptoe to give Tom a light kiss on the cheek before turning to plant one on Alston's cheek as well. The wiry guy gave her a big bear hug in return that almost left her gasping for breath. Her eyes misted with tears, and her voice was choked with the realization this might be the last time she saw either of them.

"You take care of each other—and of Nat, too."

Her heart was very well aware he had not come to say his goodbyes, but even though his pointed absence hurt her, she could not wish him ill.

"I'm thinking ye two lads better not be leaving me out of yer goodbyes, or I'll not be sending me Irish luck with ye," Mavis said jovially as she hugged each man heartily and gave them a pat on the rump, causing Alston's face to redden.

"We wouldn't be forgetting about you," Alston replied with a grin, nonetheless. "Never knew a woman who could provide so much mirth."

"Well, there's plenty more where that came from, so ye boys don't forget me when ye are in town. Ye'll find me at one of the saloons. And tell that Lieutenant Bellamy friend of yours I'm thinking I'm insulted he didn't join the two of ye in saying goodbye, but I'll come up with a way he can make it up to me." She ended with a wink and a laugh, and the two men laughed with her, peeking at Melissa as they did. Both had been surprised when Nat didn't join them to say goodbye to the two ladies. Something had obviously happened between the lieutenant and the pretty stowaway.

Mavis had started to walk back to her wagon, but turned when she realized Melissa was not following. She saw her friend looking in the direction Tom and Alston had retreated. The two men had joined Nat again, and Melissa was staring at his back.

"Go to him," Mavis said gently as she rejoined her friend.

"I can't. You don't understand, Mav," Melissa

responded tearfully.

"That I don't, lass," Mavis murmured as she followed Melissa, who had now turned to walk to their wagon.

****

Daylight was waning by the time Mavis and Melissa had secured a spot for their wagon along the banks of what Calhoune had called Cherry Creek. Several other travelers had decided to camp there as well, and the banks were now cluttered with wagons that fought for space beside the tents and tepees that had been there when the train arrived. It was a pleasant September evening with just a slight chill in the air, and the two friends sat on the grassy banks, watching the water rush over the rocks and listening to the music that spilled from the center of town, only a few blocks from where they sat. Many of the wagons were deserted, the single men having gone into Denver to celebrate their arrival. A few families were also camped there, and the women were cooking supper while the children gleefully skipped pebbles across the water. A group of the husbands stood off to one side, no doubt discussing their future plans among themselves. Melissa wondered how many of the wives would have any say in the matter at all.

"I've told ye me plans, and I know ye are thinking to find yer sister, but have ye any thoughts of how ye'll do it?" Mavis queried.

Melissa admitted she did not. She knew from a letter she had received from her sister before her parents' deaths that Alicia and Jesse had homesteaded on some land about thirty miles southeast of Denver, but she had no idea how to contact them to let them know she was here, or how to find their place even if she had a conveyance with which to do so.

"Well, ye know, ye could borrow me wagon, but I'm thinking it's not wise of ye to set out by yerself. Why don't ye come into town with me tomorrow, and mayhap we can find the telegraph office where ye sent yer sister that wire that never was answered. Someone there may know the family name. And then I'm guessing I can find ye someone who'll be more than willing to help a damsel in distress."

"Mav, what would I do without you?" Melissa marveled at Mavis's ability to come up with a logical solution to what Melissa had thought was an impossible problem. After they retired that night, Melissa clutched her mother's ring and felt a surge of real excitement for what tomorrow would hold. She'd be with her family once again—or at least what was left of it. All the trials and tribulations were behind her. Thoughts of Nat tried to creep into her mind, but she determinedly pushed them out. The cad hadn't even been gentleman enough to offer a polite farewell.

****

Mavis and Melissa trudged up the hill to the telegraph office the following morning. They had obtained directions to it from a young married couple who had a temporary tent-home along the creek. The couple had been there only two months and had never heard of Alicia or Jesse Hanks. As they walked past the one- and two-story buildings that lined Larimer Street, the town's main thoroughfare, Melissa remembered hearing Denver described as the Queen City of the Plains once, and she wondered at what the other cities out here must look like in that case. She and Mavis were constantly dodging dogs and pigs, both of which ran wild, and horses and wagons kicked up dust in their faces as the two maneuvered their way along the dirt streets. A couple of men stumbled out of a saloon and, upon seeing the two women, shouted some lewd comments at them that turned Melissa's face beet-red. Mavis just gave the men a big smile and a wink and flipped the bottom of her skirt up to reveal a trim ankle as they passed.

"Hey, I think she likes me!" Melissa heard one of the men slur after they had passed the two drunks.

"Why did you do that?" Melissa hissed. "They could have caused trouble!"

"What've I been telling ye? I know me men. Those two were too corned to do anything other than talk about it. Likely, they enjoyed the brief show I gave them, and I'm thinking it's not too early to be making friends."

Melissa shook her head in wonder. "Mav, with all the flirting you do, it's amazing you haven't ended up badly beaten or dead. I've heard men don't like to be teased."

"I can handle whatever comes me way. I always have me knife with me, and I have a bloody good aim." At Melissa's look of astonishment, she added, "What did ye think I carved those notches in me belt with? Besides, I only flirt with men I consider safe, or with men I *want* to take to bed with me. I've only had to use me knife once," she said, somewhat defensively.

Melissa quickened her pace as though to outrun the conversation. She had already heard more about Mavis's exploits than she cared to know. Shortly, she spotted the two-story brick building with the United States flag on it that served as both post office and telegraph office.

Mavis must have seen it about the same time. "Ye go on in. I'm thinking I'll go across to that saloon and see if they would like to hire a singer."

"But you can't go into a place like that alone," Melissa started to protest. Mavis was already halfway across the road by the time she finished her sentence, though, and Melissa resigned herself to the fact that she and Mavis were really very different people. Mavis would live her life as she saw fit, and Melissa could either take it or leave it. As she watched her friend enter the building across the street, a small smile formed on her lips. Mavis was a dear friend, no matter what, and a remarkable woman who got what she wanted out of life. Even if Melissa didn't quite agree with her methods, she had to admire the petite Irish girl. Taking a deep breath, Melissa entered the telegraph office, squinting as her eyes adjusted to the dimmer interior light.

"Love, Nat. Now are you sure you got the name right? Emmie Bellamy. B-e-l-l-a-m-y."

Melissa recognized his voice before she was able to see the man bent over the cage window. His words replayed themselves in her mind as she stood frozen in place. *Emmie Bellamy. Emmie was his wife!* Nat turned and almost bumped into her as he made to leave.

"Melissa?" He spoke her name as a question. She looked like she had seen a ghost!

"Melissa, what's wrong? Has something happened? Tell me!" His hands grasped her shoulders while his eyes held a look of panic.

Melissa's first inclination was to slap him, but even in her agitated state, she realized that to make a scene might not be in her best interest. A bad impression might make it difficult for her to get any information from the telegraph clerk, assuming he had anything to tell her.

"Mr. Bellamy, how nice to see you again," she said,

smiling sweetly. "No, nothing is wrong. Nothing at all. I think the bright Colorado sun just got to me a little, but I'll get used to it soon enough, I'm sure."

She observed the look of puzzlement on Nat's face as she spoke to him as though he were a mere acquaintance. The look transformed to one of anger—or was it disgust? She wasn't sure, but she smiled smugly to herself as he departed swiftly with a slight tip of his cap. She had been able to overcome her feelings for him enough to ignore the feigned concern in his voice and eyes and treat him as coolly as he had treated her during those last days on the train. With confidence born of her victory over her deepest feelings spurring her on, she stepped up to the cage and explained her dilemma to the clerk, whose youthful look did not instill her with confidence.

"Gee, ma'am, I'm sorry I can't help you. I don't remember translating that particular telegraph you sent. Wait!" His eyes lit up in his boyish face, obviously eager to be of service to a pretty woman. "Old Jim might have taken it. I'm just sorta an apprentice here and fill in for Jim when he wants to take a break." His voice was apologetic, and his glance across the street told Melissa exactly where "Old Jim" took his breaks. "But here's where we keep the telegrams never received," he said, pulling out a dusty box. "I can at least check to see if it was picked up."

Minutes later, he pulled a sheet from the file, looking like a miner who had struck gold. "Here it is. Never picked up!"

He quickly noted his elation was not matched by Melissa. "Where'd you last hear they were?" He offered, hoping to be of at least some help to the lovely lady standing there looking so desolate.

"My sister wrote that she and her husband were homesteading some land about thirty miles southeast of Denver."

She saw the young man's face briefly reflect what seemed to be alarm before he stuttered out his next question.

"Uh, when was it you last heard from her?"

"Well, it was just before my father died, so it must have been in late April or early May," Melissa responded, puzzled by why that mattered.

"Ma'am, maybe you better go see the sheriff. His office is just down the street."

The clerk seemed obviously nervous as he pointed in the direction she should take, and Melissa was perplexed. Jesse and Alicia were law-abiding citizens, so what on earth would they have to do with the sheriff? She opened her mouth to query further, but the young man had painted a welcoming—and it seemed, relieved—smile on his face as he looked over her shoulder. Greeting a gentleman who had just entered the building, he asked how he might help him. Confused, she turned, bumping into the newcomer as she set out.

The sheriff's office was housed in a one-story building, with a single window looking out onto the street. Through the window, Melissa glimpsed a large man with his feet propped up on his desk, talking to someone who was blocked from Melissa's view. She hesitated, wondering whether or not to interrupt, but her determination to find her sister won out. Assuming an air of confidence she no longer felt, she stepped into the office and was met by surprised looks from the two men who had been conversing. The sheriff looked exactly like a composite of the ones described in the several dime novels she had read. He was broad-shouldered, with the beginnings of a gut protruding from his open vest that proudly displayed his sheriff's badge. His face was a weathered brown, but not unkind. As he pushed back his chair and rose to greet her, Melissa noticed that his hat and gun belt hung on some wooden pegs directly behind him.

"Well, little lady, what can I do for you?"

Melissa felt the gentleman with whom he had been conversing perusing her with interest as she related her story to the sheriff. Before beginning, she had given him a pointed look, hoping that he would take the hint, leave, and allow her to discuss her problem with the sheriff alone. However, the man seemed oblivious to her discomfort and remained leaning against a wooden frame separating the office area from the three cells in the rear of the building. At the mention of her sister's name, she noted he pushed himself off the frame to stand erect as he and the sheriff exchanged glances.

"What'd you say your sister's last name was?" The sheriff asked.

"Hanks. Alicia Hanks. Her husband's name is Jesse."

The sheriff puffed up his cheeks and exhaled loudly as he shot another quick glance at the gentleman. "You best have a seat, little lady," he said, pointing to an empty chair that faced his desk.

Somewhat distressed by the odd looks the sheriff and his friend had exchanged with one another, she said curtly, "Melissa. My name is Melissa Sullivan," as she sat primly in the chair he had indicated. For heaven's sakes, she had told him that a few minutes earlier when she explained how she had come west on a wagon train to be reunited with her sister and brother-in-law. And the sheriff couldn't even remember what she had *just* said her sister's name was. He had asked her to repeat it! Although he seemed to be an affable enough sort of person, she was beginning to doubt his competence. This so-called Queen City and its people were not impressing her.

The sheriff lumbered back around his desk and sank heavily into his chair. "Miss Sullivan, as you might have heard, we've had some hostile Indian activity in the area recently. A few months back, a family by the name of Hungate was massacred. Their bodies were badly mutilated."

Melissa's patience was wearing thin. She began tapping her fingertips on the sides of her arms, which she had folded across her chest. She hadn't come here for a recounting of the recent history of the area. *What on earth did the Hungates have to do with Alicia and Jesse?*

The sheriff continued in a slow drawl, "Nathan Hungate lived with his wife and two children on the Van Wormer ranch where Hungate was a ranch hand. The Van Wormer spread adjoined the spread that your sister and her husband had homesteaded, and the two families became good friends. They'd come into town together for supplies sometimes. Mighty pretty woman, that sister of yours. I can see the family resemblance."

"Sheriff!" Melissa interrupted abruptly, annoyed that he seemed to be rambling on unnecessarily. She forced herself to speak in a calm voice again once she had his attention. "I'm really very sorry the Hungate family suffered such a terrible fate. Word of it spread to the wagon train I arrived on. Some of the families who traveled with us on the wagon train were also killed by Indians, so I know what unspeakable things they are capable of doing to their victims. I'm sure Alicia and Jesse must have taken it hard, having been close with the family, but if you could just tell me where I can find them, I'll be on my way and leave you to your business."

"Guess you're right, ma'am. My beating around the bush won't change the ending. I'm afraid I have to tell you you'll find them in the cemetery just east of town."

Melissa sat in stunned silence while she tried to digest the words and their meaning. When she finally could speak, she stammered, "But, but…you said the *Hungate* family…" She hoped she had misinterpreted his words.

"Your sister and her husband were, unfortunately, visiting the Hungates at the time of the massacre. Word is that Jesse Hanks was helping Nathan repair some fences while his wife visited with Mrs. Hungate. The bodies were all brought back to town and given a decent Christian burial, ma'am," he added lamely. He decided not to mention that, before the burial, the mutilated bodies that were recovered were placed on public display in Denver.

"I see." Her voice was calm—too calm—as she fingered a gold ring that hung around her neck. The sheriff and his visitor watched with stunned expressions as the lady merely got up and walked out the door without so much as a by-your-leave.

Once outside, she began to stumble back up the street. Tears flowed voluminously—tears for Mama and Papa, for Aunt Georgiana, for little Rachel and Josh, for Alicia and Jesse, and for herself. It was too much to bear. Hiking her skirts, she broke into a run, oblivious to the looks of passersby, oblivious to the pounding footsteps behind her. She struggled as she felt firm arms encircle her waist from behind.

"Noooo!" She screamed, attempting to kick backward at whoever was preventing her forward movement. She wanted to keep running until she could run no more—until she collapsed and sweet oblivion swept her away.

"Damn Barnes anyway! He could have broken it to you a bit easier." The oath muttered into her ear brought her back to reality. She stopped struggling and allowed herself to be turned to face her assailant. He held her by the shoulders at arm's length as she took great gulps of air and swiped with the back of her hand at the tears still flowing freely. He wondered how any woman with a tear-streaked face and red, runny nose could still look so beautiful as he offered her his handkerchief.

"Kent Jackson, at your service, ma'am. I'm really sorry about your sister."

The vision of the gentleman who had been in the sheriff's office swam before her. Dabbing at her eyes, she forced herself to take several deep breaths in an attempt to collect herself.

"I…I apologize. I…I don't know what came over me," she choked out, hoping to present a controlled enough image to gain her release so she could go…*where*?

"Well, I certainly do," he replied gently. "You just received some pretty bad news in a very blunt fashion. I'd like to help if I can. I will escort you back to your family if you'll let me. Where are they staying?" She hadn't mentioned any family in the sheriff's office, but he couldn't imagine her traveling all this distance alone.

He *had* wondered why she had been sent to gather the information on her sister. To his dismay, his offer only started the tears falling again.

"I'm afraid…" She inhaled deeply to find the strength to continue. "I don't have any family, Mr. Jackson. My sister was my last living relative." Her face contorted as she tried to fight another outbreak of sobbing and failed.

"Just let go. It's okay." Kent said soothingly as he pulled her into his arms, holding her as her body convulsed against his in misery. People stared curiously at the two as they passed, but the scowl that Kent gave them prevented them from lingering.

Several minutes elapsed before Melissa felt she could cry no more. Her head throbbed as she pushed herself off his chest with her hands and wiped her nose.

"Th-Thank you, Mr. Jackson. I think I'll be all right now. It was just such a shock!" She attempted a small smile of gratitude as she handed him back his soggy handkerchief.

"You know, my buckboard is right down the street, and I have nothing to do for the rest of the day. Would you like to pay your respects to your sister's grave?"

."Oh, yes! I mean, no. I mean, it wouldn't be proper." She ended, her wishes defeated by societal mores.

"Miss Sullivan, I assure you I have nothing but the most honorable of intentions. Perhaps you have someone who could act as chaperone? A traveling companion of yours?" Kent still wondered how it was she had come here on a wagon train. Single women were not usually allowed to travel alone on one. The wagon masters didn't want the grief. Perhaps she had accompanied a family she knew from her hometown.

Melissa's face brightened. "Of course! Mavis! She's down the street at the Lucky Lady Saloon, auditioning for a job. She's a singer." Melissa added the last in defense of Mavis upon noting the startled look on Kent Jackson's face.

"Well, then, I'll accompany you there," Kent said with slightly raised eyebrows. "The Lucky Lady is no place for a woman to enter alone."

Melissa frowned at the subtle slur on Mavis, but she allowed the man to escort her by the elbow up the street. They were still a couple of buildings away from the saloon when they heard cheers and shouts ring out from the Lucky Lady. Kent pushed one of the swinging doors open and allowed Melissa to enter first, keeping a firm, possessive grip on her elbow as he followed her into the bar. Once her eyes adjusted to the dimly lit room, Melissa became aware her friend had been the object of the gleeful noise. Propped atop a piano, Mavis was surrounded by a group of men, all begging her to sing another tune. Catching sight of Melissa, who had timidly stopped just inside the door, nearly causing Kent to bump into her, Mavis promised the men a quick return and hopped down to rush over and greet her. A couple of the men tried to grab her as she did so, but the piano player rose quickly to provide a shield for her, and the bartender had pulled a gun out from under the counter, threatening to shoot anyone who dared to make an ungentlemanly move toward her. Grumbling, a few men returned to the bar with their drinks, and others settled down at some of the tables.

"Miss, me friend, come meet Dan," Mavis said excitedly as she pulled a reluctant Melissa farther into the bar room toward the piano approximately positioned in the middle of the room. With relief, Melissa sensed Kent following them.

"Melissa Sullivan, meet Dan Farley. And over here is Red Donovan." She dragged Melissa over to the bartender before the piano player could do much more than acknowledge the introduction with a nod.

"Miss Sullivan," the bartender greeted her. "Your friend here is quite a piece of work. Barged right in here while Dan was practicing on the ivories and demanded an audition."

He smiled at Mavis in a way that said he hadn't found her brazenness at all offensive. In fact, if Melissa wasn't mistaken, her friend had already stolen Red Donovan's heart. He was a nice-looking man, although Melissa would not have called him handsome. She wondered if his nickname was the result of his strawberry-blond hair or his ruddy complexion. He had broad shoulders that stretched taut the cloth of his white shirt. His sleeves were rolled halfway up, revealing strong forearms covered with curly blond hair. His eyes, framed by blond almost white untamed eyebrows, were such a light blue they almost seemed transparent.

"I didn't have a chance to tell her that we don't hire ladies for that kind of entertainment here, but we surely have enjoyed listening to her belt out those songs, nonetheless." As Melissa drew closer, the bartender's expression changed, and he directed his attention to the man standing just behind her. "Something wrong here, Kent?"

Mavis looked at her friend more closely now and saw what had prompted Red's query—the puffy eyes and red nose. "Melissa! What's wrong?" She asked with great concern in her voice.

"They're dead, Mav," Melissa choked out in a whisper. She couldn't say more for fear of losing control again and was relieved when her escort filled in the details as Mavis clutched her hand in her own. Silent tears flowed down the cheeks of both women.

****

They crossed Cherry Creek with little trouble; it was only about ten feet wide and very shallow. Kent then headed his carriage east into what seemed to be an endless prairie of brown. The ride might have been boring, but Kent was an excellent conversationalist and gave the women a lesson on Denver's history, spurred on by Mavis's questions. He explained the land had originally been owned by the Arapaho and the Southern Cheyenne, who had welcomed the white man at first. Then a group of prospectors and promoters from Lawrence, Kansas came and staked a claim on the site, calling it The St. Charles Town Company. But in 1858, a man by the name of William Larimer, Jr. crossed two cottonwood sticks at the center of the large town plat he had taken over from the prospectors and renamed it Denver City. Mavis remembered that one of the streets she and Melissa had walked along was named Larimer Street and wondered aloud why the man hadn't named the entire city for himself.

"Larimer was quite the politician. He wanted to ensure Denver City would be chosen as the county seat of Arapahoe County, Kansas Territory, so he named his city for James Denver, who was then the governor of the Kansas Territory."

"Our wagon master told us Denver was once two cities, situated on either side of Cherry Creek. How and why did the two cities become one?" Melissa wanted to know.

Kent was secretly glad to find his ploy was working and Melissa was being drawn into the conversation and away from her misery. "Auraria was actually the first town at the confluence of Cherry Creek and the South Platte. It was founded by some Georgian explorers led by a fellow named William Russell. It was Russell who first found gold in Cherry Creek, and he and his followers platted the original settlement, calling it Auraria."

"The Latin word for gold," Melissa interjected.

"That's right," he responded, impressed by her knowledge. "Anyway, the Russell party headed back south eventually. Afterwards, Larimer staged a moonlight ceremony on the Larimer Street bridge—the one that spans Cherry Creek—to celebrate the merger of the two cities into one."

Seated next to him, Melissa had been studying him covertly as he talked. He was an inch or two taller than she, and his sandy brown hair was neatly trimmed, as was his matching mustache. He had shed his frock coat for the ride, and she noted his shoulders were slender, like the rest of his body, yet he seemed quite capable of taking care of himself and his passengers. He wore no gun belt, but a rifle lay on the seat between them. He had regular features—a straight nose, rounded slightly at the tip, and warm brown eyes. His teeth were straight and gleamed brightly when he smiled—which he did frequently. Her scrutiny was not lost on Mavis, who sat on the seat behind them.

When Mavis asked about the Indians, Kent felt Melissa stiffen beside him. Now was not the time to talk about the hostile tribes. Instead, he told them about Chief Chekta, a Ute Indian who, Kent said, had developed a taste for the white man's home cooking and would scare the daylights out of some of the settlers' unknowing wives, knocking at their doors and demanding one of his favorite dishes. Chekta normally stayed in the foothills southwest of Denver, he assured them.

"His appearance is enough to scare anyone." Kent chuckled. "He's at least six feet tall and weighs over two hundred and fifty pounds. He has long, stringy, graying hair, which he often tops with a broad-brimmed, dirty black hat with a red feather stuck in it. One of his more frequent requests is biscuits slathered with syrup. He's never been known to hurt a woman or child. In fact, after he's filled his belly, he often stays around and plays with the children, chasing them around the yard and putting his big hat on their tiny heads. Takes a woman some time to get used to, though."

Melissa had been thinking there were a lot of things she would have to get used to when Kent pulled the carriage to a halt at the bottom of a bare hill. "Here we are," he said as curious prairie dogs poked out of holes to peer at the visitors before scurrying away. "We'll have to hike up a bit to the graves," he explained as Melissa looked at him in disbelief while he helped her, and then Mavis, down from his carriage.

The so-called cemetery was a disorganized mess, so unlike the tidy one in which her parents had been buried; the church folk kept it in good order, vegetation trimmed and gravestones cleaned. Here, prairie dog droppings infested the land. There were all manner of grave markers—some stone, etched with names, dates, and sweet epitaphs, others carved of wood with similar markings, while many graves were marked only with a cross formed by lashing two twigs together.

"I'm thinking there be a great many graves here for such a wee community," Mavis remarked, breaking the silence as Kent guided them to the spot where Melissa's relatives had been laid to rest.

Kent acknowledged her comment with a nod. "A lot of folks are taken by disease, some are killed in mining accidents, and it's only been recently we got a jail and a sheriff and established a number of ordinances. Prior to that, Denver's streets were overrun by drunken, disorderly vagrants and bands of toughs who were able to rob, assault, and murder innocent victims at will. The bodies of both the perpetrators of such crimes and some of the victims are buried here." He stopped in front of a large wooden marker, carved in the shape of a tombstone. "Would you like some time alone with them?" He asked Melissa gently.

She nodded mutely, and Mavis and Kent moved several feet away. Melissa dropped to her knees in the dirt in front of the marker, allowing her fingers to trace the words that some kind person had whittled into the wood. "Here lies Jesse Hanks and his beloved wife, Alicia. Died June 1864. Killed by Injuns." *There aren't even any wildflowers here for me to lay on your grave, Alicia. Oh, Alicia, I loved you so. You were the best big sister a girl could ask for. I hope you've met up with Mama and Papa in heaven, and Aunt Georgina—she's dead, too, now.* Melissa's tears flowed as silently as the words she spoke from her heart. *I wish I were with all of you now.* As she clutched her mother's ring in anguish, a gentle breeze kissed her face, and Melissa, noting how the breeze was drying her tears, had the eerie feeling that it was a last goodbye from all those she had loved. She shuddered and took a deep breath. *You're all alone now, Melissa. You can wallow in misery, or you can pull yourself up by your bootstraps and go on with life. Your choice.* She argued with the voice in her head. *But how do I go on? What do I do?* The response came, *Do what you've always done. Organize your thoughts.*

Melissa obeyed the voice and concentrated on formulating a plan for herself as she continued kneeling before the graves of her dead sister and brother-in-law. Doing so made her feel better—more in control than she had felt since learning of their deaths. With a small smile, she lovingly touched the tombstone one last time. *Thank you, sweet sister—for everything.* She pushed herself up from her kneeling position with the palms of her hands, brushing the dirt from both them and her skirt as she rose. Standing, she began to recite "The Lord's Prayer" aloud. Behind her, Mavis and Kent moved closer and joined in the final "Amen."

Chapter Sixteen

Nat was still fuming as he rode into Camp Weld. Damned if he could figure Melissa Sullivan out. Worse, he couldn't even figure out his own feelings toward her. He had thought he was in love with her and had been willing to give her his heart. But she had scorned him when he'd tried to comfort her after the massacre of those travelers who had defied Calhoune. From then on, he had avoided her, trying to sort out his own feelings. When he had seen her looking so distraught in the telegraph office today, though, his immediate reaction was to console her about whatever was troubling her. Her response had been frigid enough to freeze an entire lake in an instant. He didn't know why. Nevertheless, it had felt like she was driving a knife through his heart, so he had turned and fled the scene before she could do more damage. He had almost gone back into the building and demanded she talk to him. Perhaps then he would have been able to reconcile some things—in his own mind at least. But a man had his pride. Still, he now regretted he hadn't done so. He felt as drawn to her as a bee to a flower. Even when he had been avoiding being around her, he had watched her from afar. When she walked, her graceful movements reminded him of a slender willow branch, swaying in the wind. Her luxurious mane of hair was like a waterfall, hanging in soft waves to her waist. He'd never forget the way her unique brown eyes with those tiny green flecks had shone, wide with wonder, when he had declared his love for her. She had not responded in kind, but he had attributed it to a natural reluctance to trust, given what that lecherous uncle may have done to her, and he had resolved to rebuild her faith in men. What the hell had gone wrong? And why did he care? Right now, he needed to concentrate on other matters. He entered the confines of the fort, dismounted, and began to walk his horse to the corral when a shrill whistle caught his attention. Looking up, he saw Tom waving him over to where Alston and he stood talking to a third man.

"Kenwood should have stuck with his Methodist ministry," Nat heard the distinguished-looking, dark-skinned man say to Alston and Tom as he led his horse over to where the three were conversing. "He had to have been better at that job than he is at this one."

Nat inspected the other man closely as Alston made the introductions. The man was older than what he'd appeared from a distance, but his erect posture belied his years. He wore his curly, gray-streaked, black hair longer than was fashionable, but it was neatly trimmed, as were his mustache and goatee. Despite his polished appearance, the scars on his face told Nat the man had seen his share of fights. The man's comment regarding Kenwood matched his own perception of the commander here at Camp Weld.

"It's good to meet you, Mr. Daile," Nat said. He had not missed the fact that he, too, had been under scrutiny.

"The pleasure is mine. And, please, call me Will," Daile replied as the two shook hands. "I must be getting back to the place now. Remember, drinks are on the house tonight," he said to Alston and Tom, "and,

Lieutenant, I'd be honored if you'd join us as well."
****

Melissa sat in silent contemplation on the ride back to town while Mavis drilled Kent on the particulars of his life. Kent revealed that he had come to Denver from a small town in Ohio where he had been part owner of a coal mine. He and his partner, a boyhood friend, had begun to have frequent arguments about the working conditions in the mine.

"Joe could pinch the head off the Indian on a one-cent piece, the miners' welfare be damned. I did what I could, but it wasn't enough. The mine was an accident waiting to happen, and it finally did. A shaft collapsed, burying a dozen good men. The eight-year-old son of one of them had been working for us, hauling coal after it had been brought up from the shaft. I'll never forget the look in his eyes as he flung his body across that of his dead father's when they dragged it up. I knew I couldn't continue in the operation, being thwarted by Joe at every turn. We agreed to part friends. He bought out my interest, and here I am. I gave some of the money to the families of the dead miners and used the rest to buy a stake in a gold mine out here."

"What about yer family?" Mavis inquired.

"My mother died in childbirth when I was five. The baby died, too. My father was a jeweler by trade. He saved enough to send me to college and died a couple of months after I graduated. I think he really didn't want to live anymore after my mother died but pushed on to ensure I'd have a good life. Once he was assured of that, it seemed like he decided it was okay for him to join her. He caught a cold, which developed into pneumonia and took his life." Kent shrugged in dismissal of the topic.

"Now that you've heard my story, I think turnabout's fair play."

Melissa almost shook her head in disbelief as Mavis portrayed herself as a woman who had been widowed when the Indians attacked the wagon train. Her Irish friend had a glib tongue and would have had Melissa believing her had she not known Mavis's true story. Her so-called husband had also been her agent, she asserted, and they were coming west to further her career as a chanteuse. Melissa could feel a blush rising to the surface as Mavis continued, implicating her.

"We had the Irish luck to meet up with me friend, Miss, here, in Nebraska City. The poor girl had just buried her mother and wanted to join her sister in Denver, and I convinced Seamus to let her accompany us. I was thinking some female companionship might do me good, ye see. And t'were a blessing I did, after what happened to me poor Seamus."

Melissa could feel Kent's gaze upon her. "Well, we know what Mavis plans to do. What are *your* plans, Miss Sullivan? I have had good fortune in my new mining venture and have ample enough funds to be generous. I'm more than willing to purchase you a stagecoach ticket back to Nebraska, if you so desire."

"No!" Melissa hadn't meant to shout the word. Hoping he hadn't heard the panic in her response, she stumbled over a hasty explanation. "I…uh, mean, there's nothing left for me there but sad memories. Since I'm here, I might as well make the best of it and start a new life for myself." The words sounded bolder than what she felt. A new life in *this* desolate town where foraging pigs, wild dogs, Indians, and ruffians seemed to outnumber the respectable citizens strolling the streets? Still, what choice did she have? "I shall seek gainful employment."

Kent was not unhappy to hear she had no immediate plans to leave. One thing he did miss since coming to Denver was female companionship. Sure, there were those willing enough to satisfy a man's sexual pleasures for a coin, and Kent was no stranger to the red-light district south of Cherry Creek, but he desired someone who would be a companion also.

"What type of employment?" He queried in a tone that suggested he thought her perfectly capable of doing whatever kind of work she so chose. Melissa was pleased that, for once, someone thought her able to make her own decisions.

However, before she could open her mouth, Mavis answered for her. "She's thinking she'd like to be a schoolteacher. She is an angel with children, and let no one say different. Why, ye should've seen her with Rachel and wee Joshua. Their own mum was a bloody witch, and…"

"Mavis!" Melissa admonished, embarrassed.

Kent looked at her thoughtfully. "A teacher, huh? It just so happens I have been considering bringing one into our mining camp. I've been trying to hire as many married men as I can. I've found them to be better workers and more stable than their single counterparts. As a result, the number of children has grown with the mine, and they have a tendency to run wild. In addition to my fear they will end up at the wrong end of an accident, my father's relentless lectures about the need for a good education make me want to help them get started in that direction. You seem to me to be an intelligent young woman who would be capable of filling that role if you're so inclined."

"I'm thinking ye should take the man up on his offer," Mavis put in gleefully.

Melissa did not share her friend's exuberance. It sounded like a great offer, better than she could have hoped for, but it would mean leaving behind Mavis, whom she had come to think of as a sister, and starting over again in a circle of strangers. She felt like the tall blades of grass she had observed being relentlessly tossed every which way by the wind as the train traveled across the prairie. Still…

"Might I have time to consider your generous offer?" Melissa inquired.

"Of course! In fact, I'm in Denver for a few days trying to round up more good men." Sensing she might be worried about the propriety of it all, he added, "You'd have your own place, and I think you'll find most of the wives amiable and glad to have another woman around. If you'll consent to have dinner with me this evening, we can discuss it further."

"She'd be more than happy to join ye."

Melissa was now truly exasperated with her friend's habit of responding for her. Frantically, she thought of her limited wardrobe that consisted of the three cast-off dresses, two of which were now stained and well-worn. She had donned the third this morning in an attempt to look as presentable as possible when she searched for her sister. She had been thankful she'd had the foresight to keep the best of the three dresses in reserve. It was a light-green-and-white-checked gingham, with white ruffles trimming the sides of the pleated bodice. Tiny pink embroidered rosebuds were scattered among the checks in the skirt, and a larger matching flower adorned the center of the high collar. It would have to do as her dinner dress, she decided.

"Where may I call for you?" Kent responded to Mavis's reply as though it had come from Melissa herself.

"At the moment, we're camped alongside Cherry Creek," Melissa answered before her friend could make up some improbable story.

Kent's eyebrows rose in surprise. "Two women alone?"

"Well, not exactly. When the wagon train pulled into town, several of the other wagons also chose to camp there until their inhabitants got their bearings. We situated our wagon close to the others. It's only for a few days. Mavis has already agreed to sell the wagon to one of the other families who will be venturing on to the gold mines after they have time to resupply."

"That will never do," Kent said with authority. "I'll get you a room in Mrs. Tirpak's boarding house in town while you remain here. Mavis can join you. There's no sense in your trying to find permanent lodgings when I have, hopefully, convinced you to become our new schoolteacher. The rooms are far from extravagant, but they are meticulously clean. Mrs. Tirpak is a widow and a strict Catholic, so her rules, especially for women boarders, might seem convent-like, but her Hungarian cooking is extraordinary, which is why I choose to stay there myself. However, she doesn't cook on Sundays, when she observes the Sabbath, or on Mondays."

"But…"

"We accept!" Mavis cut off any reservations Melissa might have intended to voice.

The three stopped by Mavis's wagon so the women could collect their belongings and Mavis could settle matters with Mr. Marcus, who was purchasing her wagon, rig, and what remained of her supplies. A couple of hours later, Melissa and Mavis were finally alone in a spartan, but clean, room. The twin beds with their bright, quilted covers looked inviting after all the nights spent sleeping on the hard floor of a wagon. The only other pieces of furniture were an old wooden dresser and a small table. A kerosene lamp sat on a crocheted doily on the table. Atop the dresser lay two neatly folded towels, a bar of soap, and a pitcher and bowl for personal hygiene. On the front of the pitcher a young, colonial couple were portrayed in a garden scene. The virile, white-wigged male was bowing to his lady deferentially. Upon seeing it, Melissa felt a fleeting moment of cynicism. *It may have been that way at one time, but not now. Papa seemed to love and respect Mama, but I now realize they were different from most couples. In this modern-day world, I have only observed men who have either scorned their women or were too fearful of them to stand their ground.* Her thoughts drifted to Nat, but rather than allow herself to dwell on him, she turned her attention to Mavis.

"How could you! You wove a believable set of lies about your past for Kent. I accept that. But why did you have to pull me into the web?"

Mavis was visibly dumbfounded by her friend's violent reaction. "I couldna tell him yer true tale, could I? A suspected murderess wouldna be a good candidate for a schoolmistress. And if ye think about it a bit, I dinna lie about ye. We did meet up in Nebraska City, and ye were looking to join ye sister. I just left out the uncle part of the story." Seeing she had placated Melissa somewhat, she continued. "Ye ought to be thinking heavily on

Kent's offer. 'Tis a real chance for ye to get what ye want out of life—independence. I dinna know how Nat will react to it, though."

"Nat!" Even though she had just been thinking of him, she tried to deny it, if only to herself. "What's he got to do with me? He didn't even bother to say goodbye when we parted."

Much to Melissa's disappointment, Mavis only sighed and offered no encouragement on the subject. Instead, she merely said, "I'm thinking I'd better get me backside back to the Lucky Lady ere they forget all abou' me."

Kent called for Melissa a few hours later and complimented her appearance as if he didn't recognize she had not changed attire since their venture to the graveyard. The restaurant to which he escorted her occupied the bottom floor of a three-story frame building, the upper two floors serving as one of Denver's finest hotel establishments, although Kent left out the word "finest" when describing it to her. When he told her the Broadwell House was located just a few blocks from Mrs. Tirpak's boarding house and gave her the choice of riding in his carriage or walking the distance, Melissa chose the latter.

As they approached the building on the corner of Sixteenth and Larimer Streets, Melissa observed several men in top hats and suits sitting on the porch, conversing among themselves. She steeled herself to walk past them with her head held high, realizing from their attire that her dress was far from appropriate. She needn't have worried. Kent placed his hand on the small of her back as she ascended the couple of steps, nodding to the men and greeting them by name as he and Melissa passed by.

The men returned his greetings warmly and nodded to her in greeting as well.

The dining room was more elegant than any Melissa had ever before seen. Rich wood paneling lined the walls, and a small, beautifully etched glass kerosene lamp sat on each white-clothed table. Prior to ordering for the two of them, Kent asked if she had any adverse reactions to any particular food, which surprised and pleased her.

As they waited for their meals to be served, he entertained her with additional stories about the beginnings of Denver and the colorful characters involved. She remarked on the strange-sounding street names she had observed as they had walked the short distance from the boarding house to the hotel. Many of the streets, he told her, had been named for the Indian wives of a Scottish mountain man in return for his willingness to convey his wives' relatives' land rights to Denver City. There was Wewatta, Wazee, and Champa. Additionally, the man had requested a street be named after him and another after what he claimed to be his ancestral castle in Scotland, Glenarm Place. The Scotsman also claimed to be the son of the Lord Mayor of London.

"If the last is true," he told her as the waiter approached with their meals, "my guess is the Lord Mayor shed no tears when his son decided to put an ocean's distance between them. At his best, the man can only be said to be in a state approaching sobriety, and some of this city's founding fathers are ready to buy his passage back. He's become a source of embarrassment for them."

Whether it was because she was famished or the

Broadwell House had a talented cook, Melissa didn't know. She knew only that she had to force herself to eat like a lady, taking small bites rather than devouring her meal in one gulp. The venison was moist and tender, and the vegetables were perfectly cooked in a rich, brown sauce. She made an audible sound of delight and immediately turned as red as one of the beets on her plate. *He is really going to think I'm some country bumpkin!* Noting her chagrin, Kent sought to dispel it.

"Everyone here appreciates having fresh vegetables on the menu again. Last year the area experienced a bad drought that made the price of vegetables dear—that is, if you could find any at all," he told her, as though her reaction had been commonplace.

It wasn't until dessert had been served—apple dumplings smothered with freshly whipped cream—that Kent broached the subject of her employment.

"I do hope you will say yes to my offer. Everyone will be better off—the children will benefit from your knowledge and the added structure to their lives; the parents will be happier knowing their children are receiving an education and are not in danger of being in the way of some mining mishap; and you will have a responsible position that, hopefully, will somewhat take your mind off your recent losses. I come to town every three to four weeks for supplies, and I promise to bring you with me so you can visit with Mavis. Although—I want to be perfectly honest with you—sometimes it's longer when the snow flies hard. The roads between here and Cold Creek are not passable then, and we're pretty isolated. But you'll find the brilliant sun comes out and melts the snow quickly in this part of the country, so it's usually not too long a wait, even under the worst circumstances. What do you say?"

"Mr. Jackson, it's an offer I can hardly refuse, but…"

Before she had a chance to answer, he continued with his sales pitch. "Of course, you'd have your own cabin, fully furnished, and I can advance you your first month's salary so you can buy any other supplies you deem necessary. We do have a company store at the camp where you'll probably be able to find any necessity you might forget. We don't have a cook like most of the other mining companies. We're one of the few operations that hires mainly married men, and we believe private meal-time conversations make for happier employees, so we give our miners food credits in addition to their wages. They can then spend these credits at the store as they so choose. As an employee, you'll receive these credits as well. When I'm coming to town, the store manager provides me with a shopping list based on the requests she receives. It seems to work well."

Melissa's head was reeling. She'd have her own place, with furnishings included, a large portion of her food bill covered, money to spare, and, most importantly, independence. She'd be insane to say no. "Yes," she said simply. "I accept your offer."

Kent felt like whooping with glee, but he restrained himself, sensing that any display of exuberant emotion would scare the girl off as easily as a doe gets startled when it sights a human.

"It's settled then," he stated in a perfunctory voice. "And here is the advance I promised," he continued in the same businesslike tone as he placed the Union currency on the table between them.

Melissa's eyes widened. It was far more than she had expected. Kent Jackson must be a prosperous man, indeed, to be able to advance her so much. Left speechless, she silently vowed she would not let this man down.

****

Nat, Alston, and Tom were enjoying Will Daile's hospitality at his farmhouse-turned-saloon on the outskirts of town. Daile had just finished giving them a brief account of his very colorful past. Like Tom, he had also been born a slave in Frederick County, Virginia, not far from where Tom had served the Bellamys. His mother had been the slave of the Doyles, another family of Irish aristocrats. Will, the product of a union between his mother and Sir Aidan Doyle, had been freed at the age of 24, well before the War Between the States. In the years that followed, Daile had roamed the country. He'd done some blacksmithing, ridden with Kit Carson, fought the Cheyenne and Blackfoot Indians, and had even become a war leader of the Crow Indians.

"Mind if I pick your brain about the current Indian situation?" Nat queried.

"What do you want to know?" Daile responded.

"Well, being brand new to the territory, I don't know much, but Kenwood briefed me on the increasing frequency of Indian raids on the ranches and stage stations along the South Platte River. So any light you can shed will be good."

Daile studied Nat and his companions for several seconds before responding. He sighed deeply. "Regardless of what your commander would have you believe, Indians are not dissimilar to any other race of people. There are the good, who try to keep the peace, and there are the bad, who prefer fighting to negotiating."

"How do we tell which is which?" Alston posed the question.

"Sometimes it's difficult. But Lone Wolf—"

"Is a war monger," Nat interjected. "Kenwood told me Lone Wolf was responsible for the massacre of the Hungate family."

"I greatly doubt it." Daile shook his head. "Lone Wolf has been an outspoken advocate for peace from the time he was selected to the Council of Forty-Four, the ruling body of the Cheyenne nation. In fact, rumor has it that even when that idiot sergeant John Simpson and his troops attacked Lone Wolf's own village this past May, while they were camped near Fort Lyon, Lone Wolf tried to dissuade his warriors from fighting back."

"Maybe he had second thoughts, which is why he attacked the Hungate ranch," Tom supplied.

"It's possible," Daile admitted. "But knowing Lone Wolf as I do, I don't believe it."

The night was still early when they bid Daile goodnight, thanking him for both the information and the free drinks. Nat suggested a stop at one of Denver's many saloons on the way back to the fort.

"What's your opinion?" he asked the two men after the bartender had deposited their drinks in front of them.

"Seems like a straight arrow," Alston readily responded.

Chapter Seventeen

The large meal had made Melissa drowsy, but the walk back to Mrs. Tirpak's in the crisp autumn air restored her senses somewhat, for which she was grateful. She didn't see the three men as they exited one of the town's saloons and gaped at the image of her taking an evening stroll with a gentleman supporting her elbow. Nor did she hear the muffled expletive as one of them kicked the beam of a hitching post.

"Don't that beat all!" A second of the three said.

"Shut up, Alston."

Tom and Alston exchanged knowing looks. They had both endured Nat's foul mood all evening, and Alston, never one to mince words, decided he might as well take the bull by the horns then and there.

"You know, Nat, in most ways you're one of the smartest men I ever met up with. But when it comes to matters of the heart, you're too damn dumb to pour piss out of a boot with the directions on the heel!"

"And just what's that supposed to mean?"

"It *means* that Tom and I know how you feel about that little lady. You couldn't keep your eyes off her the whole trip. And if'n' I don't miss my guess, she feels the same way about you. You gonna just let your chances slip through your fingers because of some dang misunderstanding that's cropped up between you two?"

"*Misunderstanding!* Hell, I bumped into her today

at the telegraph office, and the look she gave me could have frozen the entire Atlantic Ocean. A man has his pride."

"Pride don't keep you warm on a cold winter night, my friend. Hell-o-billy, I'd be a-crawling on my hands and knees if it'd bring my Trudy back."

Nat shook his head as if to clear the cobwebs from it. Whether it was the alcohol they had consumed or the aftereffects of the raging jealousy he had felt when he saw Melissa with another man, he wasn't certain, but Alston's words rang true. He still remembered how he had found Alston in the gutter overcome with such grief over his wife's passing that the man had sought death from the bottle he had clung to so fiercely. Tom had had to knock him out, and the two of them had carried the inebriated male to their room, piled blankets on his nearly frozen body, and let him sleep off the effects of the liquor before trying to reason with him. Normally, Nat would have stepped over the drunk and gone on his way, but he had recognized him from earlier in the day when, only slightly corned, Alston had stood up to a couple of no-accounts who had been heckling Tom while Nat was rounding up some supplies. Not that Al hadn't done more harm than good in his less-than-sober state. Nat had had to pull the men off both Alston and Tom when he returned. But Melissa wasn't Trudy. Melissa was…well, truth was, he didn't know what Melissa was. She certainly hadn't wasted much time in finding another man to wield her charms on.

"I'm riding back to the camp. You two coming with me?" he asked, his voice dripping with disgust.

"Could have been her brother-in-law, ya know. I sure wouldn't be hanging up my fiddle just yet," Tom muttered as he untethered his horse, but his comments were met only with silence.

****

The sun was streaming in from the window when Melissa finally awoke the next morning from a deep sleep. Looking over at the next bed, she saw a lump that must be Mavis. Her quilt completely covered her head. She must have slept soundly, Melissa thought, for she had not even heard Mav come in that night. Quietly, she slipped out of her own bed and padded over to the dresser. Pouring cold water from the pitcher into the bowl as silently as she could, she splashed the water on her face. It was like ice. Gingerly, she splashed some on her neck and the area of her chest that was left uncovered by her undergarments. It was all she could do to keep from uttering a sound. She longed for a hot bath, but this would have to do.

After she had finished and was slipping into yesterday's dress again, she heard Mavis rousing.

"Miss, what time is it?" Mavis asked groggily.

"Way past the time when I should have been up. The sun awakened me."

Mavis struggled to a sitting position and patted a place on the bed beside her.

"Sit ye here and tell me how ye fared with Mr. Jackson last evening."

"He's a very nice gentleman, and I accepted his offer."

The pronouncement was followed by a loud whoop and a big hug from Mavis. "I'm thinking it couldn't have happened to a nicer person. I'll be missing ye, of course."

"I'll miss you, too, Mav. But Mr. Jackson told me he would bring me with him when he comes to town for supplies, so we could visit. He's very kind and considerate. He even gave me a healthy advance on my salary, so I plan to go shopping today. Lord knows, I can't wear this same dress every day, and the other two are ready for the rag pile. Kent also suggested I try to find the warmest coat imaginable and some sturdy boots. When I went to live with Aunt Georgina, these brogans were nearly new, but I wore holes in their soles with all the walking we did."

"*Kent*, is it now?"

Ignoring Mavis's interjection, Melissa continued. "And how was *your* evening? Did you convince Red to give you a job as a singer?"

Mavis's eyes sparkled. "Aye, but not without a fight, mind ye. He said the Lucky Lady were no place for a lady such as meself. Can ye imagine? It's been a long while since even I have thought of meself as a lady. But when I told him of my plight and my dearly departed Seamus, he grumbled that he figured I needed someone to watch out for me, and it might as well be him. Said since he spent his days and nights at the Lucky Lady, he could best do so if I were there, too. He's a good mon. I'm thinking it's too bad he's not rich as well."

Melissa groaned. "Mav, do you ever believe in telling the truth?"

"Of course I do. When it suits me purpose!" Mavis popped out of bed. "Do ye want some company while ye shop? I'm wide awake now, and Red won't be expecting me at the Lucky Lady for a few hours. Besides, he's only agreed to let me sing in his bar if I agree to wear clothes that don't show me tits as much. Of course, he didn't say 'tits.' He's too much the gentlemon for that, and his face turned as red as his vest when he was speaking to me about it. Can ye imagine? I'm thinking a mon who owns a bar like the Lucky Lady would bloody well be used to seeing a bit of chest. 'Tis kind of cute, really."

****

It took every ounce of strength Nat had to lead the men through their morning drill. He hadn't slept at all the night before. The vision of Melissa on another man's arm kept floating before him, and Alston's words reverberated in his mind. Images of Melissa's being stripped naked by that Indian, waking to find Melissa's luscious, nude body draped across him protectively, and gazing at the wonderment in her eyes as he declared his love to her haunted him. He knew he was sometimes too stubborn for his own good. Hadn't Emmie often teased him about that? But damn it, on the other hand, he *had* professed his love to Melissa, and she had been aloof ever since. What in the hell was on her mind? And who was that man she had been hanging on to? If it was her brother-in-law, as Tom had suggested, then where in the hell was her sister? Maybe Alston was right. Maybe it was time to take the bull by the horns, as his friend would say, confront the woman, and get things settled between them one way or another. He sure as hell wasn't going to be good for anything until he did. But first, he had to find her, he realized. He had no idea where this sister of hers lived. Mavis would probably know, though, and she had told Tom and Alston to come looking for her in one of the town's many saloons.

After the evening drill, he rounded up his two friends, who had been avoiding him and his foul temper the entire day. They happily agreed to accompany him.

"Must've et some brain food today," Alston muttered to Tom.

185

Nat had lost count of the number of bars they had searched—six…eight?—when they heard the singing as they stumbled up the street.

"That be Mavis's voice, 'less I miss my guess," Tom exclaimed, grabbing an inebriated Nat's arm as he pulled him toward the swinging doors with Alston shoving Nat from behind.

"Hey, we was here first!" Angry voices shouted as the three tried to push their way through the crowd surrounding the piano. A burly, redheaded man quickly appeared before them with a shotgun.

"You boys here to make trouble?"

"Red! It's okay. These lads are friends of mine!" Mavis intervened when she noticed the cause of the commotion. "Show's over for a wee bit," she explained to her admiring fans. "I'm thinking me voice needs a break."

"You heard the lady," Dan Farley announced, rising from the piano to stymie any thoughts some of the more unruly patrons might have of grabbing Mavis, while Red made the crowd give way on the other side. Red wore a ferocious frown as Mavis hugged each of the three soldiers with exuberance.

"I'm thinking I'm happy to see the three of yer ugly faces again. What brings ye to the Lucky Lady? It can't be more liquor you're looking for. The fumes from the three of ye are enough to burn down the town. Red, can you be getting these corned gentlemen something to sober them up?" she requested as she led her friends to a vacant table.

"Wher's Missa?" Nat asked. "Got somethin' to settle with her, but don't know where her sist'r lives." He looked at her through bleary eyes. "Don't believe I've ever seen you quite so…cov'rd, Mav. What gives?"

"Oh, Red here likes my singing just fine," Mavis replied as Red returned with three cups of coffee and slammed them down on the table with a scowl, "but I dinna think he likes my feminine attributes quite so well."

Red said nothing, but stood a few feet from the table with his big arms folded across his chest, looking like some guard dog and ignoring a patron's call to him for another pint.

Seemingly oblivious to the disapproval of her employer, Mavis continued in a softer tone. "Yesterday Melissa learned her sister was dead, and her brother-in-law as well. Indians killed them. The poor lass was devastated, but she seems to be holding up. Now, ye'll be telling me what it is ye have to settle with her."

The news had somewhat of a sobering effect on Nat. He felt like he had been doused with cold water, but his voice still wasn't working all that well. His countenance took on a theatrically sad look.

"That esplains why she looked so strik'n when I saw her in the tel'graph offish." The look suddenly turned angry. "If her brother-in-law ish dead, then who the hell wash that man we shaw her with las' night?"

"Oh, that would be Kent Jackson," Mavis replied nonchalantly. "He owns a mine in Cold Creek. He's offered Melissa a position as a schoolteacher for the children in his camp. I'm thinking she'll be a good one, don't ye?"

It was obvious from Nat's expression he didn't agree.

"Where ish she now?" He demanded to know.

"I won't be telling you that now, given the state

you're in, Nat Bellamy." Mavis said.

"Mavis…!" Nat reached forward as though to shake the information out of her. Unafraid of her old friend, she didn't shrink back, but Red was at the table in an instant.

"Party's over, soldiers, unless ye be wantin' me to call the sheriff."

"Go home," Mavis said more gently. "Come back when ye're feeling more like yerself, and I'll be giving ye Melissa's whereabouts. Don't be long about it, though, for I'm thinking she'll be moving on soon. Good to see ye again. Don't be strangers," she said to Tom and Alston as she pushed back her chair and took her place beside the piano amid hoots and howls from the patrons who quickly gathered around her again.

"Lads, I'm thinking I'll dedicate this one to me old friend sitting in the corner over there. It's an old Irish folk song that Dan and I worked on this afternoon, 'The Parting Glass.' "

The three men finished their coffee and left just as Mavis was belting out the chorus, nodding to them, "…the parting glass… goodnight and joy be with you all."

Chapter Eighteen

Nat awoke to a splitting headache with Mavis's final words to him ringing in his ears. *Don't be long about it. She'll be moving on soon.* With an urgency, he dressed in civilian attire, obtaining permission from Captain Dvorsky to be relieved of morning drill duty to spend the day in town. Dvorsky had seemed surprised at the request, since few of the men asked permission for anything, and he readily granted it without question.

When Nat arrived at the Lucky Lady, he saw no sign of Mavis. Only the redheaded bartender was there, polishing the bar. He didn't spare the customer a glance as he informed him, "Bar's closed, cowboy. Come back in an hour."

"Where's Mavis?" Nat inquired, undaunted by the barkeep's unwelcoming tone of voice.

Looking up at the mention of Mavis's name, Red broke into a grin. "Well, ye're lookin' none the worse for wear. Name's Red Donovan," he continued, extending his hand. "Mavis told me all about ye last night. Sorry I was a wee bit unfriendly toward ye, but I have to protect the little lady, ye understand."

Nat almost hooted at the thought that Mavis needed any protection but thought better of it. "Nat Bellamy," he said, shaking Red's outstretched hand. "I guess I didn't make any great first impressions, either."

"Women'll do that to ye," Red commented

189

knowingly.

"Speaking of which, when will Mavis be in? I have something to settle with one particular woman, but I don't know where she is."

"Mavis told me all about it." Red nodded. "I'm thinkin' I can be of some help. Yer lass and Mavis are rooming together temporarily—Tirpak's Boarding House, over on McGaa Street. Want something to bolster the courage before ye leave? It's on the house."

Nat declined with a grin. "No, I think I'm going to need all my wits about me when I get there."

"Good luck, then. Kent Jackson's a good man, but may the best man win. Bellamy's an Irish name, is it not?" When Nat nodded, Red continued, "Well, I'll be placin' me bet on a fellow Irishmon any day."

****

Perhaps the so-called "luck of the Irish" was indeed with him, Nat thought as he followed Red's directions and easily found the well-marked house. Then again, maybe not, he thought as the stern-looking, round woman who had answered his knock informed him the women boarders were not permitted male callers in their rooms and that Melissa was not yet up. His hope surged again as he heard her familiar voice drifting down the stairway.

"Mrs. Tirpak! The *palachintas* smell delicious!" Melissa exclaimed, stopping suddenly in her descent as Nat came into her line of vision. "Nat! What on earth are you doing here so early in the morning?" Surprised by his appearance, her voice lacked the aloofness she had promised herself she would display toward him if ever she saw him again.

"I tell him the rules, Miss Sullivan. He vill be

leaving now."

"No!" Melissa nearly shouted. "I mean," she softened her voice, "he was a friend of Jesse's, Mrs. Tirpak. My brother-in-law, you remember. I hope to hear more news of my sister's life here," she lied convincingly. The words coming out of her mouth shocked her. *I'm becoming like Mavis*, she thought despairingly. *That was too easy!*

Nat's elation at Melissa's obvious willingness to talk to him was quickly doused by the appearance of another gentleman whom he recognized as one Kent Jackson. Jackson's hand briefly touched Melissa's shoulder as he approached her from behind, stirring possessive feelings in Nat, who clenched and unclenched his fists in an effort to restrain himself.

"Melissa, I'm so glad to have caught you before you left on your morning errands. I haven't time to stay for Mrs. Tirpak's delicious breakfast, but if you have a minute, I'd like a private word or two with you," he said, his pointed look at Nat revealing he had obviously overheard at least some of the previous conversation.

With a nod to Kent, Melissa glanced at Nat. "If you'll excuse me," she said as she allowed Kent to lead her by the elbow down the stairs and into the drawing room just to the right of the entryway. Kent's subsequent closing of the heavy wooden pocket doors to ensure the privacy of the conversation was almost enough to undo Nat's intentions, but he held his ground, even as Mrs. Tirpak stood scowling before him.

They seemed to be in a stare-down contest when the woman suddenly flung up her meaty arms exclaiming, "*Yoi estinem*! My *palachintas*!"

As she hurried toward the kitchen, the drawing room

doors slid open.

"I understand Mrs. Tirpak's famous chicken and dumplings is on the menu for tonight, and I will most assuredly finish my business in time to partake of that. She makes the dumplings different from what we find in America. She uses eggs in her recipe, and the result is better than anything even the chef at the Broadwell House can produce. I hope to see you at the table as well. A well-cooked meal shared with a charming and beautiful woman. What more could a man ask for?" Certain Jackson's parting words were intended for his ears, Nat seethed. Melissa's sweet reply didn't help.

"With such a recommendation, how can I afford to miss it?"

In the few seconds it took the two of them to emerge from the room, Nat was feeling angrier than a bear whose cub had been stolen from it. Nor was his rage abated when Jackson confidently tipped his hat at him as he left the building and Melissa's expression toward him resumed the icy nature to which he had become accustomed of late.

"I'd like to talk to you. Please," he said, barely quelling his anger.

Melissa closed her eyes briefly and allowed herself a deep breath. She *would not* allow herself to be hornswoggled again by those cerulean eyes that seemed to darken just a shade to feign a look of sincerity. When she reopened her eyes after a moment, she felt in better control.

"I don't know that we have anything to discuss, Mr. Bellamy," she replied coldly.

In response, he seized her by the arm and pushed open the door, shoving her through it. "We have *everything* to discuss, Miss Sullivan," he growled, turning her to face him as they stood on the front porch. "And if I have to hog-tie you to get you to talk to me, believe me I will, because until I do, I've discovered I'll be no good to anybody."

His last words had the effect of a sockdologer on Melissa. She heard the desperation underlying his anger, and…his expression… *Was that a flash of fear she saw?* It made no sense. Her curiosity was aroused. Still, she was cautious.

"All right. Let's talk then," she said, shrugging out of the light grip he had on her shoulders and folding her arms across her chest as she prepared to listen to his words.

"Not here." Her acquiescence abated his anger somewhat. "Ride with me?"

Melissa had spied the army supply wagon when she was forced onto the porch and assumed correctly that it was the means of conveyance he had in mind.

"Yes." The response came out almost before she realized she would agree to his request. "Just let me get my wrap." She turned and started to reenter the house but was halted in her progress as his hand snaked around her wrist.

"You *will* return."

Incensed by what seemed to be a command, Melissa opened her mouth to give him the tongue-lashing he so certainly deserved, but as her eyes collided with his, she was shocked at the bald pain she saw in the sapphire depths. Could she have mistaken the meaning behind the harsh, raspy tone in which those last words were spoken? She recalled an all-too-frequently-needed admonishment from her mother: *Remember, Melissa, the benefit of the doubt is the kinder road to follow*. Holding his gaze, she gently removed his hand from her wrist and forced a small, reassuring smile.

"Before you even realize I'm gone."

If only you knew, Nat spoke silently to her retreating back.

Melissa returned shortly, as promised, and an awkward silence ensued. Nat helped her step up into the wagon and proceeded to tuck her into a woolen blanket he had thought to bring, spreading it across her lap and around her legs. Even through her layers of clothing, which included her new gray woolen cottage cloak, Melissa felt flames licking through her body at his touch. For his part, Nat was thankful his military trousers were as loosely cut as they were or he would have embarrassed himself by splitting them as he climbed into the driver's seat of the wagon. The subsequent concentration required to dodge the pedestrians, pigs, dogs, horses, and other conveyances as he steered his team out of town provided him with at least temporary alleviation from his physical needs and stymied conversation.

"I was sorry to learn about your sister and brother-in-law," Nat said as they finally left the congested town behind them and the horses had assumed an even gait. The words came out sounding stilted and formal, but it was the only thing he could think of to say.

"Is that what this talk is about, then?"

"No. In fact, I just found out about it from Mav last night. I wish I had known when I bumped into you in the telegraph office. No wonder you looked so upset. I would have liked to have been of some help."

"No one, not even you, can bring the dead back, I'm afraid," Melissa replied, choosing not to correct his misconception about the source of her distress the previous morning.

Nat heard the slight crack in Melissa's voice as she spoke, and, out of the corner of his eye, saw her fingering her mother's gold ring. Her mouth was twisted oddly, and she looked as if she were desperately trying to collect herself. As much as he wanted to stop the wagon then and there, sweep her into his arms, and promise her he'd make everything in her world all right again, he refrained from doing so. For one thing, he wouldn't make a promise he couldn't keep, and at this point in time, he had his obligation to the federal government. Not that he was sure what that obligation entailed, given the lack of leadership at Camp Weld. Shortly after reporting for duty there, he had learned that Burrows, the officer whose company he, Alston, and Tom were to have joined up with, had been given orders to depart with his men for a fort farther north, Fort Laramie, to help with Indian troubles there. For another, he sensed it wasn't what she wanted from him right then. So instead he continued to steer the horses in silence and pretended not to notice as she struggled to keep her emotions in check.

Melissa could not say what exactly had brought on the sudden feeling of overpowering grief. While she still experienced an aching feeling in her heart and stomach when her thoughts drifted to all the loved ones she had recently lost, she had thought she had spent the last of her tears. But the caring and concern she heard in Nat's voice, which spoke so much more loudly than his words, seemed to be her undoing.

"Here we are," Nat announced as he maneuvered the horses off the trail. Setting the brake, he came around the wagon to help a still-pensive Melissa down before he secured the reins to a nearby pine tree. "I'll never forget the long talk we had as you were standing guard over me while I was trying to decide whether to live or die from that arrow wound. The words between us flowed as easily as the water in Cherry Creek. Remember? So I thought maybe that would work again, seeing as how things got messed up between us somewhere along the line," he said as he took her hand and led her through a maze of pine trees that appeared to end at a steep wall of jagged rock.

Melissa was busy watching her step lest she trip over an exposed root or some rocky debris as she dragged behind, half regretting that she had agreed to this outing but curious all the same. Looking up when Nat suddenly stopped, she was left momentarily breathless by the beauty of the scene that lay before her. Rather than butting up against the cliff as she had imagined, the trees opened into a flat, grassy area. There she viewed a narrow stream snaking its way through the landscape near the base of the bluff. From the top of the precipice, a cascade left a wet, sinuous trail before joining forces with the water rushing through the rocky creek bed. A squirrel chattered at her from the nearest pine tree as though welcoming her to his piece of paradise.

"I found this place accidentally the other day," Nat said as he led her to a nearby large, flat boulder and motioned for her to sit. "It seemed too pretty not to be able to share it with someone, and I couldn't think of anyone I'd rather share it with than you. But for some reason, you've been acting like you don't want much to do with me," he continued as he hunkered down beside her and took her two hands in his much larger ones, forcing her to turn her body partially toward him. "I don't know what happened, but I miss you, Melissa Sullivan. And, I admit, I got angry at the way you were treating me and decided to give you a taste of your own medicine, which is why I didn't come over and talk to you and Mav before Al, Tom, and I left for Camp Weld. I tried to convince myself it didn't matter, that you didn't matter. But, as Al would say, I could put as many wings as I wanted on that pig, but it still wouldn't fly, so I figured I had to at least try to fix whatever got broken." He flashed her a sheepish grin. "Okay, since I've promised myself I'd be nothing but purely honest with you, I have to admit that Al and Tom gave me more than a little bit of prodding in that direction."

Melissa absorbed his words in silence as she watched the water flow rapidly over the craggy bottom, parting around a particularly large rock and rejoining at the other side. Indeed, she did remember their conversation by the river—as well as a lot of other things she and Nat had shared. All too well and all too often. Forcing those memories from her mind had been a daily struggle. She knew he awaited a response from her. She supposed she risked nothing in agreeing to a friendship since she would be going off shortly and would probably never see this man again. In time, she hoped, the memories would fade.

"Nothing needs fixed since nothing is broken," she finally answered without looking at him. "The events of the last several weeks have been quite stressful, and my actions and reactions were, no doubt, the result of the strain. Please don't consider that they were anything more than that. I regret I may have given you some wrong impressions about me."

The strained calmness in her voice was Nat's

undoing.

"Oh, hell!" He tugged on her hands, forcing her body to turn toward him even more. She looked up sharply and green-flecked brown eyes collided with those matching the color of the sky above them. "Melissa Sullivan, I don't know where my present obligations will take me or what the future holds in the near term. But I do know that I need you, and I love you. I admit I don't have much to offer you at the moment, but Camp Weld does have facilities for married soldiers, and although I may have to be away some of the time, at least I'll know you're protected."

Abruptly, Melissa jerked her hands from his, clenching them tightly in her lap and swiveling back to face the creek. The echo of Nat's words washed over her, spreading an uncomfortable warmth throughout her body. She should never have allowed herself to come here with him, she thought ruefully, as conflicting emotions surged through her. Anger won out. "I think I've told you before I don't need a protector." She spoke in a controlled voice. She did not look at him, but he could see the color rising to her face, and her chin was thrust upward in what Nat had come to recognize as a defiant gesture of hers. "As a matter of fact, in the short time I've been in Denver I have secured a stable position as a teacher in a nearby mining community. So, you see, you're not the only one with pressing duties. I have obligations to fulfill myself. You needn't worry about me or my welfare. I can take care of myself." She smoothed her skirts with the palms of her hands. "And besides," she flung the words out before she could stop herself, "I believe bigamy is illegal, or did you think to keep me as your mistress at Camp Weld?"

For a few brief seconds, she thought she had won the battle. Her proclamation was met with total silence. So why did she feel more hurt than relieved?

"Bigamy! What the hell is that supposed to mean?" He boomed, grabbing her wrists and jerking her to a standing position. An arm quickly snaked around her waist and pulled her against him when she stumbled and almost fell into the turbulent creek waters.

She pushed herself back from his chest with the palms of her hands, but he continued to hold her loosely captive. She could feel the warmth of his hands on her waist.

"So it was the latter proposition you had in mind?" She asked rhetorically, her eyes downcast. "Please, let me repeat my earlier statement. I realize I may have acted in an untoward fashion in the past. Regrettably, more than once. I suppose my actions suggested that I would be amenable to such an offer, but I assure you, I am not." She could feel her face becoming redder, and tears began to well in her eyes as she realized what this man must think of her. *And justifiably so*, she thought sadly.

"Melissa," he said gently, as he tilted her face up and forced her to look at him. "I'm asking you to *marry* me!" He gently wiped away the tears that had begun to spill onto her cheeks with his thumbs. "How could you think I'd have so little regard for you I'd ask you to be my mistress?"

Confusion was evident in his cerulean eyes as she stared into them—as was love, as he bent his head to place a tender kiss on her lips.

"B-but you're *already* married!" Her words were muffled against his mouth.

"Then you sure as hell know something I don't!" Pulling her body closer, he invaded her once again with his tongue. Incensed that he treated her declaration so cavalierly, she bit down on the intruding organ.

"Ouch! Daaammmit!" He released her quickly and stepped back. "Is that any way to treat your betrothed?" He asked as he retrieved a handkerchief and applied it to the injured part.

"I don't recall agreeing to your proposal," she shot back, folding her arms across her chest. "Maybe Emmie finds arrogance in a man attractive, but I certainly don't."

"Emmie! What's she got to do with this?"

"Everything, I would think, given that she is your wife."

"My *wife*?" He stared at her and then burst out laughing. His laughter was deep and resonant, and would have been infectious had she not been so startled by it. Melissa realized she had never heard him laugh before. She stared, dumbfounded, at the tears flowing down his cheeks and could not think what he found so humorous. It was at least a full two minutes before he regained his speech.

"Emmie's not my wife." He choked out between a couple of lingering chuckles.

"But...you spoke of her in your delirium. You sent a telegraph to her from Denver." Melissa shut her mouth abruptly as she realized her poorly veiled accusations were revealing more of her emotions than she wished.

"Sweetness," Nat approached her again and encircled her waist with his large hands. "Emmie is my *sister*! My kid sister, although she's now reached the ripe old age of seventeen and wouldn't cotton to that title much. Not that she ever did, independent little cuss that she is. Is this what all this has been about?"

Embarrassed, Melissa opened her mouth to deny it, but was cut off as he continued. "I admit it. I love Emmie dearly, and I'm hoping to bring her to Denver where I can keep an eye on her. I think you'll love her, too. And, like you, she would have no use for an arrogant male."

Melissa's head was reeling as she pulled away from his hold and returned to sit on the rock. Nat made no attempt to restrain her, obviously realizing her need to absorb these new facts. As she stared blankly at the water, she sensed he had walked up to stand behind her. A brightly colored mallard floated by beside his dull brown mate. *Nat had asked her to become his wife!* It was so tempting to say yes. No, to *scream* yes! Wasn't this the fulfillment of the dreams she'd had only a few short months ago? There would be no white picket fence at first, but she was certain there could be one in the future. Nat was the type of man who could make things happen, she was sure. It would be so easy to succumb to the temptation of being taken care of by this man who stirred feelings in her she had never known existed. But she was no longer the fresh young girl who had become instantly infatuated with a handsome young soldier as she sat on her uncle's wagon. She had seen so much, and at times she had felt too much like the leaf she now observed bobbing willy-nilly, taken wherever the current directed it. She didn't want to turn out like Aunt Georgina, although she didn't at all think Nat was like John Hund. Nor would he be cruel like Annie's husband—but would he be supportive of *her* dreams? She had already observed his overbearing nature more than once. He seemed to view himself in the role of a guardian of womankind. Hadn't he said he was bringing

Emmie to Denver to protect her? Perhaps, for Southern women, independence had a different meaning. She had heard they were of a different ilk.

It struck her that this was the first time in her life she had really been given a choice. Ever the dutiful daughter, she had always subjected herself to her parents' wishes, and her escape from her uncle had been one of necessity, not choice. Choices, which were always something she had thought she would someday embrace gleefully, given the chance, were not exactly easy, she realized ruefully. She could now easily agree to marry the man she loved—or, at least, thought she loved. Did she even know what love was? Or she could continue on her path of self-determination that had so excited her only a day before—a path that would allow her to make her own decisions in all aspects of her life. She raised her hands and rubbed her temples with her forefingers. Several minutes passed before she spoke.

"I ca-can't marry you, Nat." Even as she spoke the words, she thought she had never before felt more wretched. She had no idea whether she was making the right choice.

"Why the hell not?"

His words spilled out as an angry growl from behind her, reinforcing her decision. She leapt up and turned to glare at him.

"That's precisely why," she spat out.

"What's that supposed to mean?" he asked, his voice fraught with frustration, his arms stretched out, palms up, in a gesture of total bewilderment.

"It's quite obvious to me that your so-called marriage proposal was more a command than a question." Tossing back her hair, she stood akimbo.

"You never once gave a thought to what I might want. No doubt you thought this poor, orphaned girl would jump at the chance to be married to you. Unfortunately, you thought wrong. Now, if you will please return me to Mrs. Tirpak's, I have some errands to run before I leave to attend to *my* obligations."

Her words struck him like rocks. His initial shock quickly turned into anger.

"If that's what you *want*, Miss Sullivan, I'm *more* than happy to oblige you."

****

Interminable. That was what the ride back to the boardinghouse seemed to Melissa. She was constantly scooting to reestablish the small space between them as the wagon lurched over the bumpy terrain. She found herself wishing they had not ended their conversation on such a hostile note. She had much more enjoyed the ride out of town, during which she had allowed her thigh to rest against his, thrilling at the warmth that spread through her at his nearness. In fact, she reflected, she had never felt so utterly miserable as she did right now. Nat had not spoken to her since he had agreed to take her back, but then, of course, she had made no attempts at conversation either. Perhaps she had been too hasty in her decision. She chanced a sideways peek at him. He sat erect on the seat. His tightly clenched jaw quickly dispelled her of any notion she might have had to right matters. Silently, she scolded herself for so soon doubting herself and forced herself to turn her thoughts to the adventure awaiting her in Cold Creek. It was not an easy task, and relief washed over her as the wagon finally came to a stop in front of the boardinghouse. Nat remained erect as he held the reins, and she realized he had no intention of assisting her off the conveyance. Her heart felt as though it had shattered into a million pieces. Wanting to end things on a more civil note, she felt compelled to say something, anything.

"Nat, I—"

"Stop right there, Miss Sullivan." He interrupted her, turning to pierce her with icy blue eyes. "I think you've said quite enough already. Now, if you'll please step down, I, too, have a life to attend to."

Melissa's feet had no sooner touched the ground than the wagon rumbled off.

****

Rather than heading back out to Camp Weld immediately, Nat drove the vehicle a couple of blocks into the main part of town. He wanted to check to see if he had any more news from Emmie. Normally, the telegraph operator, Jim Jeters, or his assistant, Calvin, were pretty good about delivering what they considered to be important messages to the fort as soon as they could. Sometimes, however, "as soon as they could" meant a couple of days. More than ever, he was thankful he had hidden a bag of Union money on the plantation before he had been thrown off the property by Alfred. While any Confederate currency Emmie could come up with might be useful and accepted for some of her traveling needs, all but the staunchest Confederates had already begun to view their own currency as worthless. Had he not hidden his stash, he might have had problems getting the Union currency to her. The Virginia bank he and his family had always used was owned by a man whose four sons were fighting against the uniform Nat now wore. Nat doubted he'd have been able to turn there for help in getting funds to Emmie. If things got so bad in Virginia that Nat felt Emmie should chance what could be a dangerous trip to Denver, at least things were in place for him to be able to move on it.

Nat collided with Calvin as the young man came storming out the door.

"Lieutenant Bellamy! I was just riding out to deliver a message we'd received for you," the apprentice exclaimed as he recognized the face that accompanied the hard body he had encountered so abruptly. "Talk about coincidences, huh?"

Seeing the scowl on the lieutenant's face, Calvin quickly decided the soldier was in no mood for small talk and handed over the folded paper he had been carrying. Remembering the message it contained, he beat a quick retreat into the office, wishing he had someplace to hide for the time being.

Nat STOP Mother is dead STOP Funeral tomorrow STOP Advise STOP Love Emmie.

To the apprentice's relief, when the lieutenant entered the office, he seemed too preoccupied with the detailed message he was composing to bother with him. After handing him the return message and some coin, the soldier left abruptly. Calvin watched as he crossed the street to the Lucky Lady.

The saloon was almost empty, except for the few regulars who never seemed to leave the bar. Nat didn't see any sign of Mavis.

"Nat, good to see yer ugly Irish face again," Red called cheerfully from behind the bar where he was washing up some glasses in preparation for the next wave of customers. "Mav's not here just yet, but she should be soon. Come share a shot with yer fellow countrymon till then."

Red poured two fingers of Taos Lightning into a shot glass and slid it toward Nat as he approached the bar. Nat took a big swig that burned all the way down.

"What was that?" he choked out as soon as he could speak again.

"Taos Lightning. One of Uncle Dick's creations," Red responded, using the nickname bestowed on Richens Lacy Wootton, a familiar character in Denver. "Uncle Dick swears it's a concoction using only the highest quality of whiskey, but there are those who judge it could kill a man at forty yards."

"Count me among the latter," Nat responded.

"Speaking of killing, what do ye hear about the Indian situation these days?" Red asked as he refilled Nat's glass with the house brand.

"Hopefully, things are turning around. Remarkably, Lone Wolf is still interested in peace."

"Even after that bloody idiot Sergeant Simpson and his troops attacked Lone Wolf's village while they were camped near Fort Lyon in May? Of course, I'm thinking the Hungates and Melissa's family paid with their lives for that fiasco the following month."

"Those who know Lone Wolf don't believe he could have been responsible for that massacre," Nat responded. "And, if you think about it, it doesn't make sense that he'd commit such an act and then seek peace. Major Wynkoop just received a letter signed by Lone Wolf in which he and the chiefs of several of the other tribes are agreeing to an exchange of prisoners."

"Might it have anything to do with the new regiment of 100-day volunteers Governor Evans got the War Department to approve?" Red asked.

"It might, but it's my understanding Lone Wolf has

been an outspoken advocate of peace for years, ever since he was selected to the Council of Forty-Four, which Daile tells me is the ruling body of the Cheyenne nation."

"I haven't talked to Will lately meself, but I be betting he's ready to spit nails over this latest development."

Nat laughed. "I doubt you'd find anyone to bet against you. There are plenty who are not as sympathetic to the Indians as Daile is."

"Who gets to define 'hostile'?" Red asked.

"You got me. For all Indians' sakes, I hope it isn't Colonel Kenwood."

Nat knew by the look on Red's face Mavis had arrived before he heard her voice.

"I'm thinking she's the prettiest lass I ever have seen." Red spoke the words almost to himself as Mavis ran up to Nat and gave him an excited hug.

"I'm hoping this is a pleasure visit, Lieutenant Bellamy," Mavis proclaimed, only half teasing.

"Too late. I've had my pleasure talking to Red, here. If you'd get out of bed earlier, you wouldn't miss out on all the fun," Nat responded. "Now I'm ready to talk business."

"But me granny always said, 'Get the name of an early riser, and you can sleep till noon.' It sounded like good advice to me." Mavis pouted prettily.

Red threw back his head and laughed at that one. "Yes, but, love, ye forgot to heed the first part. Ye've not yet established the reputation of being an early riser." He came around the bar and planted a kiss on the top of her head.

"A wee detail," Mavis muttered. "So, what brings ye

to us, Nat? Have ye talked to Miss, yet?"

"Yes, but never mind that." The scowl that flashed across Nat's countenance told Mavis and Red the meeting had not gone well. "I've come to ask you a favor in another area."

Chapter Nineteen

The sun shone brightly through the window of the schoolhouse, creating the deceptive image of a warm spring day, belied by the patches of snow still on the ground. Melissa sat at her desk, pencil poised in her hand, mesmerized by the fingers of melting ice as they formed ever-changing patterns on the windowpanes. As one finger dissolved, another slid gently, aimlessly, into place. She had been trying to prepare lesson plans for the coming week all morning but seemed to be able to find one distraction after another in her surroundings. First, reasonably enough, a fire had to be built in the potbellied stove in the middle of the room to make the room comfortably warm enough. Then, a good sweeping of the rough wood floor had seemed called for. After she finished that, she had decided the four rows of desks, three deep on each side of the stove, could stand a solid scrubbing to rid them of the fine layer of chalk dust. That had entailed retrieving a bucket from her own little cabin, scooping snow into it, and heating the bucket on the schoolroom stove. Finally satisfied with the tidiness of the classroom, she sat down to tackle the task at hand, but still she found her mind wandering. With a sigh of resignation, she laid down her pencil and pushed back from her desk. Deciding a walk in the brisk, cool air might clear her mind, she snatched her coat and scarf from a peg on the wall and retrieved her gloves from the coat's pockets, pulling them on as she trudged along.

The mining community was fairly deserted. Most had gone into Denver for the weekend, taking advantage of the fact the roads were once again passable. How quickly the snow melted remained a source of amazement to Melissa. The first time the community had been covered with sixteen inches of the pristine, white blanket in less than twenty-four hours, she had been certain she would not be leaving the camp again until spring. Not that it wouldn't have been worth it, she had thought at the time, ignoring a couple of threads of despair that tugged at her heart. But already the camp had received two such heavy snowfalls, as well as one that had produced half as much powder, yet she had been able to visit Mavis twice in the seven weeks since her arrival. A snowfall here was so breathtaking it was worth any minor inconvenience, in her opinion. She would never forget that first snow. It had begun on the night of a full moon, and she had happened to glance out her tiny bedroom window as she prepared for bed. Her breath had caught in her throat as she gazed on what looked like thousands of tiny diamonds falling soundlessly against a black velvet landscape. She had been as excited as a little girl on Christmas morning and had stayed up for hours, enthralled by the scene. The next morning, she had shared her excitement with one of her student's mothers, who was experiencing her second winter in Cold Creek, and had received a gentle scolding.

"It is beautiful, yah. But the weather can be a very powerful adversary, too, Miss Sullivan," the large Danish woman had told her. "Best you not be too quick to forget it." Mrs. Anderssen had given her a pat on the shoulder, as if to say she forgave the younger woman for her foolishness, while waving goodbye to her daughter, Christina, with her other hand.

Today, the married workers had taken their families into town with them to give the wives a chance to do some shopping and the children a change of pace. Kent had offered her a ride to town with him, but Melissa had declined at the last minute. He was partly responsible for her lack of focus this morning.

Not that she blamed him at all. Kent was everything he had represented himself to be. He was a strong, determined man, but kind and caring. Upon their arrival in Cold Creek, he had immediately provided her with her own little cabin, allaying any fears she might have had of less-than-honorable intentions on his part. It had been deserted by a miner and his wife who had left it to return East, he had explained. They had left a lot of their belongings behind, and even then it had the warm and cozy look of a home. He'd left her to get settled, telling her to prepare a list of any other items she felt she might need for her new home or for the school, which lay only a few yards from her cabin. A wooden walkway had been built between the two structures.

Later, he had returned to escort her around the camp. They first stopped at a two-story wooden building that served as a meeting hall for the miners when the occasion arose, and he pointed out the large medical supply storage closet just off the hall. The company store was housed in the same building, taking up the remainder of the lower level as well as the entire upper level, and he introduced her to Elizabeth Krehlik, a miner's wife who ran the store.

"I keep an ample stock of staples on hand: flour, sugar, coffee, tea, and spices. I have fruits and vegetables when they're in season, too. Some of the miners hunt their own meat, and many have chicken coops behind their cabins. The price of meat is dear these days. You'll also find some non-food items on these shelves: cooking utensils, yarns, threads, bolts of cloth, hand tools, small toys, and other odds and ends. Come 'round when you have more time, and we can visit while you check out the inventory," she encouraged as the two were leaving to continue the tour.

As they proceeded past the camp's church, a white clapboard structure with a brown cross painted across its double front doors, Kent explained worship services were held once a week, with one of the miners leading them whenever a traveling preacher or priest was not available. Those first couple of days, he had also introduced her to the families whose children would be under her charge, and he had spent most of his free time since then entertaining her with stories about the area and teaching her how to play chess. She had considered him a good friend and an interesting companion. Until last night's kiss.

She had recognized something was on his mind from the moment he entered her cabin. His mood was more somber than usual, which she attributed to a problem with the mine. The most recent snowfall had further weakened the timbers at the entrance of shaft number three, and he feared it had created the potential for an accident. Even after the conversation had changed directions, she sensed his continued distraction as the evening progressed.

"I've been considering teaching some of the older students this game," she told him, waiting for his input.

"Good idea," was his only response as she noted he

carelessly moved his bishop where it was threatened by her knight.

"I know it's not part of the traditional three Rs, but I've found it to be good training for the mind," she continued as she captured his bishop after assuring herself her knight was safe from attack in its new position.

"You'll get no argument from me. I'd even argue it's good training for life," Kent concurred as he puzzled over the new predicament he was faced with on the board. "In life, just as in chess, you're wise to consider the moves your opponent might make several steps ahead, not just his next couple of moves. My father taught me that when he first introduced me to the game, and I've found it to be a good lesson." Kent then castled, moving his king two squares toward his rook and placing his rook on the opposite side of his king to afford his king further protection.

Not too many moves later, Kent's state of mind, or lack thereof, revealed itself. While he could have continued to move his remaining three pieces—a king, a rook, and a pawn—around the board, avoiding checkmate for a while on the chance Melissa might make a mistake in her play, he laid his king on its side, signaling his acceptance of his defeat.

"Of course, Dad never warned me there might be different problems when dealing with a beautiful opponent," he commented with a wry smile.

Embarrassed by the compliment, Melissa rose hastily and excused herself to make brandy toddies, which had become an evening ritual. The combination of brandy, hot water, and sugar generated a warm, relaxed feeling, and they often discussed their plans for the next day while they enjoyed the drinks. Last night had been no exception—in that regard, at least. It was later than usual when Kent finally stood to leave. Melissa sensed his reluctance to do so. As she stood to accompany him the few steps to the door, he had placed his hands firmly on her shoulders, holding her in place while he spoke as though fearful she'd run away.

"Melissa, you've been an asset to this camp. The children love you, the miners and their wives love you, and, well…I love you, Melissa." Ignoring her sharp intake of breath, he continued as though he were desperate to get the words out without interruption. "I've probably loved you from the first, but I wanted to be certain before I declared my intentions to you. I am asking you to become my wife." Not waiting for a reply, he hurried on. "You don't have to give me an answer yet. I realize this may have come as a surprise to you. But think about it, Miss. We're good together, you and I."

Any response she might have made had been thwarted as he gently cupped her cheeks in his hands and pulled her mouth to his, lightly brushing his lips across hers as their brandy-sweetened breaths mingled. He then slid his arms around her, pulling her closer, his kiss deepening as she opened her mouth to voice a protest.

"I'd best go before I get into trouble here." His parting words were husky as he released her and set her away from him. He was out the door before he could see the moisture forming in her eyes.

She had feigned illness when he stopped by to pick her up for the trek into Denver this morning. Concerned, he had been willing to delay his trip, but she had encouraged him to go without her. Reluctantly, he had. After he had departed, she had thrown herself into work, trying to run away from her thoughts.

Suddenly, those thoughts came to an abrupt halt as she found herself flat on her rump. One minute, she had been trudging furiously along, oblivious to the surroundings she normally found such delight in. The next minute her feet had gone out from under her. Momentarily stunned, she looked down to see the patch of ice beneath her. Her boot must have caught it just right. Two squirrels scampered by in front of her, chasing each other up a tree. They looked down and chattered at her, as if to scold her for her lack of vigilance.

"Miss Sullivan, are you all right?"

Melissa turned her head in the direction of the voice to see Pete Bodnar lumbering toward her.

"Are you hurt?" Pete asked again as he drew closer.

"Only my pride," Melissa responded, forcing a small smile for her student as he positioned his hands under her armpits to help her stand.

"You were moving real fast when you took your fall, Miss Sullivan! I thought some wild animal was chasing you."

Not far from the truth, Melissa thought wryly, as she brushed off the back of her coat.

"What are you doing here, Pete? I would have thought you'd go into town with everyone else."

"No, I didn't feel like it today, ma'am," Pete responded, ducking his head to hide what Melissa knew was his embarrassment.

He probably suspected she knew the real reason he hadn't accompanied his dad into town. His dad hadn't wanted him tagging along. Clifford Bodnar didn't like his son very much and picked on him even more than the other children did. Melissa had managed to enforce rules of respect for each other among the children when they were in the classroom, but thus far her influence hadn't extended any farther than that. And she had no control over his father's behavior toward him. Melissa had heard Clifford call his son a "mama's boy" more than once.

Pete was about average height for his thirteen years but was very overweight. Melissa suspected he used food to comfort himself and provide some relief from all the harassment he endured. He had the face of an angel, with rounded pink cheeks and light, sky-blue eyes. Eyes that were frequently filled with tears at the teasing he took. With his wavy blond hair and naturally pink lips, he would have made a very pretty girl, Melissa thought. Although she had really wanted to be alone with her thoughts, the boy tugged at her heart. Kent had told her Pete had lost his mother, to whom he had been very close, a year ago. Given his father's attitude toward him, Pete had essentially been orphaned by her death. He was as alone in the world as she. But she, at least, had friends.

"Tell you what, Pete. I think I'm ready to go back for some hot cocoa. And I baked a batch of sugar cookies yesterday morning. They're still fresh, if you'd like to join me. I could probably use a steady hand next to me in case I should slip again," she added, in the improbable case the boy would turn down the cocoa and cookies.

Pete's eyes lit up as he nodded his agreement. "I'll stay right beside you," he said importantly, taking her elbow as she carefully picked her way back down a steep incline, avoiding any more icy patches.

Melissa stepped onto her tiny porch ahead of Pete and opened the front door to her cabin. Entering the small space that served as her parlor, she was glad to note warmth still issued from the fire she had banked earlier that morning. A brightly colored, braided rag rug covered a large portion of the puncheon floor, compliments of the couple who had returned East. Two chairs, one a slat-backed rocker, the other an old, but solid, Windsor chair, flanked the fireplace occupying the left wall of the room. A battered trunk Kent had secured for her from elsewhere was positioned between the chairs, serving as both a table and extra storage. His chess set sat on top of the trunk. Kent had also constructed three parallel shelves on the right-hand wall of the room, next to the doorway leading to her bedroom, so she would have a place for what she hoped would be a growing collection of cherished books and magazines. Charlotte Bronte and Nathaniel Hawthorne were two of her favorite authors, and she enjoyed the variety of the articles offered by *Home Journal*, *Harper's Monthly Magazine*, and *Ponder*, too.

"Just hang your coat here if you like," Melissa said as she hung her own coat on one of the four pegs by the entryway and stashed her scarf and gloves on the shelf above. "You can stoke the fire up again while I prepare our snack," she directed as she exited through the doorway on the back wall of the parlor that led to her small but efficient kitchen area.

There were still red embers from the fire she had built in the woodburning stove to make her tea that morning, so Melissa had only to feed it a couple small pieces of wood to get it going again. Satisfied with the results of her effort, she opened the door at the rear of the kitchen and fetched the container of milk she kept there, buried part way in a mound of snow she had built for just that purpose. She poured the milk into a kettle and set it on the stove to heat while she removed four sugar cookies from a large, glass jar and put them on a small plate. Once the milk was hot, she measured small amounts of cocoa and sugar into two cups and added the milk. Loading everything onto a small tin tray, she carefully carried it into the next room where Pete awaited her return.

She found him sitting in the Windsor chair by the fire, studying a wooden chess piece he held in his hand.

"Would you like to learn how to play?"

"Yes, ma'am," he replied with boyish enthusiasm.

She positioned the rocking chair across from him and began to explain how the different pieces moved, thankful for the diversion.

"Chess is a lot like life," she found herself echoing, "and you're wise to consider the moves your opponent might make several steps ahead, not just his next couple of moves."

Pete proved to be a quick learner, and as Melissa observed him and his enthusiasm for the game, a plan began to form in her mind.

Hours later, after Pete had returned to his own cabin, Melissa sat in that same chair and tiredly tilted her head back, stretching the muscles in her neck and upper back where tension seemed to have nested, sucking her strength like a thousand leeches as she rocked and mentally refined her plan.

****

The man dropped his single piece of baggage on the floor and sank down on the edge of the bed, pulling out a dirty bandana, which he used to mop the beads of sweat dripping profusely from his forehead. The short walk from the station to Planter's House had left him winded.

He needed a drink. But first, he'd take a nap. That brat on the stagecoach had cried continuously, making sleep impossible. Its overwrought mother, somewhat of a looker, had blamed it on teething, and he had even supplied some of his good whiskey for her to rub on its gums—anything to get some shuteye—to no avail. The bitch hadn't even shown her appreciation. In fact, she had given him a dirty look when he had brushed her breast with his hand as he extended his flask, and she had even asked the man sitting in the seat opposite to trade places with her after his gesture of affection. That *after* she had liberally applied his precious liquid to the toddler's gums, of course. In the end, he had finished the bottle himself, hoping it would render him oblivious to the kid's screams. Yes, he'd take a nap, find a saloon, and go visit the sheriff. In that order.

Chapter Twenty

Melissa was startled out of her reverie as she recognized the familiar knock. Sighing, she got up and opened the door to her visitor.

"Feeling better?" Kent's voice exuded its usual warmth.

"Much, thank you," she responded, hating the awkwardness that permeated the room as she stepped aside and motioned for him to come in.

"Can't come in right now. I have some business to finish up in the office yet. Just stopped by to bring you something I picked up in Denver."

She almost stopped breathing when she noted the hand he held behind his back. *Please, no. Not another proposal,* she thought frantically. She hadn't had time to sort things out in her own mind yet. She had instead been focused on devising a method she thought would help Pete. Kent smiled as he held out the latest edition of *Ponder*. Melissa's face relaxed in a joyful grin.

"Th-thank you," she stammered, feeling somewhat embarrassed, as though he could read her thoughts. "Are you sure you don't want to come in?" she asked, holding the magazine to her breast.

"I'm sure. Thanks for the invite, though. Enjoy," he said nodding to his gift as he turned to depart.

Melissa felt doubly troubled as she gently closed the door behind him and leaned against it. She sensed the real motive for his quick departure. He knew she needed to be alone to ponder her thoughts. Unlike Nat, he didn't try to suffocate her with his presence or demand her acquiescence. He put her feelings first and tried to make her feel comfortable. He was kind, sensitive, caring, and intelligent. And handsome. He was a man most women would be thrilled to marry. She had even observed some of the younger wives of the married miners flirting with him scandalously. He had always politely deflected their advances in a manner that left them preening with what they perceived was a high compliment, which never ceased to amaze her. Perhaps she was actually just frightened of this ability of his to charm, afraid she was merely being expertly seduced without realizing it. A stupid reason to reject a proposal from a man who had given her no reason to doubt him, she recognized. And if his kisses didn't stir her as Nat's had? Well, there was a big difference between love and lust. She had learned that much from Mavis. Tomorrow, she would tell him she would gladly become his bride—first thing in the morning, she vowed, throwing another log onto the fire before she settled back down in the rocking chair to enjoy her soon-to-be betrothed's gift to her.

She noted this month's *Ponder* contained a biographical sketch of the famed poet and abolitionist, John Greenleaf Whittier, accompanied by one of his poems, "Maud Muller," and eagerly turned to it first. After reading the article and the poem, Melissa sat staring at two lines from the poem emblazoning themselves in her heart: "For of all sad words of tongue or pen, / The saddest are these: 'It might have been!' "

They seemed to reverberate through the room, suffocating her. *It might have been.* What might things have been like had her parents not died? As she fingered the ring on her necklace, she wondered whether she could have talked to her mother about the indecision she now faced. She felt herself flushing as she quickly realized there were some details of the relationship between herself and Nat that she would have been uncomfortable divulging to her mother. Perhaps even to Alicia. And most definitely to Aunt Georgina. What "might have been" had she accepted Nat's proposal, or if she had at least not lashed out in anger at him? Given her strident reaction, he no doubt now thought her a shrew and was probably relieved she had not, in fact, accepted his proposal.

As she rose abruptly, the magazine fell to the floor from her lap, its pages as tumbled as her thoughts.

No sense living in the past, she scolded herself. *The past is dead. Everyone I loved is dead. Except Nat,* she thought briefly. *No, he's dead to me, too. Best to go on from here.*

****

Although groggy from a restless night, Melissa had a newfound determination as she faced her class of twelve students, ranging in age from six to fourteen, the following morning.

"Good morning!" she greeted them cheerfully. "We're going to start out with our math lessons today." At the collective groan, she offered a potential reward. "And as soon as you finish, I have another new story I've written for you," she declared.

The students loved her stories. She incorporated several of their names into each one, along with some of their more positive attributes, and they were delighted to hear themselves being cast as heroes and heroines. She made them intriguing enough even the older students listened attentively as she read the tales she had penned.

At the prospect of the reward, the students soon quieted down and set to work. She first helped the youngest ones, whom she had already paired in teams, in their practice of addition and subtraction. She instructed the first of the couple to write a sum or subtraction problem on his or her individual chalkboard and the second to write the answer on his or hers. They were then to switch roles. Any disputes would be settled by her. The nine- and ten-year olds were given a similar assignment, except with multiplication problems as the focus.

She approached Pete, with Kent's chessboard in hand. "While I supervise the activities of the younger students, would you be willing to instruct this group in the rudiments of the game?" She inquired. The proud look on Pete's face was swiftly quelled as complaints were registered from some other members of his group.

"Mama's Boy don't know nothing. Thought you was the teacher," one of them muttered disgustedly.

"I ain't gonna learn nothin' from him," another proclaimed.

"I seen my uncle play this game back when I lived in Indiana," a boy named Steve said. "I think I'd like ta learn how it goes."

"Well, Steve, here's your chance." Melissa hopped on the only positive response, deciding not to correct the grammar of the speakers as she normally would. "You two can practice doing long division if you'd prefer," she told the first two students. "It's up to you."

She kept a stealthy eye on this oldest group of students as she helped the two youngest with their assignments.

"Miss Sullivan, ain't eight plus seven fifteen?" Bobby queried as he glared at his partner, Susie, who was insisting that it was sixteen.

"*Isn't* eight plus seven fifteen," Melissa automatically corrected. "Let's check to find out." Melissa went to her desk and retrieved a bag of small stones she had collected on one of her hikes around the community. "Bobby, you count out eight stones, and Susie, you count out seven. Then we can count them all to see what they total."

She moved away from that pair as Bobby proclaimed his victory and was threatening to make up a really hard addition problem for Susie to solve, as revenge.

"I just can't remember the nineses," ten-year-old Amanda complained.

Melissa moved to stand beside her. "Let me show you a trick. Hold up both hands," she instructed Amanda and her partner. "Now, tuck down your thumb," she said demonstrating for them. "See, nine times one is nine— exactly the number of fingers you have left up. Tucking down two fingers, she showed them that eight fingers remained up. "Nine times two is eighteen." She repeated the process, explaining that the number of fingers left up would be the ones digit and that the tens digit would always be one less than the number that nine is being multiplied by. "Until you get to nine times eleven. Then the first two digits of your answer will be *two* less than the number you are multiplying the nine by."

"I want to play next."

Melissa looked over and saw all three of Pete's classmates had become interested in the game after listening to Pete's instructions to Steve and watching the two of them battle it out on the chessboard. Pete had won, of course, having had the advantage of playing three games with her the previous evening, but instead of lording it over his opponent, he was using the opportunity to instruct him in the notion of looking several moves ahead. She headed toward the boys with a smile.

"I'm going to ask Mr. Jackson if we might get another one of these chess games so you four can take turns competing against each other. *After* you finish your other lessons," she quickly added. "Right now, I've promised everyone I'd read them my latest story, though, so let's put the board away. I'll make certain each of you other two boys get a chance to play the game with Pete after lunch. Okay?"

None of them looked too happy about it, even though they did like her stories. However, the prospect of playing the game in lieu of formal lessons kept even Jesse, the unruliest of the bunch, from voicing any objection.

Chapter Twenty-One

"Gimme another of the same, barkeep," the distasteful-looking man commanded as he swallowed his third shot of Taos Lightning in one gulp and slammed the glass down on the bar.

"Might want to be careful with these," Red advised as he finished drying the glass in his hand and moved to fill the man's request.

'Jes' leave the bottle here," the man slurred, pulling some coins out of his pocket and throwing them on the bar. "Good looker," he commented, nodding toward Mavis, who stood by the piano chatting with Dan while he tuned the instrument.

"She's taken," Red replied curtly as he scooped up the coins and deposited them in the cash register behind the bar before he greeted the new customers who had just entered.

"Well, if it ain't the three ugliest men in Denver come to visit," he called out to Nat, Tom, and Alston jovially.

Mavis was already greeting each of them with a warm hug and a kiss on the check.

"What brings ye three handsome soldiers here?" She queried as she sauntered with them up to the bar.

"Emmie's due to arrive today, Mav. You still okay with the idea of her staying with you?"

"Anything for ye, luvie," Mav responded sweetly.

"Hey!" Red interjected playfully, no longer feeling threatened by Nat and Mav's relationship.

Mavis leaned across the bar and planted a big kiss on Red's lips. "There be more where that came from," she promised as the bartender's face turned several shades more crimson than its natural state. None of the group noted the man at the other end of the bar ogling Mavis's breasts as they pressed against the polished wooden surface.

"Don't know how long it will be for," Nat warned. "Kenwood is being pretty closemouthed about everything, but we all know something is up. And Emmie *is* a handful."

"And I would be thinking nothing else, given she's yer sister, Nat," Mavis observed.

"We'll take good care of her," Red promised. "I'll not be lettin' Mavis be a bad influence," he said, grinning at the object of his insult, who was now pouting prettily in mock anger. "She'll not be workin' here," he declared as he slid three glasses and a bottle of Kentucky bourbon in front of the men.

"I've already checked with Mrs. Tirpak. She's needing some help these days, and I'm thinking maybe Emmie could take on some of those tasks while she's acquainting herself with the town," Mavis supplied as Red moved to refill the glasses of the four miners playing cards at one of the eight tables in the joint.

Nat grimaced as he recalled the dour boardinghouse owner who had almost turned him out when he'd tried to talk to Melissa. At least Emmie might not get into too much trouble under that woman's watchful eye.

"Heard from Melissa?" He tried to sound casual in his inquiry.

"I'm thinking I should just be banging the two of ye's heads together," Mavis responded in exasperation. None of the three friends noticed the alert reaction of the man seated a few bar stools away. "Ye're always askin' after her whenever ye come in, and when she was last in town, she'd be looking out onto the street, not heeding a word I said, doubtless hoping to catch a glimpse of yer ugly mug."

"What'd I tell ya, Nat?" Alston butted in before Tom delivered a sharp elbow to his ribs to remind him of how quickly Nat's mood could turn sour whenever Al felt compelled to give the lieutenant his opinion on his love life, or lack thereof.

"Ye'd best be minding him, Nathaniel," Mavis said seriously. "That lot over there work for Kent," she explained further, indicating the four poker players, "and one of them was tellin' me, earlier, rumor has it their boss may be planning on marryin' me friend."

"I'm thinkin' it be more than a rumor, Nat," Red supplied, having returned to hear the last bit of the conversation. "For the past couple of weeks, the miners comin' here have been placing odds on whether or not Melissa will give Kent the mitten, and the odds are weighin' more heavily in Kent's favor."

"Oh, oh," a deep groan escaped Tom at the news.

Alston wisely kept his silence as they all observed the stricken look on Nat's face.

"It's about time for Emmie's stage to be arriving. Coming, Mav?" Nat inquired stoically.

"It's sorry I am I can't join ye right now, but bring that sister of yours on by, on the way to Tirpak's," Red said to Nat as Mav kissed his cheek before leaving with the three men.

Red's smile changed into a frown when he noted the drunk had left his bar stool and was staggering toward the miners, the now almost empty bottle of Taos Lighting clenched in his fist. He coughed, and the piano music stopped abruptly before resuming more softly as Dan recognized the signal to be ready for trouble. Red's hands gripped one of the guns stashed on a shelf under the bar.

"You boys min' if I joi' you?"

The four players eyed the drunk suspiciously for a couple of seconds. "Pull up a chair," one of them said finally, no doubt thinking the man would be easy pickings. "You got money to lose, I'm willing to take it." The other men laughed.

"Yep, Cliff's been the beatingest man these couple of hours," another one warned the newcomer.

Red released the grip on the gun, and the piano began playing more loudly when it seemed there would be no confrontation. It was a slow time at the bar, so the drunk and the four miners were the only occupants at the time. With a relieved sigh, Red resumed washing up glasses in anticipation of the larger crowds he could expect this evening when Mavis began singing.

****

As soon as Nat left the room Mavis would now share with Emmie, Mavis decided to get down to business. She had taken an immediate liking to Nat's younger sister and quickly determined that if anyone could get Nat set in the right direction, Emmie could. She had observed the love between the brother and sister and had also noted that Emmie was easily able to deflect any attempts at high-handedness on Nat's part. When Nat would have stayed a bit longer, Emmie had shooed him out, telling him she would be quite all right negotiating details of her employ with Mrs. Tirpak on her own and assuring him she would neither be underpaid nor overworked.

"I'm thinking Nat's needin' your help," Mavis said abruptly, deciding not to mince words.

"My help?" Emmie inquired, clearly stunned by the statement.

"It's a long story, and I'll be tryin' to make it short, but mind ye, I've got the gift of blarney in me," Mavis said as she began to fill Emmie on the details and a plot she was essentially devising as she spoke. Emmie listened silently in fascination.

"I think I'd like this Melissa," she said finally, when Mavis had ended her tale an hour later. "And it's obvious she'd be good for Nat, which is why he's so attracted to her, even though I doubt he realizes that. He's used to women without a brain in their heads throwing themselves at him, and while he's never had any use for that sort, I don't think he knows how to deal with a woman who has a mind of her own and refuses to succumb to his bullying tactics, however well-intentioned they might be."

"Ye seem to handle him well enough," Mavis observed, pleased that the younger woman was receptive to helping her in her plot to bring Melissa and Nat together once and for all.

Emmie laughed. "I've eighteen years of experience. *And* he's not in *love* with me, though he loves me well enough, as I do him. He's all I have in the world now," she finished sadly, making Mavis feel a bit guilty about pouncing on her with this problem so soon after her arrival.

"I'm sorry for yer losses, lass."

"Thank you, Mavis," Emmie responded, her eyes filling with tears. "But," she continued more cheerfully, "I think helping you in this plot you've laid out will be the best medicine I could take to relieve my sorrows."

****

He had lost more money than he'd intended, but it had been money well spent, the man decided as he sat on the edge of his bed, holding his throbbing head. Maybe that barkeep knew what he was talking about when he had warned him to go easy on that whiskey. At least he had been wise enough to stop drinking after he entered the game with those four miners. He had wanted to be able to recollect any information he could get from them, and it seemed he had struck the Mother Lode. He'd even gotten directions to the mining camp where it seemed that bitch niece of his was playing schoolmarm. He had been going to enlist the help of the sheriff to find her, telling him the same story he had told the sheriff in Nebraska City: she had murdered his wife and stolen his money. But this was even better, given that other sheriff's reaction to his story back in Nebraska City. Just dismissed him, he had, like he wasn't worth shucks.

He had learned, too, that his niece was all alone; that her sister and brother-in-law had been killed in an Injun raid a few months ago. He grinned as he thought about how smart he had been in extracting that piece of information. The barkeep had come up and asked about the most recent odds of that wedding he had heard talked about earlier, and he had slyly put in that they should be considering any family objections to the bride's marriage when placing their bets. That's when he had found out the bride-to-be had no known living relatives. Got a thorough accounting of the massacre, he did, though he could have cared less. 'Course he'd have to deal with this Kent fellow who had designs on her. He wasn't too worried about that soldier boy. Seemed like he had just accepted defeat at the hands of the mine owner, so he'd be out of the picture. He thought briefly about finding another saloon to whet his whistle in but decided he needed to lay off the stuff for a while in order to form a plan of action. *It'll be worth it*, he promised himself as he lay back down on the bed, deciding to get a good night's sleep. His stomach rumbled, reminding him he hadn't fed it since morning, but he was too tired to acknowledge it.

Chapter Twenty-Two

"Somethin' just don't smell right about this," Tom commented as he, Nat, and Alston rode to rejoin their company after forcing yet another stagecoach to stop its journey. The drivers had been none too happy, especially when the soldiers were unable to provide any explanation other than that Colonel Kenwood had commanded it, and the four soldiers who had ridden out with them had been left behind in pairs of two to ensure that the drivers obeyed the orders. Other troops had been assigned to detain mail carriers along the road, and still others had been ordered to surround the ranches in the area and cordon them off.

"I couldn't agree with you more. I wish there were some way one of us could speak to Will in private."

Will Daile rode in front of the troops alongside Kenwood, and while he had remained alert to any possibility, Nat had not been able to catch the older man out of the earshot of his commanding officer. Two days ago, Kenwood had directed them to be ready to ride but had gruffly refused to answer any inquiries from the men under his command. They had ridden south from Denver to Booneville where, as the commander of the Colorado Military District, Kenwood had assumed control of the Colorado Third Regiment.

"'Pears we're heading southeast," Alston noted, looking up at the sun.

"To Fort Lyon, then, is my guess," Nat surmised, still puzzling over the events of the last few days.

Since late September, Kenwood had been more or less uninvolved in military matters, concentrating instead on his bid for Congress. Indeed, it had seemed that the concern over hostile Indians attacking Denver was over. Near the end of that month, Lone Wolf and other Cheyenne and Arapaho chiefs had met at Camp Weld with Kenwood, Governor Evans, and Major Edward Wynkoop, the commander of Fort Lyon. They were directed to surrender to Major Wynkoop at Fort Lyon if they truly desired peace, and they had done just that. Wynkoop had treated them fairly and had even issued them rations from time to time, as did his successor, Major Scott Dillard, when he had replaced Wynkoop earlier this month as commander of the fort. The disappearance of the buffalo from the area had left the Indians starving. Lone Wolf's Cheyenne and Running Bear's small band of Arapaho were now peacefully settled forty miles north of the fort at the Great Bend of Sand Creek. Little Raven's Arapahoe had moved down the Arkansas River, some seventy-five miles away. The Third Regiment of Colorado Volunteers, those 100-day volunteers that Evans had raised in August, had even been dubbed the "Bloodless Third" in *The Rocky Mountain News*. So what was all this about?

Four days later, Nat had still not had the opportunity to find out what Daile knew about the troops' movements when matters became worse. They arrived at a ranch owned by John Watson, who had the misfortune of being married to a Cheyenne woman. Upon learning this, Colonel Kenwood went on a tyrannical rampage. He began roaring orders for the troops to disarm the man's seven ranch hands and place Watson under house arrest. As they departed, Kenwood commanded some of his men to stay behind as guards.

It had sickened Nat to have been a part of it, but he was compelled to follow orders. If he did not, he, himself, would be incarcerated, with no hope of helping if Kenwood's actions became more violent. It was only a small consolation that no real harm, other than injured pride, had come to anyone. A similar situation occurred later that day at the ranch of one of the most powerful white men in the region. It was common knowledge that the rancher had married an Indian woman, and, in Kenwood's eyes, therefore, could be counted as an enemy. He, too, was confined to quarters under guard, while his son was pressed into service by the colonel. Will Daile had taken ill and had to be left behind, so Kenwood needed a new guide. The son, being a half-breed, knew the area and the Cheyenne language. Nat was dismayed to learn of Daile's fate. He had counted on his being able to be a voice of reason with Kenwood if things became too ugly.

As he spotted the flag signaling their arrival at Fort Lyon, a feeling of relief washed over Nat. Even though Kenwood outranked him, it was possible that Major Dillard could talk some sense into the man Nat was certain had become maniacal. A seemingly surprised sergeant greeted the troops as they rode up. Kenwood was inexplicably hurried as he dismounted and asked the sergeant if it was true that Lone Wolf was camped at Sand Creek. When the sergeant answered affirmatively, Kenwood inquired about the whereabouts of Major Dillard and strode to the building to which the sergeant had pointed with as much haste as his bulky six-foot, four-inch frame allowed.

He reappeared less than thirty minutes later, barking orders for his men to resupply their rations and be ready to ride again in four hours. Dillard directed some of his officers to round up the men under their command as well as two howitzers and prepare to move out. Kenwood called his top officers to a meeting. The other soldiers under the colonel's command looked as bewildered as Nat felt but moved to obey the orders.

It was eight o'clock in the evening when they left Fort Lyon, stronger by another one hundred twenty-five men and two cannons, picking their way in the dark across the rugged landscape. It was chill-you-to-the-bone cold, Nat thought, as he struggled to reposition the wool blanket he wore over his shoulders as further protection from the relentless wind. There was not the usual chatter among the riders. While the officers wore overcoats for added protection, none of the enlisted men or 100-day volunteers was as lucky, and most were struggling with their blankets as well, Nat observed. He decided to concentrate on happier thoughts. He knew Emmie would be charming Mrs. Tirpak and wondered how big a handful Mav and Red must be finding her. The latter brought a grin to his face that threatened to crack his cheeks in the cold. Mav's image quickly morphed into Melissa's, however, and he found himself pondering Mav's revelation that Melissa had been looking for a glimpse of him when she was in town. Maybe there was some hope after all. When he returned to Denver, he'd seek her out and try to set things right between them once again. He'd make her see he was not the cad she thought him.

****

Melissa felt cold, even as she stooped to remove the Brown Betty, her contribution to the mining camp's Thanksgiving dinner, from the hot oven. In the prior year, 1863, President Lincoln had proclaimed the last Thursday in November as a day of Thanksgiving, and it seemed that people throughout the nation were especially happy to spend the day this year celebrating the good and forgetting all the bad going on around them. The president had declared it a day to be used to praise and thank God for guarding them from their enemies, and the morning and early afternoon had been spent doing just that in the camp's small church. When Kent had asked if she would help some of the miners' wives organize a potluck for the evening meal to extend the celebration, she had eagerly agreed.

She had had a series of long arguments with herself the past couple of weeks and had decided just last night that today she would accept Kent's proposal. *He's a good man*, she repeated the mantra. *He'll make me happy. He does make me happy.* She pushed aside the unwanted thoughts of Nat that crept into her mind. How was he spending the day? With someone else who had captured his attention and was now doting on him? *Stop it!* she reprimanded herself as she sucked the finger she'd just burned in her carelessness.

"Ready to go?" Kent called out as he entered her cabin. "Smells delicious!" he said, leaning over to sniff the savory apple-and-bread-crumb pudding Melissa had managed to set on a brick on the table before injuring herself further.

"Just about," she responded from the sink where she had dunked her burned appendage in cool water. "But before we join the others, there's something I have to tell you."

She wiped her hand on a clean rag and took a deep breath.

"I do," she blurted out before she lost her nerve. Her words sounded brisk and businesslike to her ears, and once they were spoken, she immediately set to the task of placing the somewhat cooler dessert she had made in a basket and covering it with a cloth. She couldn't seem to look at him as she awaited his response.

"You do?" Kent questioned, hoping she meant what he thought she meant.

Finished with the task at hand, Melissa reprimanded herself for acting like a silly, naive schoolgirl and forced herself to look directly into the eyes of the man she planned to marry. His warm, brown eyes seemed to plead with her.

"Don't make this harder for me than it already is," she scolded with a smile, noting how his eyes always offered comfort, emitting a gentle softness that cocooned her like a warm blanket. "I do agree to marry you."

"I'll ignore the first part of that statement, if you don't mind," Kent said gleefully, as he picked her up and twirled her around, breathing in the fresh scent of her hair. "I promise you, Melissa. I plan to make you the happiest woman in the world," he said more somberly as he set her back on her feet and lightly gripped her shoulders.

"And I, Kent, hope to make you the happiest man in the world," Melissa responded, looking directly into his smiling eyes.

"When?" Kent wasn't a man to let this opportunity get away.

Melissa's chest tightened a notch. Agreeing to the proposal was as far as she had gotten in her thought process. She hadn't actually envisioned a wedding day.

"Well, when would *you* like it to be?" Melissa asked quickly, in hopes of concealing her momentary discomfort.

"*I'd* like it to be tomorrow! But our wedding day should be special. We can go to Denver next week, and I can take you to Miss Hattie's so you can pick out some material and have her sew you a wedding dress."

"But—"

"I'd do it sooner, but I have given the men these last two days off, so I really need to be here to oversee that the operations are resumed smoothly before leaving for town. Is that okay with you?" he asked, releasing his light grip after seeing what seemed to be a look of dismay flash across her face.

Melissa had started to object to a wedding dress and had been about to tell Kent she had one or two nice dresses to wear, but as he was speaking, she reconsidered. At least this would give her time to get used to the idea.

"That sounds fine," she said, giving him a smile. "And, Kent, thank you for being so generous and thoughtful."

"We can also pick out a ring when we're in town," Kent added.

Melissa's hand immediately went to the ring she still wore around her neck.

"Would you be terribly disappointed if we used my mother's wedding ring? It's always been very special to me."

"Done!" Kent declared, pulling her into his arms

239

again for a tight hug before letting her go. "As much as I'd like to savor the rest of the day alone with you, I think we'd best go now and join the others." Helping Melissa into her coat, he added, "Besides, I can't wait to accept all their congratulations."

Melissa's stomach felt as though several mice were using it as a playground as she walked through the door Kent held open for her, and her grip on the basket she carried tightened ever so slightly.

Chapter Twenty-Three

"We will be charging directly into the village," Kenwood instructed, as he rode amongst the troops and reminded them of all the white women and children who had been murdered at the hands of the Indians. "Then one company will veer to the east, and another company will flank the village on the west to block off any chance of escape," he continued. "Half the westbound company will break from the unit to secure the far side of the camp, effectively surrounding the enemy." Sand Creek was less than an hour's ride away, he informed them.

A lot of the men were cheering, even after the long, cold ride through the night, eagerly thirsting for the blood of the savages now that they had been informed of their destination. Others remained silent. Nat, Al, and Tom exchanged looks, and Nat knew his friends were looking to him for leadership. He felt impotent and confused. While he was required to obey orders, he couldn't understand why they were attacking Indians he had understood were peacefully settled under the protection of the flag of the United States. Perhaps, he considered, there were facts of which he was unaware. Even though he had long ago lost faith in Kenwood's ability to make a rational decision regarding the Indians, surely Major Dillard would not have lent his support to an unjust cause. Hadn't he even supplied the Indians with rations when he could have allowed them to starve? He gave a slight nod to his two friends in affirmation of the order.

Kenwood's forces began their attack on the village shortly after first light on the 29th of November. Some Indian women who had awakened early to gather firewood for cooking breakfast mistook the loud sound of the charging horse hoofs for a stampeding herd of buffalo. As the rumbling noise drew closer, Lone Wolf and White Buffalo came out of their lodges. Spotting the advancing troops, they unfurled the six-foot by twelve-foot American flag, which they had been told would ensure their safety.

The first thing that caught Nat's eye as the Indian camp came into sight was that American flag waving. He could make out Lone Wolf standing by it, and as the troops grew closer, he heard the Indian chief cry out to his people not to be afraid, not to run, that the troops would not attack their village. Women and children were huddled near the chief, screaming in fear as bullets began to fly. Another Indian, whom Nat recognized as White Buffalo, ran toward the soldiers with arms raised over his head to show he was unarmed, singing a song in his native tongue that sounded like a dirge. At his advance, heavy firing broke out from all sides of the surrounded village. White Buffalo fell seconds later, cut down in the storm of gunfire. One soldier dismounted and scalped the seventy-five-year-old chief.

Bullets flew thick as locusts, aimed at women and children as well as the warriors, who were few in number but who had now equipped themselves with bows and arrows. Unarmed women, children, and old men ran every which way in an attempt to escape the onslaught as the dust from the advancing horses' hooves and the smoke produced by the gunfire burned their eyes and throats. Some women and children ran towards the soldiers, getting on their knees for mercy, only to have their heads bashed in.

Five women attempting to hide under a bank begged for mercy when they were discovered, to no avail. Screaming expletives at them, the three soldiers who had found them shot all five before dismounting to scalp and further mutilate their bodies. Even the howitzers' roar could not drown out the screaming.

An attractive young Indian woman watched in horror as her new husband was gunned down, along with her grandfather and father. Spying her, one of the soldiers stayed behind and tried to tear off her clothes, but she fought him off. Finally able to break free, she managed to get to a buffalo gun her grandfather had received from two gold seekers and killed her attacker.

Nat caught Lone Wolf out of the corner of his eye as the chief and another man headed for the upper end of the village, running through a gauntlet of bullets while dodging the numerous bodies that lay strewn on the ground, some dead, others close to death. He said a silent prayer that the peace-loving chief would escape, even as he galloped forward with the rest of his company.

"Do *not* fire!" Captain Dominik Dvorsky ordered the men under his command. Nat heard the order and observed Dvorsky positioning his men between Nat's company, which was being led by Kenwood himself, and the fleeing Indians.

"Hold your fire!" Nat yelled over the chaos to Tom and Alston before pulling up his regulation kerchief to protect against the assailing smoke of the battle as he moved to join Dvorsky's troops, beckoning his friends to accompany him.

A small Indian boy, about nine years old, Nat guessed, ran toward him with outstretched arms and a look of terror on his face. Nat leaned down and, encircling his arm around the boy's waist, swept him onto his horse. Seconds later an arrow Nat assumed had been meant for him struck the young boy in the back, and he fell from the horse.

"Injun lover!" Someone snarled from behind him. It was the last thing Nat heard before slumping forward on his horse, hit by a bullet fired directly at his back.

Chapter Twenty-Four

Hattie McClelland was behaving like a hen with a new chick under her wing, for which Melissa was grateful. Kent had deposited her in Hattie's care, informing the middle-aged proprietress to spare no expense in outfitting Melissa for their upcoming wedding before he left to handle the numerous errands he had in town. The widow's eyes had sparkled at the news, and having spent the last hour with the woman, Melissa was convinced the sparkle had less to do with monetary gain than with the opportunity to transform Melissa into a stunning bride. She had almost begged off this trip to Denver. She had, in fact, felt sick to her stomach this morning, but finally convinced herself it was nerves, and that the trip would be made sooner or later so she might as well get it over with. Although she knew nothing about current fashion and suspected Mavis would have been delighted to help her, she was hoping to avoid her old friend on this particular visit. She just wasn't ready to deal with Mavis's all-too-insightful questions and comments at this point.

Hattie had begun by showing Melissa several fashion plates featured in the most recent editions of *Godey's Lady's Book* that she thought could be the beginnings of a wedding dress. If the widow sensed Melissa's lack of interest, she made no mention of it but made up for it with enough enthusiasm of her own.

"This style will be beautiful on you," she exclaimed, indicating one of the plates. Jumping up from her seat, she retrieved a bolt of pure white velvet from among the many bolts lining the left wall of her shop and placed it on the table between them. "This will be perfect for the skirt, don't you think?" she said as she lovingly caressed the fabric. "I'll add flounces trimmed with white satin ribbon bows—or would you prefer a contrasting color? And here..." Without waiting for an answer, she began pulling out another bolt of cloth. "This white gossamer satin will make an elegant bodice. I think the sleeves should be in the same white velvet as the skirt, though. No, no. Wait. I have an excellent idea. I can use the same material as the bodice for the sleeves and then trim just the wrist portion of it in white velvet. This leg-of-mutton sleeve is timeless," she pronounced with satisfaction, tapping her fingers on the puffed-out shoulders of the sleeve on the fashion plate. "I'll also use the velvet to trim the high neck and maybe secure a white satin bow to the center of it and on each of the wrists. Now, let's just get some measurements."

The tiny bell on the door of the shop rang, announcing another customer, just as Miss Hattie had led Melissa behind the dressing screen at the rear of her shop and unhooked the top hook on the back of her dress.

"Good morning, Miss Bellamy," the proprietress greeted cheerfully as she poked her head around the screen. At the name, Melissa started. The dressing screen crashed down as her elbow collided with it, and she stood facing a young woman with features all too familiar.

"I'm so sorry," she apologized, her voice sounding distant as she stared into those glorious blue eyes, wide with surprise, and noted the thick coffee-colored hair that hung in natural waves to the younger girl's waist. While her features were more delicate than Nat's, there was no mistaking this was his sister. "I'm really not feeling well," she mumbled to the widow, who was busy setting the screen to rights while assuring Melissa that no harm had been done. "I'd best leave this for another time."

"But…"

Melissa didn't hear the rest of Miss Hattie's words as she snatched up her reticule and stumbled to the door past the girl, who, bewildered, turned to witness her rather inelegant departure. She moved quickly to seek the solitude of the alleyway behind the shop, clutching one arm to her abdomen as she leaned against the cool brick of the building. Seeing the girl had been like looking at Nat again. She concentrated on taking deep breaths in an attempt to regain her composure so she could think more clearly. *Was she being fair to Kent in agreeing to marry him when she clearly still had feelings for Nat? Didn't Kent deserve better?*

"Miss Sullivan?" Melissa looked up at the sound of her name. "Emmie Bellamy." The young woman announced with a shy smile, extending her hand to Melissa.

"How…?"

"Did I find you?" Emmie let the untaken, proffered hand fall back to her side. "Simple. I just thought of where I might go after I had staged such a retreat. Truly, you needn't have been so embarrassed. If you had witnessed some of my clumsiness, you wouldn't have had a second thought about toppling over that screen. I was an eternal frustration for my family."

The sad pitch in the girl's voice as she uttered the last dissolved Melissa's initial anger at what she had felt was presumptuous behavior on the girl's part.

As if reading her mind, Emmie continued. "I know you probably would have preferred being left alone, but after Miss Hattie told me who you were, I just had to seek you out. I believe you may be the only person who can help."

"Help…?"

"My brother is in love with you. Mavis has told me all about it. Maybe you can motivate him to get well again. I know it's a lot to ask. Miss Hattie informed me you were there to be fit for a wedding dress, and maybe you don't feel the same way about Nat as he does about you, but if you ever felt anything for him, I implore you to help him…" She grasped Melissa by the shoulders as her words shot out as fast as a Gatling gun's bullets. Tears glistened in her eyes, threatening to spill over. "He's all I have left!"

Melissa fought for composure. *Help Nat get well again? What ailed him?* She wanted to scream the questions and demand answers, but the other woman's tears stayed her. Putting her hands over Emmie's, she gently removed them from her shoulders, but kept them in her own.

"Let's go somewhere we can talk," she said as calmly as she could. "I will help if I can. But first, I need to return to Miss Hattie's to tell her where we are going so Kent will not be worried when he returns to collect me."

The Lucky Lady would not have been Melissa's choice, but she reluctantly followed Emmie into the saloon. Given that it was before noon, Mavis was not around, and Melissa breathed a silent sigh of relief. Few customers were in the bar at this hour, and Red greeted both women as though they were close family. With a scowl at any man he thought might be tempted to get out of line, he settled Emmie and Melissa at a back table that overlooked the street and was well away from the riffraff.

Melissa's head was reeling as she listened to Nat's sister recount how her brother was injured at Sand Creek and how he was being guarded while in the infirmary at Camp Weld, awaiting court-martial for defying orders. Emmie spoke with derision about Colonel Kenwood's return to a hero's welcome after so many innocents had been slaughtered.

"They've even put Indian scalps and body parts on display at the theater down the street. I overheard some men making lewd comments about some of the items in the exhibit and laughing about some others."

Horrified at the mental picture, Melissa asked, "And Nat's being brought to trial for refusing to participate in this atrocity? Is he the only one?"

"No. Al and Tom said there were a couple of other officers who ordered their men to cease fire when they saw they were fighting mostly old men, women, and children. They face the same fate as Nat. Some, however, feel the Indians are nothing but savages and support Kenwood wholeheartedly. Not even the betting man will take odds on the outcome of this one."

"I don't understand." Melissa shook her head in frustration. "You know Nat better than I, and I would have sworn he would be willing himself to get better so that he, too, could testify against this monster," she declared vehemently.

"Even the strongest man has his limits," Emmie replied with a wisdom that seemed beyond her years.

"Did Nat ever tell you why he came West?"

In the next thirty minutes, Melissa learned all about Nat's life, including how he became a family outcast, the boyhood friend he had tried to save on the battlefield, his revulsion for unnecessary violence from that point on, and his dedication to his youngest sister and hers to him.

"He seems to have concluded," Emmie finished, "that his vision of what life should be like is nothing but a fantasy and that he would prefer to leave this life rather than to live anymore. To quote: 'I'm tired of fighting.' And that statement is about all any of us—me, Mavis, Al, and Tom—can get out of him during his lucid moments. The camp's surgeon is baffled. He's been giving my brother better care than he would normally provide for someone facing the charges Nat faces because he grew to like and admire Nat before this incident and because he sides with those who feel the Sand Creek attack was a massacre of innocent people. He thinks Nat's infection should have already run its course, and he attributes the fact that Nat still lapses in and out of consciousness to what he calls 'the loss of will to live.' My hope is that you can reinstate that will."

Images of Nat flooded Melissa's mind as his sister finished her plea—Nat suffering from the arrow wound and the subsequent bonding conversations they had shared as they awaited rescue; Nat saving her when she lost control of the horses during the hailstorm and his gentleness thereafter; Nat's look of hurt when she rejected his proposal; his brilliant smile that always warmed her heart as though it had been pierced by a ray of sunshine, no matter what the weather…

"Will they let me see him?" she finally asked Emmie.

"You shouldn't have any trouble, although I should warn you that you may have to endure some rude comments, depending on who's on guard duty there. I truly believe that some of those who support the colonel enjoy our grief as we watch Nat languishing toward what everyone suspects is a slow death."

"I don't know how much good I can do," Melissa responded, "but I will try. I will need to talk to Kent first, of course. He's probably already waiting for me. Give me some time to explain the situation to him, and I will meet you in front of Miss Hattie's in an hour."

Emmie's smile was almost as brilliant as her brother's as she grasped Melissa's hand. "Thank you," she whispered hoarsely, tears fighting her smile for control of her countenance.

Waving goodbye to Red, the two women walked back to Miss Hattie's together. Emmie had to complete her errand for Mrs. Tirpak before reuniting with Melissa. As they approached the shop, Kent could be seen standing outside, looking first in one direction and then another, obviously hoping for some sight of his fiancée.

"I think it's time I exit," Emmie murmured to Melissa before quickening her pace and slipping quietly past Kent into the shop. He had just noticed Melissa's approach and began moving toward her. Melissa forced a smile in greeting.

"Have you been waiting long?" she asked in what she hoped was a normal tone of voice.

"Not too long. But I was about to come to the Lucky Lady looking for you. I assumed you wanted to have a private conversation with Mavis, so I delayed to give you some privacy, but I admit I was getting a bit worried," he responded with a warm smile.

Apparently, Miss Hattie, bless her heart, had kept her own confidences.

"Actually, I never saw Mavis—it's much too early for her to rise," Melissa revealed in a tone she hoped resounded with nonchalance. Nervously, she massaged the ring around her neck. Kent, ever attuned to her emotions, apparently noted it.

"There's a problem," he said flatly.

Melissa's heart sank as she knew that what she had to say was going to hurt him, but Emmie had done a good job convincing her she was Nat's only hope. And, she recognized, given her feelings for Nat, she should not be marrying Kent, good man that he was.

"Yes," she replied softly. "Walk with me?"

****

If Emmie had been surprised to see Melissa drive up with Kent, she had not let it show. She sat twisting a handkerchief in her hands during the short ride to Camp Weld, responding politely but succinctly to Kent's attempts at conversation. The entire trip was draped in a heavy cloak of silence for the most part. Melissa was busy attempting to construct mentally the conversation she would have with Nat. She considered several different greetings, trying to decide how Nat would respond to each of them, discarding some when she didn't like the imagined reaction. Having settled on the one she liked best, she moved on to ponder the conversation that might follow.

After having been directed to Nat's bed in the small makeshift infirmary at the back of the stockade, she decided it had all been for naught. Emmie had stayed behind with Kent, explaining that she thought it best if Melissa visited her brother alone. Nat's eyes were closed when she approached the bed and took a seat in the chair that sat beside it, but she observed the pain and weariness etched on his face. Seeing him in this state, she forgot everything she had rehearsed.

Tenderly, she took one of his hands in hers and began stroking it. *Such strong hands, yet so gentle*. She became so involved in tracing the curve of his thumb to his wrist and each long finger in turn that she didn't know exactly when his eyes opened, but she was drawn to them as she felt their stare. They were as blue as ever, but the brilliance had dimmed.

"Hello, Nat," she managed, her voice catching in her throat.

"What are *you* doing here?" Hostility was evident in his voice.

"I-I heard you had been injured. I wanted to see you," she replied defensively.

"Why?"

"Because we were once close. Because I miss that closeness as I've missed you these past months. Because I want things to be right between us again. Because I love you, Nathaniel Bellamy."

"Too late."

"It's never too late for love, Nat," she said, hoping the panic she felt wasn't revealed in her voice.

"I didn't have much to offer you before, when I asked you to be my wife, and I have even less now. I'm facing a court-martial for doing what I believed—what I still believe—was right. If I don't die first, that is. And that's what I'm praying for just now, so go away, Melissa. Leave and never come back." He closed his eyes as if wearied by the conversation and, struggling, rolled over, putting his back to her.

"I never took you for a coward, Nat, and I don't believe it of you now," she said, not budging from her seat.

No reply. Not even the slightest body movement.

"In the last year I've lost my father, my mother, my aunt, my sister, and my brother-in-law. I don't want to lose you, too, Nat. Please, please, talk to me." This time she couldn't keep the panic out of her tone.

Nothing.

"You want to die while unprincipled men like Kenwood go on to procreate the world with others like him? If the good people on this earth let men like the colonel beat them, where will the world be a few years hence?"

"I'm tired of the fight, Melissa. Let other good men take it up. Men like that miner you've been cavorting with," Nat replied flatly, still turned away from her.

"Kent *is* a good man," Melissa affirmed, "and he has asked me to marry him. I said 'yes' initially, but I broke off our engagement this morning. And, no, it is not because of you, or at least not in the way you might think. I had been considering it for a quite a while—when I realized I still loved you and that I could never love him as I love you. To marry him just wouldn't be fair to him. So even if you choose to give up and die, I still couldn't marry Kent. Maybe someday I will meet someone I can love as much as I do you. I'm here in a new place, and I have high hopes of making a good life for myself." She stood, pacing the area around his bed, her voice growing stronger with conviction. "I'd like to have children someday. Children who will grow up to be fine citizens to lead the city of Denver and thwart those who look to serve only their own needs and prejudices at the expense of others. And my children will have children who will carry on the role after they pass on."

Silence.

Melissa stopped pacing and stood still beside the bed for several more minutes before giving up on getting any reaction from him. Sighing softly, she left the room.

Sensing she was gone. Nat struggled onto his back again.

"How many children, Melissa?" He whispered to the empty room.

****

Melissa stared sightlessly at the flickering flame that danced inside its multi-faceted crystal prison, casting shadows on the pristine white tablecloth. Kent had insisted she eat something, reminding her that her last meal had been at breakfast, but she didn't feel the slightest bit hungry. The day's events had sapped her energy, and even the delicate china teacup seemed heavy as she lifted it to her lips. She would have liked nothing more than to retire to the hotel room upstairs that Kent had arranged for her.

"I'm sorry?" She raised her eyes to meet Kent's as she realized he had asked her a question and was obviously awaiting a response.

"I think that's at least the tenth time you've apologized to me today. I'll give you two minutes more to beat yourself up, and then no more. Agreed?"

Melissa looked down at the table and shook her head in bewilderment. "I can't believe you're being so kind and understanding about all this," she exclaimed.

"Do I have a choice?"

"A lot of men would be enraged and hurl insults, and—"

255

"I'm not a lot of men, Melissa," he interrupted as he placed his large hand over hers.

She looked up into those warm brown eyes again and sighed in acceptance of his statement. "I know that. You're a good, decent man, Kent, and I wonder if I'm making the biggest mistake of my life."

"Much as it pains me to say it, I suspect Nat's a good man, too, Melissa. I had quite the conversation with Emmie while you were in there pleading your case with her brother. It's very telling of a man's character to have two such beautiful, intelligent women devoted to him the way you and Emmie seem to be. I should be so lucky."

"I'm sor—"

"Don't say it again," Kent cut her off, raising his hand to put a finger to her lips. When he was assured of her silence, he removed his finger and continued. "What, really, do you have to be sorry for? For being honest? Look, I won't lie and say I'm not disappointed, but I would have been more disappointed had you chosen to marry me while you loved another man more."

"But I—"

"Would have been a devoted, loving wife," Kent finished the sentence for her. "I know that, but maybe *I* want more. I'm not perfect, Melissa. No man is. And if you were to marry me feeling as you do for Nat, the day could come when I might inadvertently do something to anger or frustrate you, and then you might very well wonder how it might have been different had you married Nat instead. Sure, he has his faults, too, but, over time, you would have idealized him in your mind. Oh, you would never throw him in my face. You're not that type. But there would be subtle things—maybe a wistful look about you—that would be telling. A rift would begin, like a small crack in a rock, but it would gradually widen with time, just as the constant circle of ice and thaw causes the crack in a rock to expand until the rock is eventually split in two."

The waiter appeared with a platter of succulent roast beef, surrounded by roasted potato wedges and carrots basted with brown sugar. Beside it, he set a bowl of peas in a delicate cream sauce. Melissa digested Kent's words as the waiter sliced off pieces of the roast, putting a portion on each of their plates, and then spooned up ample portions of each of the vegetables, artistically arranging them beside the slices of beef.

"Will that be all, sir?" he asked Kent as he efficiently refilled Melissa's teacup from the matching china pot on the table. Kent raised his brow in silent query to Melissa.

"Yes, thank you," Kent replied upon seeing Melissa's affirmative nod.

"Friends?" Kent queried after the waiter was out of earshot.

"The best of," Melissa replied with a tired smile.

"Good. I'm starved," he said as he began attacking his food enthusiastically. Melissa watched in amazement. Men were able to stomach emotional upheavals far better than women, she decided, as she herself picked meagerly at the enormous serving before her, mulling over the day's events.

When she had told Kent she must go to Nat, the dear man had quickly masked whatever feelings he might have had out of concern for her. She had tried, unsuccessfully, to put it all on Emmie's shoulders, coward that she was, but Kent was too perceptive.

"You love him, don't you?" he had quietly asked.

She couldn't, wouldn't deny it. She felt to do so as Nat lay dying would be the ultimate betrayal of what she now accepted was her deep, abiding love for the stubborn soldier.

"And I love you," had been all she could muster in response.

"But in a different way," he had countered with no apparent hostility. "Not in the way a woman should love a man she has promised to marry."

Unable to think of a response, she had remained silent.

"I'll accompany you," he had said decisively, breaking the few minutes of awkward silence. "I think you could use a good friend right now."

How much easier he had made it for her than had Nat. With Nat, she had failed, and he would probably still die on her, she thought as she struggled to swallow the piece of beef she had forced herself to eat. It sat like a lump in her throat. Still, she couldn't regret what she had done, what she had said, to him or to Kent. Kent deserved to marry someone who loved him as much as she loved Nat. And she could never have lived with herself if Nat had died before she told him her true feelings.

"We haven't discussed whether or not you will be returning to the mining camp to finish the school year," Kent's voice interrupted her thoughts. "I promise you that I will refrain from any romantic overtures toward you, and I know the children will be very disappointed if you do not, but I will understand, either way."

"Of course I shall. There's nothing more for me to do here anyway," she replied sadly. "Like I told you and Emmie on the ride home, I couldn't get through to Nat.

There's no sense staying around when I'm not welcome. And Nat made it perfectly clear that I'm not." She had stopped by the Lucky Lady to visit Mavis before she met Kent for dinner and told her of her failed attempt to roust Nat out of his melancholy state. Mavis had been dismayed at the news but didn't try to convince Melissa to continue her efforts.

Chapter Twenty-Five

"Reckon heaven wouldn't have you, and the devil didn't want the likes of you, either," Al said as he waited for the guard to unlock Nat's cell. "Glad to have you back!"

It had been a full week since Melissa's visit. Nat had slipped in and out of consciousness the first few days, but willed himself to prolonged periods of lucidity, determined to fight the inflammation that raged through his body. The camp's surgeon had expressed amazement at the recovery that now seemed to be taking place.

"Decided to live to fight another day," Nat replied as he struggled up from his cot and embraced his friend. "Glad you were able to come. I need someone to fill me in on what's been going on. Guess I've been a bit out of touch recently. Tom okay?"

Al nodded as he pulled up the single chair in the cell and sat facing Nat, who had repositioned himself on the cot. "He would have come, too, but soon as the doc let it be known you might be up and kicking again, the guards were instructed to keep visitors away. Luckily, Johnson pulled guard duty this week, and I was able to convince him to give me a few minutes with you. Thought we might be pushing it to get him to let both of us in. Think Kenwood's getting worried."

"About what?"

"Well, seems the War Department is sending some

people here to investigate the matter at Sand Creek. While Kenwood still has a lot of supporters— bloodthirsty bigots, the lot of them, if you ask me— there's them who are disgusted by the Indian scalps and other body parts that've been put on display at the Denver Theater. And Daile says Major Wynkoop was infuriated when he learned about the attack since he had just negotiated an accord with Lone Wolf in September while he was still the commanding officer at Fort Lyon. He was there when Kenwood and Governor Evans agreed to allow the Cheyenne and Arapahoe to settle at Sand Creek in peace under the American flag. He fired off telegrams to Congress and President Lincoln, demanding an investigation. Reckon Washington listened."

Nat closed his eyes as the atrocities he had witnessed before his injury once again marched through his mind as they had so many times in the past month.

"The boy?"

Al shook his head sadly. "A soldier rode by and shot him point-blank in the head while he lay there with the arrow in him."

"Lone Wolf?"

"Alive. He and some of the others were able to escape. Daile reports they're now camped at Smoky Hill. Lone Wolf's wife survived, too, though I don't know how. Daile says she was hit by nine bullets. Says she played dead, which might have been what saved her. It's lucky she escaped scalping or maiming at the hands of some of the lunatics we rode with. There's a lot of us will have nightmares the rest of our days over what we seen that day."

"You can skip those details. I think I saw enough.

But tell me how I got back here."

"After you was hit, Tom and me dragged you back behind the lines to tend to you. The lunatics were too hell-bent on seeking blood and collecting more souvenirs to pay any notice. Tom and me watched from where we were, but weren't nothing we could think to do. There were others holding fire, too, when they seen what was happening. Most of those that did resigned from the Volunteers shortly after we got back to Denver."

"Will they be subpoenaed to testify?"

"Don't rightly know. Hear tell many of them up and left the area—whereabouts unknown. Some of the ones that have stayed ain't talking. To my mind, it's fear that's keeping their mouths shut. One former soldier who was overheard talking in a saloon about what he saw was found beaten near to death in an alley. There's those that don't want their actions at Sand Creek known in case this investigation goes against Kenwood. They don't want to share his bed." The footsteps of the guard sounded, and Al rose from his seat. "Tom or me'll try to finagle another visit soon," he promised over his shoulder as Johnson motioned him out of the cell.

****

With Christmas just a few days away, a lot of the camp's occupants had gone into Denver to get some supplies to celebrate the holiday. Not feeling very festive, Melissa had declined Kent's offer to ride in with him and had, instead, taken the opportunity to give the schoolroom the thorough scrubbing it sorely needed. It was impossible to keep the wooden floor clean on a regular basis, with the children tracking in snow on some days and mud on the days after the snow had melted. When she had finished, it was nearly time for dinner.

After pitching the final bucket of dirty water outside, she gave her back and shoulders a good stretch before donning her cloak and trudging along the wooden walkway that led from the schoolroom to her own cabin. Returning the greeting that a couple of passersby called out to her, she suddenly felt exhausted. And she couldn't shake the feeling that someone was constantly watching everything she did—a feeling she had been having all too often recently. Which was preposterous, she knew. Perhaps just a cup of tea, along with a couple of the gingerbread men she had baked to decorate and give as ornaments to each of her students, would calm and restore her.

After hanging her cloak on the peg by her doorway, she poked at the embers of the fire she had banked before she departed earlier in the day and threw some pieces of kindling on it. Satisfied the wood scraps had caught, she dragged into the adjoining kitchen to brew some tea. She poured a cup and stole a satisfying sip before adding it to a tray with some cookies she had snatched while the tea steeped. Setting the tray on the chest by her rocking chair, she strategically placed a couple of bigger logs on the now-hot fire and prepared to relax.

But her mind had other ideas. As she sipped her tea and watched the flames lick at the logs, her thoughts turned to Christmases past. Happier days. Days spent surrounded by friends and family. How different this Christmas would be! Although she had made the acquaintance of many of the miners' wives and everyone had been welcoming and friendly, she didn't feel especially close to any of them. Their lives were busy taking care of their husbands and children, providing them with fodder for conversation among themselves—

conversations to which Melissa could contribute little. She was thankful she was still able to visit Mavis every so often, but there were times she wished her friend was available to share her thoughts with whenever, wherever.

Had she not broken her very short engagement to Kent, she would have at least felt a part of something, like she belonged, she reflected. Retrieving a gingerbread man from the tray beside her and biting off his head, she scolded herself. *Don't I have exactly what I said I wanted? Independence? Is this the price I must pay for it—a lifetime spent on the outside looking in?*

She thought about Mavis, probably one of the most self-sufficient women she had ever met. While Red had fallen head over heels for her friend almost immediately, it was apparent that Mavis was more than a little smitten with him as well. *Is it possible to have your cake and eat it, too, contrary to what the well-known proverb says? What would Mavis say to that?*

And then her thoughts drifted to Elizabeth, the miner's wife who ran the company store. On several occasions, she had engaged in short conversations with the petite, black-haired woman with lively brown eyes. Elizabeth seemed to have the best of both worlds. From what Melissa gleaned, Elizabeth and her husband worked together as a team, each respecting the other's contributions, and when she observed them in church together, it was clear they were deeply in love.

Like her mother and father. They, too, had been devoted to each other and operated in tandem. Her mother had been the hand—the nurturer—while her father had been the glove—the protector.

The protector. She thought of Nat. How different her life might have been had she accepted his proposal those few months ago! Based on what she had learned about Nat from Emmie, he wasn't the unreasonable, autocratic man she had believed him to be. Perhaps if she had communicated her feelings and needs to him instead of behaving like a shrew, he would have understood. *Too late now. He wants nothing to do with me,* she thought sadly.

****

Nat was surprised to see both Tom and Al accompanying the camp's surgeon when they entered his cell. If he didn't feel so much like his old self again, he would have suspected they had come to say their final goodbyes—but that couldn't be right. Still, after greeting him, his two friends stood silently as the doctor examined his wound for the final time.

"You're good to go," he declared.

"What does that mean?" Nat asked, observing the wide grins Tom and Al now sported.

"You're a free man," the surgeon responded. "The powers that be, in Washington, received a number of complaints about the attack on the Cheyenne and Arapaho Indians and have mandated that any soldier being held for disobeying orders be released immediately, pending a thorough investigation of the matter. There is some concern that those who would testify against the actions of Kenwood might come to harm, given the violence that has already ensued between those supporting his actions and those supporting Captain Dvorsky and others who failed to execute the colonel's orders."

"Daile asked us to meet him at The Lucky Lady once you got the doc's go-ahead," Al put in. "He said he would have invited us to meet him at his place, but what he wants to discuss is best done out of earshot of his wife. You feeling up to it?"

"Never better," Nat replied, thinking he had never meant those words more.

****

"Good to see you up and about," Daile greeted Nat with an outstretched hand. "And many thanks to you for standing for what is right and good and not blindly following Kenwood's commands."

"No thanks necessary," Nat replied. "I could do little else in good conscience once I saw what was happening."

"Tom and Al have said you might be willing to testify against him and his second-in-command, Stevens, if it comes to that, and it's looking more like it will. Chief Justice Benjamin Hall, Lieutenant Colonel Samuel Tappan, and Indian agent Samuel Colley have added their complaints to those issued by Major Wynkoop and Captain Dvorsky. Hall's voice, in particular, is too loud to be ignored. No doubt that's what spurred the release of those facing court-martial for disobeying orders. But if Kenwood, Stevens, and others think that will be the end of it, they have another think coming. I've word the Cheyenne, Arapaho, and Sioux have all banded together now and are planning attacks on the white villages in the area in retribution for what happened at Sand Creek."

"More innocent victims," Nat replied sadly.

"Well, lookie who's here!" Al exclaimed, breaking the mood as he spied Mavis entering the saloon.

Hearing his voice, Mavis ran up to the table, giving each man a hug in turn.

"Al and Tom have kept Emmie and me updated on your health progress, but no one was telling us you'd be out walking the streets!" she exclaimed.

"We didn't want to get your hopes up," Tom said, a bit defensively.

"Well, for sure it is that I'll be telling Emmie!" Mavis said excitedly. "Red, I'll be seeing you back here shortly," she called out to the bartender as she left to tell her new friend the good news.

"Excuse me. I didn't want to interrupt your conversation, but I'd like to have a private word with you if I might." Nat recognized the man who had approached the table as the mine owner who had stolen Melissa's heart away from him. He was tempted to reject the man's request outright, but his curiosity wouldn't let him.

"There's a vacant table in the back there I think will be private enough," he responded instead.

After the two were seated and had ordered drinks, perhaps as courage-boosters, Kent spoke first. "I'm glad to see you looking so well."

"Are you really?" Nat replied sarcastically.

"I realize this may be hard for you to believe, but yes, I really am," Kent responded. Observing the look of disbelief on Nat's face, he continued. "Look, I fell in love with Melissa. Who wouldn't? You did yourself. I even asked her to marry me, but she broke off our engagement—because you are the one she loves, not me. And I've gotten to know all about you through your sister over the past couple weeks. From what she has told me, I know you are a good man and worthy of Melissa's love, and loving her myself, I want her to be happy. Besides," he said somewhat abashedly, "I have my eyes on another equally good, equally smart, equally beautiful woman— one who has captured my heart and made me forget all about my lost love—and I ask your permission to continue to court her."

The object of his affection ran into the saloon on cue as he made this proclamation. Taking just seconds to adjust her eyes to the dim light, Emmie darted toward her brother's table as soon as she spotted him, embracing him in a deep hug when he stood to greet her. Turning from him, she gave Kent an equally ardent embrace.

"I was just asking your brother's permission to continue our courtship," he said as he pulled up another chair at the table for her.

"And what was his response?" Emmie queried impishly, ignoring the fact that Nat was sitting right there.

"I hadn't given one," Nat interjected. "Not that I guess it matters much. You have always done whatever pleases you anyway. But I have to admit, if it pleases you, it pleases me. I just want you to be happy." Turning his attention to Kent, he warned, "But if I ever hear that you mistreat her, I will find you and make you pay dearly. You can count on that."

"Deal." Kent replied amicably, extending his hand to Nat. "Mavis," he called across the room, "bring us a round of drinks, and please join us if Red can spare you for a few minutes."

Chapter Twenty-Six

Damnation, it's hard to breathe in this godforsaken place, John Hund thought for what must have been the hundredth time since he had come to the Colorado territory. After learning his niece's location, he had rented a buckboard, bought supplies, and headed toward the mining camp. In the process of scouting it out, he had found an abandoned shack to hole up in while he waited for the ideal time to spring into action.

Pretending to be interested in looking for work, he had visited the company store. It had been easy enough to get information from the friendly, talkative woman who ran the place, he thought derisively. Women could always be counted on to run their mouths.

She was full of praises for the new schoolmarm when he had hinted he had a child he wanted to do his best to raise, widower that he was. It was all he could do to keep his hatred from showing on his face as the woman expounded on all his bitch niece's attributes. But he had done so. And he had learned that she resided in the cabin just beyond the schoolhouse—alone. He had expected that would make her easy pickings.

He had been wrong. In planning her abduction, he had visited the camp numerous times since his arrival, taking care Melissa didn't spot him. During the day, she was usually surrounded by the schoolchildren, and a couple of the boys were double the size he thought he would be able to beat in a fight. The man the company store woman had pointed out as the owner of the mine spent the evenings with her and, for all he knew, stayed the night, defiling what was his to take, he thought angrily. He always left after a couple of hours, deciding he needed some whiskey to calm his nerves. He could wait a bit longer for his revenge.

When he observed the camp's boss man leaving for town along with some of the miners and their families this morning, he recognized his chance. Melissa hadn't been among them. Once they had passed by, he set out for the camp. Leaving his buckboard in a copse of bristlecone pine, he crawled up to the rear window of what he had learned was her cabin and, raising up on his knees, peered inside. Not sensing any movement within, he was about to crawl through the window when he heard her voice responding to others. Apparently, a number of miners had stayed behind this morning, but it was now or never. He would just need to create a diversion that would draw the attention of anyone who had remained in the camp to ensure there would be no one to come to the bitch's rescue when he made his move. As he crawled stealthily back to his wagon, he devised a plan he considered quite brilliant. Everyone knew mine shafts were often accidents waiting to happen.

Driving around the deserted backside of the camp, he tethered his horse to a tree near one of the pitheads and lumbered off, axe and rope in hand. He'd think of something after he had a chance to check this one out.

This is going to be easier than I thought, Hund said to himself as he recognized that one of the shaft timbers was already weak. Once he weakened it further with the help of his axe, he could tie a long rope around it and return to his buckboard, rope in hand. The extra tug that would occur as he drove off should cause the shaft to collapse, at which point he could simply throw the rope off his wagon and race to capture his niece while those who rushed to the scene tried to piece together what happened. *Merry Christmas to me*, he thought with a grin as he swung his axe.

Clifford Bodnar hadn't gone into Denver with the others. Since his wife had died, Christmas meant nothing to him. His boy looked so much like her it pained him to look at Pete with those same rosy cheeks and sky-blue eyes. He tried to put as much distance as he could between him and his son, even calling him names so Pete wouldn't want to hang around him. Pete hadn't gone into town, either, though, and Clifford needed to get out. Explaining he was worried about one of the supporting timbers, Kent had temporarily closed mine shaft number three and had asked Cliff to take a look at it when he had the chance. *Now's as good a time as any*, Cliff decided.

Hearing what sounded like an axe as he drew closer to the pithead, Bodnar picked up his pace. "Hey," he called out as he approached and observed a man he recognized as the drunk at a recent poker game swinging at the timber Kent had indicated was compromised.

"Son of a bitch!" Hund muttered. He was so close to finishing his task. If he hadn't had to stop to catch his breath so often, he might have already been on his way. He wasn't about to let this intruder stop him. Pulling the axe out of the timber, he threatened the unwelcome meddler with it. "Get the hell out and mind your own business, or you'll have no business to mind," he warned.

Hund's shortness of breath and the beads of sweat on the man's forehead were not lost on Bodnar. "This here *is* my business, and I'll not let you destroy it," he declared as he continued to advance on the trespasser, thinking he could easily overcome this stranger who seemed to be exerting great effort as he attempted to menace him.

As Bodnar entered the shaft opening, Hund used every ounce of strength he had to raise the axe over his head and bring it down on Clifford's head. Cliff parried to one side, and Hund's swing landed wide, the head of the axe landing squarely against the damaged timber. It splintered, but continued to support the entry, compromised as it was. Clifford had dropped to his knees to avoid being struck, and he now lunged at the stranger from that position, wrapping his arms around the man's legs. Losing his balance, Hund swung his axe wildly, hitting the weakened support again as he fell to the ground.

"Noooo!" Bodnar shouted as he sprang up and attempted to reach the supporting beam before it gave way completely, but Hund's last swing was the final blow. Clifford tripped over the large man's body and fell backward as the entire shaft collapsed, burying the two men under a mound of dirt, timber, and other debris.

The rumble reverberated throughout the camp. At the sound, the few folks who had not made the trip into town came running. Melissa and Pete arrived from opposite directions. One of the first miners on the scene cried, "There's at least one person trapped under this wreckage, maybe two. I can see a couple of limbs. I don't know if they're alive, though. Everyone start digging!

The order had been unnecessary. The people there had already begun throwing pieces of wood and sod from the top of the rubble aside and were digging with bare hands through the dirt to try to get to those entrapped. Luckily, the last couple of weeks had been warmer than usual, so the ground was not frozen and hard as it might have been otherwise.

"Dad!" It was Pete's voice. Recognizing the hand that had become slightly visible through the rubble as his father's, he began digging more furiously than ever, scooping up armloads of loose debris and throwing them aside. Others shifted to focus their efforts on digging out Bodnar as well.

"We'll get him out, Pete, don't worry," one of the diggers consoled.

"Dad!" Pete repeated, sobbing as his father's grimy, battered face was uncovered, knowing he might just have lost the only parent he had left. "I love you, Dad," he said anyway, cradling his father's head in his hands, gently brushing some of the loose dirt from his face, his tears forming streaks in the more caked-in dirt.

"Son," Clifford managed to whisper through his pain. Opening his eyes, he attempted to smile, but his mouth wouldn't work. There wasn't one part of his body that wasn't in great pain—except maybe his heart. Seeing the beautiful, gravely concerned face of his son, now his rescuer, had done much to heal it. "Thank you."

Pausing briefly to witness the poignant moment between father and son and exchanging smiles, the others returned to clawing through the other dirt and debris to uncover the second body they had discovered as they were digging out Bodnar. When the face she had come to despise appeared, Melissa fainted.

****

"What the…?" Kent exclaimed as the buckboard he was driving approached the camp and he saw the gathering of people around mine shaft three. "Hold on tight," he instructed Emmie, sitting beside him, as he urged his horse to a faster pace.

Nat, who had been riding beside the wagon on his own horse, raced forward. Seeing Melissa lying on the ground amidst all the rubble, he dismounted quickly and ran toward her. A miner, not knowing Nat, attempted to block his path as one of the wives knelt over Melissa and began to loosen some of her clothing.

"Let him pass," Kent called out when he drew close enough to be heard.

"Please don't be dead," Nat pleaded as he edged the miner's wife away and knelt beside Melissa's still body, taking her hand in his. "I am so sorry—for everything!"

A bit confused, the others at the scene looked at each other, wondering if and how they might tell this stranger that their schoolmarm was unharmed and had just fainted. One of the miners approached his boss's wagon as it pulled up to inform him about the goings-on. Upon hearing that Melissa was uninjured and had only passed out, Emmie climbed down from the wagon and ran to her brother's side while the miner filled Kent in regarding Clifford Bodnar's injuries and other details.

"Nat, she's okay, really she is," Emmie said, putting her hand on her brother's back in a comforting gesture. "We've been told she just fainted. She wasn't around when the shaft collapsed." Nat's tear-streaked face broke her heart as he turned to look at her, her words sinking in.

Hearing their voices, Melissa slowly regained consciousness and tried to lift herself up on her elbows. At the rustling sound, Nat turned back to her.

"No, Sweetness, please just lie there a few minutes

more, and then we'll get you to someplace more comfortable. I'll be right here beside you," he added. "Now and always."

Melissa closed her eyes again, recalling what had happened immediately before she passed out. Surveying the scene, Nat saw a face he recognized in the wreckage and put two and two together.

"He's dead, Sweetness," he assured her. "Your uncle can't hurt you anymore."

Chapter Twenty-Seven

After all the debris was removed from atop Clifford's body, it was determined that, miraculously, he had suffered only a broken arm, a couple of black eyes, and a split lip, although red and purple bruises were forming on almost every part of his body. He looked like he had been run over by a railcar. Someone had already gone to retrieve some medical supplies from the closet designated for emergency purposes such as this one. Another had gone to the ice house for ice. When the items arrived, Kent fashioned a sling out of a clean piece of cloth while Pete applied ice to his father's eyes and lip. A few of the men helped Clifford sit up, bracing his back as he did, so Kent could tie the sling around his neck and carefully place his arm in it. Once Pete's father was able to stand, a miner assisted Pete in getting him back to their cabin where Pete could tend to him.

After Melissa's uncle's body was fully uncovered, Nat took Kent aside and informed him of John Hund's identity and what he knew of his relationship to Melissa. A couple of the miners' wives had helped Melissa to a sitting position, and the two men returned to her side. Kent told her he could have her uncle's body buried in an unmarked grave in the cemetery located just outside the mining camp if she wished, or he could transport the body to Denver and bury it in the cemetery where her sister and brother-in-law were buried.

"No, not that!" Melissa immediately rejected the latter idea. "He does not deserve to share the same soil. I realize it's very un-Christian of me, but I feel even an unmarked grave is too good for him after the way he treated my dear Aunt Georgina." Her eyes filled with tears at the memory of her aunt. "Nevertheless, I know it's the proper thing to do."

Nodding in agreement, Kent directed some of the men to load Hund's body into his wagon as Nat helped Melissa stand and began walking with her to her cabin.

Kent was in the process of suggesting Emmie go with her brother and Melissa while he took care of the burial when one of his men called out, "Hey, Boss, why don't you let me n' Zeke handle the body whilst you show that pretty lady around the place?"

Grinning, Kent was only too willing to acquiesce. "Thanks, Jake. I'll owe you one."

"You don't owe me nothing, Boss. You do enough for all of us," Jake replied, tipping his hat to Emmie.

****

"Pretty nice place you've got here," Nat said as he entered the cabin that Melissa called home. "Mighty comfy."

"Yes. I was really fortunate," Melissa said as Nat helped her out of the cloak she had donned quickly before running to the site of the crash. "The miner and his wife who lived in this cabin decided to return East, and they left some of their belongings, like this beautiful rug that I've been told the wife braided herself," she said, pointing to the rug that added bright color to the rough plank floor of what she referred to as her sitting room. "Kent put in those shelves to hold my books and other reading material, and he added a few pegs for me to hang things on the wall nearest the door," she said as she motioned to one on which Nat could hang her cloak.

Suddenly realizing how Nat might take her obvious gratitude to the man who had once been her fiancé, however short-lived, Melissa abruptly stopped talking.

Nat sensed her discomfort and was quick to put her at ease. "Kent is a good man, Melissa. I am more than thankful he was here for you when I was not. He and I have had a couple of long conversations. As have Emmie and I. The two of them have convinced me what a dunderhead I have been, not that I hadn't come to that conclusion myself at some point." He added the last with a sheepish grin.

"Nat, I—" Melissa began to interrupt with her own confession.

"No, Sweetness, let me finish. Then you can have your say and speak as long as you want, and I will listen as though my life depended on it—because, in a very real sense, I know it does."

"Then let's have a seat," Melissa said, indicating the two chairs flanking the fireplace in which burning embers remained. "I'm fully recovered from the shock of seeing my uncle's face again, but I'm not certain I'm capable of handling much more while still standing."

Nat stoked the embers and threw another couple of logs on the fire before he began speaking again. He didn't want to get this wrong. Once he thought he might have the words organized in his head, he began.

"Okay, please hear me out, because I want to be perfectly honest with you, even though I worry you might be offended by some of what I say initially. Nevertheless, I think good relationships are based on honesty, and I want our relationship to be even better than good." Sensing her accord, he continued. "I must admit I considered it a great inconvenience to find a stowaway, pretty as she might be, in my wagon. And you have to realize I knew nothing about you at that point. I was focused on my mission—getting Tom, Al, and myself to Denver to join the forces at Camp Weld. Still, I had observed your uncle's behavior toward you the day before when the two of you were in town. You probably didn't realize that I saw what I saw. I considered stepping in to object to such salacious public behavior, but how was I to know you two weren't husband and wife? It seemed unlikely, but I decided it wasn't for me to judge. You don't know how many times I wished I had—but then I wonder, to what avail?

"Still, when I discovered you were my stowaway, I had options. I could have instructed Tom or Al to accompany you back home and rejoin the wagon train afterwards. That didn't set right with me, given what I had seen the day before. When I learned that the preacher needed help with his family, I thought it would be an ideal situation that would enable you to accompany the wagon train without compromising your reputation, as it might be if you continued on in the company of Tom, Al, and me. I realize now that I should have consulted you on the matter. Okay, Emmie pretty much hammered that point into my thick head," he admitted with a wry grin.

"In my defense, I will say that I was raised as a Southern gentleman to believe women need protection. The way you managed all the adversities you faced along our westward journey with courage and resolve clearly disputes that idea. And Emmie was quick to remind me of how she had always rebelled against my interference whenever I tried to shield her as she stretched her wings to try new things. At the same time, she also reminded me of our parents' relationship. Mom and Dad were a team. They didn't always agree on everything, but they respected each other's opinion. Dad despised the fact that I joined the Union forces. I sensed Mom was not that opposed, but it was a point on which she felt his view should prevail. Still, I think she was mainly responsible for the fact that Emmie was not poisoned against me.

"I want to have that kind of relationship with a woman—and with only one woman—you, Melissa. I think I loved you at first sight, if there is such a thing. But, more importantly, my love grew with the admiration I felt as I observed your actions and reactions regarding each and every challenge along the trail west. I confess that my stubborn Irish pride kept me from admitting these things until now. Emmie managed to give me a tongue-lashing on that point, too. That baby sister of mine seems to have grown up to be sharp as a whip in addition to being extremely observant," he continued. "She admonished that life's too short to let pride stand in the way of our relationships with those we love, reminding me of how pride tore our family apart."

His voice cracked. "She mentioned our father. She told me that as angry as he was at me for joining the Union forces, he loved me until the day he died, but he was too proud to admit it. As glad as I was to hear that, I was overcome with sadness, too. Perhaps there might have been something I could have done toward reconciliation, too, had I not been so bumptious. Our family might not have become fractured. My brother Albert might not have taken to drink—"

"I have lived in the world of 'what might have been' for a while now," Melissa interrupted. She moved from her chair to kneel before him and give him a tight embrace. Pushing away slightly, she captured his eyes with hers as she spoke. "What might have been if my parents had not succumbed to typhoid? What might have been had my sister Alicia and her husband Jesse not been murdered by Indians? What might have been had that young Indian woman who had suffered such brutality at the hands of a white man not been shown equal kindness by a different white person? Would she have helped me—us—in our escape from the Indian camp? And, yes, what might have been had I not been so quick to pre-judge you and reject your initial proposal to me? I have decided I don't want to look back at what might have been anymore. It is a senseless endeavor. I want to embrace the future. And I want to apologize to you for some baseless assumptions I made about you. Emmie is, indeed, wise beyond her years. While fear played a part in my rejection of your initial proposal—along with my outrage at the fact you might be cheating on a wife back home," she added abashedly, "pride also played a part. I didn't want to be beholden to anyone ever again after I found myself, along with my Aunt Georgina, under the thumb of John Hund. I allowed that experience to poison my opinion about relationships, and my opinion became further entrenched as I observed the manner in which some of the men on the wagon train treated their wives. Annie Miller died because her husband insisted they leave the train and forge forward by themselves. She was given no say in the decision."

"Would you want to stop looking back and move forward together, Sweetness?" Nat asked, pushing his chair back to kneel beside her and take her hands in his. "As my wife?"

"Nothing would make me happier!" she exclaimed. "I love you, Nathanial Bellamy," she affirmed.

"And I love you, Melissa Sullivan. As I will forever."

****

A knock at the door interjected itself into the tender moment. Emmie didn't miss the rapturous look on Melissa's face as she welcomed Kent and Nat's sister into the cabin. Seeing her brother with a similar expression, Emmie broke into a delighted grin.

"Congratulations!" she exclaimed. Observing the puzzled look on Kent's face, she explained, "These two have finally found their way to each other."

"I haven't been able to pull one over on you for a number of years now," Nat said, grinning back at his baby sister as he put his arm around Melissa's waist. Turning to Kent, he explained, "Melissa has agreed to marry me, and Emmie and you had everything to do with it, for which I will be eternally grateful. It took the two of you to do it, but I finally had some sense knocked into my thick skull."

"Congratulations!" Kent responded sincerely, moving to shake Nat's hand.

"And just when are you two planning to tie the knot?" Emmie wanted to know.

"We haven't had a lot of time to think about it, much less make any plans," Melissa explained, laughing a little at the exuberance of her future sister-in-law. "Not that we want or need a lot of time to prepare."

"Let me know what I can do to help," Emmie replied. "I will finally get one of the things I have wished for all my life."

"And just what is that?" Kent wanted to know.
"A sister!" Emmie responded enthusiastically.

Chapter Twenty-Eight

The small white church overlooking the camp held more people that Christmas morning than ever before. At Kent's invitation, Al, Tom, Mavis, and Red had ridden in earlier to celebrate the holiday with the miners. They were all eager to escape the desecration of the meaning of Christmas that had been occurring in Denver, and fortunately, Mother Nature forestalled any snowfall, making it possible. "Peace on earth and good will toward men" seemed to be absent in the Queen City. In its December 22nd issue, *The Rocky Mountain News* reported, "Cheyenne scalps are getting as thick as toads in Egypt. Everybody has got one, and is anxious to get another to send east." And yesterday, Christmas Eve day, the paper reported that a Navajo blanket found "on a defunct Indian at the Battle of Sand Creek" was being raffled off.

Standing in front of the scarred wooden pulpit decorated with pine boughs and red ribbons, Kent introduced his guests to the other attendees prior to the Christmas service. The traveling preacher wasn't going to make an appearance, so one of the miners gave a brief but worthy sermon, emphasizing how the current gift-giving tradition had evolved from God's greatest gift to us—His son, Jesus Christ. Afterwards, Mavis led the congregation in a variety of Christmas songs. She followed the traditional Christmas melodies of "Silent

Night," "Joy to the World," and "O Holy Night" with a couple more recent ones, "Jingle Bells" and "Up on the Housetop," which the children delighted in singing, snapping their fingers or stamping their feet to the words, "Click, click, click."

Afterwards, Kent, Emmie, Nat, Melissa, Tom, Al, Mavis, and Red celebrated with other attendees in the meeting hall of the camp, feasting on wild turkeys stuffed with celery, mushrooms, onions, bread cubes and spices, as well as ham, pickles, sweet potatoes, and a variety of honey and sorghum-sweetened Christmas cakes, with apple cider and eggnog to wash everything down. Melissa presented her students with her gifts for them at the potluck and watched with pride as each one gleefully added his or her ornament to the Christmas tree that stood in the large hall, already adorned with ribbons of popcorn and paper snowflakes the children had made in Melissa's classroom.

After whispering something to Mavis and some of her students' parents, she filled a couple of plates with the Christmas fixings while Mavis filled two jugs with cider and eggnog. Laden with their basket of treats and accompanied by the students, the two women excused themselves from the frivolity temporarily and made their way to the Bodnar cabin. Mavis began leading the children in song, and a startled but obviously happy Pete swung open the door even before Melissa was able to knock on it. His father remained sitting at their table with his arm propped up and his head bandaged, but he smiled and raised his undamaged hand in greeting when Melissa entered the cabin. His eyes filled with tears as she opened her basket and laid out the Christmas fixings before him.

"Merry Christmas, Mr. Bodnar," she said while the

children's singing continued in the background.

"Merry Christmas, Miss Sullivan. And thank you—for everything," Clifford replied. "Despite all this," he said, his good hand indicating his battered face and damaged arm, "this is the best Christmas I've had since my Tillie died. And I hope Pete and I will enjoy many more together."

"He's a good boy, Mr. Bodnar, and a smart one, too."

"That, I know. Takes after his mother, he does," Clifford replied, taking a long swallow from the cup of eggnog Melissa had poured for him and raising his cup in toast to her words. "And I'm going to make sure he knows how proud I am of him from this day on," he vowed.

Pete was still waving to his fellow students and clapping after each of their songs when Melissa left to join the others. She presented him with the ornament she had made for him as she passed by. Seeing it—a crocheted knight chess piece strung with a red ribbon—he broke into a broad smile and unabashedly gave his teacher a big hug in full view of his fellow students without worrying about what they might think, as he once might have.

****

Having had their fill of food and gaiety and contributed to the cleanup, the miners and their families departed for their individual cabins shortly after Melissa, Mavis, and the student carolers returned to the meeting hall. Kent, Emmie, Melissa, and Nat were finally alone for the first time with the Denver guests, who had arrived only that morning.

"Mav, I have a serious favor to ask of you." Melissa

said after bidding farewell to the last of the miners. Her friend's solemn tone took Mavis aback, but it didn't delay the Irish lass's response.

"I will be doing whatever you're asking, me friend. Surely you know that."

"And will you do the same for me, Tom and Al?" Nat questioned.

Clearly confused, Nat's two friends glanced at each other briefly before offering their simultaneous responses: "Yessir!"

Nat moved to encircle Melissa's waist as he announced their intentions to wed.

"We'd like the three of you to stand as our witnesses," Melissa added.

Mavis was only a little more subdued than Tom and Al when it came to the celebratory cheers.

"We're hoping to have a small ceremony at the church here," Nat continued. "Kent says when the traveling preacher told him he wouldn't be able to make it to the camp for Christmas, he said he thought he could make it here to usher in the new year with a prayer service. Melissa and I can't think of a better way to begin 1865.

"Tom, Al, and I will be able to muster out of the Third Colorado Calvary of 100-day volunteers in January, when our 100-day enlistment period will be up," Nat informed everyone. "Kenwood and his cohorts will be able to muster out at that time, too, making it next to impossible to punish them for the despicable crimes they committed at Sand Creek. At best, we can hope to tarnish their reputations so none of them will ever again hold a position of power that will allow them to do anything similar. I, along with others, will testify against him when the trial begins, even though we will no longer be part of the Third Colorado Cavalry."

"I have offered Nat a position here at the mine after he musters out, and I'd be pleased if the two of you would consider signing on, too," Kent said, turning to Al and Tom.

"Don't reckon we need to think much on that offer," Al responded for the two of them. "Nat and us are a team."

"He's saying it right, Boss," Tom affirmed.

Chapter Twenty-Nine

True to his word, Preacher Goss arrived on December 31, 1864, to lead a prayer service for the new year. He was delighted to learn he would also be officiating a wedding. He had witnessed too much hatred and violence over the past several months, and a celebration of love seemed like a good way to begin the new year for him as well. Fresh pine boughs had replaced the ones adorning the pulpit on Christmas Day, with more added throughout the church. White ribbons to represent purity had replaced the red ones.

The day after Christmas, Melissa had accompanied Nat, Tom, Al, Mavis, Red, and Emmie when they returned to Denver while Kent stayed behind to supervise the reconstruction of mine shaft number three. She and Nat had agreed they would use her mother's wedding ring to seal their vows, and while she would have been happy to wear one of her better dresses for the ceremony, Nat wanted to purchase a new one for her— one of her own choosing. Although it could not be a custom-made one at this late date, Mavis suggested she might find a suitable pre-sewn dress at Miss Hattie's, and Mavis hoped to find a dress befitting her role in the wedding there as well. As it happened, Miss Hattie had recently created a beautiful white taffeta gown with white velvet trim and a short flounce on the back for a customer whose fiancé had died in the battle at Sand

Creek. It was a little snug and too short on Melissa, but Miss Hattie said she could easily alter it to fit Melissa by letting out a couple of seams. The dress had originally been designed to be worn with a hoop, which Melissa didn't own and didn't care to own, so only one row of velvet trim would be necessary to add to the length of it. Mavis found an emerald green hoop dress she thought befitting of both her position as witness and her Irish ancestry. Although Hattie would have to let out the darts in the bodice, the gown otherwise served to accentuate every aspect of Mavis's impressive figure.

The mining camp seemed to pulsate with as much excitement on the day of the wedding as it had on Christmas Day. Kent, Emmie, and Red sat in one of the front pews. Pete and his dad arrived early enough to claim the other front pew, along with Mr. and Mrs. Anderssen and their daughter Christina. The other miners and their families filled the remaining nine pews lining the aisles on each side of the church. Hardly noticed as the attendees continued buzzing in conversation, Preacher Goss took his place at the pulpit. The chatter paused only slightly when Nat, Al, and Tom followed shortly thereafter and stood just to the right of the pulpit.

The sound of a single bell ringing at even intervals finally caught their attention. Turning, they watched as Mavis, stunning in her emerald gown, rang the bell to ward off evil spirits in the Celtic tradition as she approached the pulpit. Red's gasp, quite audible when he saw her elegantly performing her role as the bride's witness, was not lost on Mavis, who smiled brightly and nodded in his direction before taking her place to the left of the pulpit.

A hush filled the church as the attendees watched Melissa proceed up the aisle next, her eyes locked with Nat's, and a hair wreath clutched in her hands. Some of her students had made bouquets of paper flowers, which they tossed at her as she passed by, earning them a grateful smile. She felt more nervous than she ever had before in her life—more nervous than when she had been taken captive by the Indians, which she found hard to believe. Her legs were shaking as she neared the pulpit where the vows would take place, even as she continued to focus on the countenance of her beloved. Sensing her discomfort, Nat took a couple steps forward and grasped her hand in his, giving it a quick, encouraging squeeze as he whispered in her ear, "How many children, Sweetness?"

Author's Notes

This is a novel, and, as such, the main characters are creations of my imagination. However, numerous incidents described within these pages are real. My descriptions of them are based on a compilation of historical accounts I have read, not all of which are in total agreement with each other.

Indian attacks on wagon trains were happening at the same time the Civil War was raging, and it was, in fact, the case that the army was forbidding any wagon train to proceed west unless it was one hundred men strong. This said, Fort Kearny was never a target of an Indian attack, much to the puzzlement of some historians. I used poetic license in describing the attack in this book; nevertheless, my description of the treatment of the hostages by the Indians is a composite of actual occurrences.

The Hungate massacre happened much as described. However, ranch hand Nathan Hungate, his wife, and their two children were the only victims. They were not entertaining any visitors when the attack occurred. I again employed poetic license when I included Melissa's sister and brother-in-law as other casualties there.

I tried to be true to historical accounts in my description of the Sand Creek Massacre, but there are different versions of what happened on that bloody day in late November. Three official investigations were held—one by the Army and two by Congress. The Army's investigation concluded there was no justification for any court-martials because the investigation was unable to get "an honest, impartial determination of facts." Congress had the same issue.

The testimonies of various eyewitnesses contradicted each other. Some said they saw a U.S. flag flying along with a white flag of surrender at Sand Creek; others claimed they saw no flag. Anywhere from 69 to 600 Indians were killed that day, depending on whose account you believe, and there was no agreement on the relative numbers of Indian men, women, and children or on the number of mutilated bodies. Because of all the inconsistencies, to protect the innocent I have used fictitious names for all who participated in the battle and the events leading up to it.

A word about the author…

After spending 25 years in academia, teaching finance and authoring finance textbooks as an independent contractor for major publishing companies, Marianne retired early to devote more time to her lifelong dream: writing a novel and having it published.

What Might Have Been, her debut novel, was inspired by the rich history of the Denver, Colorado, area she discovered while living there. She currently resides in western North Carolina and enjoys hearing from her readers.

Connect with her through her website:
https://marianneplunkert.wixsite.com/
marianneplunkert-4

Thank you for purchasing
this publication of The Wild Rose Press, Inc.

For questions or more information
contact us at
info@thewildrosepress.com.

The Wild Rose Press, Inc.
www.thewildrosepress.com